Y12

The Secret Of The Ancestors

"As a thinker and planner, the ant is the equal of any savage race of men;
as a self-educated specialist in several arts she is the superior of any savage race of men;
and in one or two high mental qualities she is above the reach of any man..."

--Mark Twain

Chapter 1.

"Blue Team, go to formation Arizona", the team leader whispers coarsely as he inserts a fresh magazine of ammunition, and moves the slide back to load a round into the chamber. The squad of young men, armed with state of the art, gas powered rifles, stealthily move into predetermined positions burned into their brains through months of practice. Silently, each individual crouches as he quickly paces into place. The Blue Team leader, employs hand signals to communicate with the other members of his team, fine tuning their positions on the battlefield to gain a strategic advantage over the adversary.

The point man of the Blue Team signals back to his leader that the opposing force has been spotted ahead. The team leader motions to the two outside wing positions to move to encircle the opposing force, identified by their red uniform markings. The Blue leader sends the point man to begin his thrust into the center; a move designed to create confusion, and focus the attention of the opponent toward his attack and away from the outside wings.

The point man sprints into the opening in front of the Red Team, a hail of projectiles whistling past his ears. The enemy shooters are now intent upon stopping him as he dives behind a half wall, unable to see them, but knowing that his team members are successfully approaching from the sides. He looks back to see his team leader flashing the signal to attack, and rolls to his right, away from the protection of the half wall. Using the two finger trigger technique his team has perfected, he eliminates one enemy combatant, and another, and a third.

Seeing flashes of blue rushing in from the flanks of the opposing fighters' positions, he jumps up and runs straight at the now weakly protected center. Gun spewing, he sprints toward the Red Leader's position and dives behind a small protected ridge. He quickly pops his head over the ridge to spot the opposing shooter and then immediately ducks back down again. Visualizing the other's position in his mind, he prepares to stand up and fire. He counts to himself "One, two...three", and stands to fire. Before he even fully stands, he is hit. His face shield is splattered with thick, red goo, making it impossible for him to see. He unenthusiastically raises his hand, acknowledging that he is out of the game.

At the same moment the point man is disqualified, his fellow team members have routed the opposing Red Team members and captured the flag. High-fiving and back slapping, the Blue team members all congratulate each other, as they ridicule the point man for being the only one to be hit. "Way to take one for the team, Clark", says the grinning team leader. "Way to draw their fire."

The group members recount the highlights of the day's game as they remove their gear, and plan for the evening's celebratory dinner at the local hangout. "You're just not lucky, Clark", says his friend Henry. "You had those guys; that Red guy was just spraying and praying, and got you with a random shot. It really was a good move. We couldn't have won without you." "Story of my life", Clark replies. "Close, but no cigar."

"Do you two guys need a ride home?" another team member asks Henry and Clark, who are loading their gear on to their bicycles. Clark looks at Henry and then answers, "No thanks. We'll probably beat you to the Institute anyway." Henry says to Clark, "Hey, thanks for riding here with me. I probably would have just driven if you hadn't talked me into it." Clark replies, "You're welcome. No big deal to me; I ride everywhere."

As the two begin down the trail, Clark yells to Henry, "I'm going to go to the lab and get some work done. There's something I need to do before Monday." Henry nods that he understands. The trail is not very technical; mostly just dirt with some paved sections prepared by the city's Parks and Recreation department. Trees line the path, and there are quite a few very old and large ones that tower above the riders.

Within sight of the campus, Clark pulls ahead of Henry on the single track trail. Henry thinks to himself, "Clark always has to go for it at the end. He just has to win at even the smallest things." As Clark pulls ahead by about twenty yards, suddenly, his rear wheel goes up into the air, and the bike flips over on its front, with Clark still hanging on to the handlebars. He lands on his head, his neck contorting in an almost elastic motion, then flops like a rag doll on to his back, the bike resting on top of him.

Henry jumps off of his still rolling bike, and runs up to check on Clark. "Clark, are you OK?" Clark is unconscious and motionless, breathing shallowly. Henry quickly pulls his phone from his trunk bag, and calls 911. "Yes, this is Henry Lee, and my friend has crashed on his bike and landed on his neck. No, he's unconscious. Yes, he's breathing, but it doesn't sound right. We're on the bike trail, about a quarter mile south of the parking lot of the Research Lab at the Institute. Yes, I'll stay here with him. Hurry."

As Henry watches the motionless Clark, his eyes rolled completely back in their sockets, his body rigid and frozen stiff, his jaws clenched together tightly, Henry thinks back to the first time he and Clark met. It was the first day of orientation at Oak Ridge, and Henry and Clark were the only two students who had been chosen for the special cooperative program that had been sponsored by the U.S. Army. It offered multiple PhD degrees, while guaranteeing salaried laboratory research fellowships after their four years of service, all the while offering promising contacts with influential industry executives.

While each of them pursued slightly different paths, Clark going more toward his strengths in math and computers, and Henry to Biology and Earth Sciences, their time at the Institute went by quickly as they moved toward their career goals. What little free time they had, they enjoyed doing things like intramural paintball games.

The paramedics hurriedly check the still unconscious Clark. Their practiced poker faces betray no signs of the seriousness of his condition. As one carefully positions the neck collar, another enters vital signs into the computer that relays the information to the waiting staff at the hospital emergency room. Into the radio, one paramedic announces, "Breathing is labored; initiating respirator now."

Henry gathers up all of Clark's scattered belongings that he can find, and jogs with a bike in each hand back to the parking lot. He quickly puts the bikes on the rack on top of his car, and speeds toward the University Hospital. After what seems like hours, a doctor walks to the reception desk and asks the nurse something. She points toward Henry, and the doctor walks up and begins, "Are you the friend that was with Clark Shepherd?" "Yes", Henry answers tentatively. "How is he?"

The doctor pauses for a moment, and carefully answers without even the slightest smile, "Clark fractured his C5 vertebrae, and pieces of the bone have pierced the spinal column. He's in surgery now, but it is too early to tell if there will be any permanent paralysis." "Paralysis?", Henry almost gasps. "How bad?" The doctor, maintaining the exact same facial expression, responds, "Currently, total paralysis below the collarbone. Some times, such paralysis is only temporary, caused by pressure from increased fluid inside the spinal column. We'll know within a day or two if the surgery will relieve that pressure and improve nerve response."

"What if it doesn't?", asks Henry. "Then life will change dramatically for Mr. Shepherd", answers the doctor unflinchingly.

Henry shakes his head slightly, realizing that he has been staring at his computer screen while thinking about Clark's accident. "Three years ago seems like yesterday", Henry says to himself. "A lot has happened since then."

Now in the fourth year of his four year service requirement, Henry reflects back upon that day, and his time at the Oak Ridge Institute. Every night and weekend, he attended classes, did extra lab work, and studied toward the multiple doctorate degrees he was offered. Henry knew that he would never have another such opportunity to advance his career, and completed degrees in Arthropod Endocrinology, Biological Anthropology, Ecological Entomology, and Evolutionary Ecology. Henry often wondered if this unusual combination of disciplines would pay off.

Henry wasn't alone in this rigorous schedule. Clark was just as busy, just as focused on his studies. Henry often thought about how the two of them were well suited as friends; who else could have put up with their schedules? While his friend Clark's studies moved in the direction of computer simulations and brain chemistry, specifically degrees in Bioinformatics, Computational Biology, Molecular Biophysics, and Neurobiology, the two had enjoyed their years at Oak Ridge Institute, and were optimistic that their unique experiences would open up interesting opportunities.

One day, in a meeting with two of the Institute's professors and the U.S. Army Research Laboratory director, their career paths were validated. "Henry and Clark, the work you are doing here will not only yield findings that will benefit the human race, but will also guarantee you a secure and celebrated career. Keep doing what you are doing. We are already fielding inquiries for candidates for post doctoral fellowships from several very important research institutes, and you two are at the top of the list of candidates."

They were right, of course, but no one could have known just how different Clark's path would be. It has been three years since the accident, and Clark spent the first year getting used to the new way of life he would lead. While still holding out a glimmer of hope that he would some day be able to have a more normal life, he gave his total attention to learning how to use the technology provided to him by the Institute to study toward his degrees. No one would have blamed him for giving up and just studying for his own personal gain, but Clark fulfilled his responsibility to the program and not only continued with his studies, but became one of the Institute's most valuable assets.

It wasn't easy; just learning how to breathe with the diaphragm pacer was difficult at first, and then learning to move his motorized chair with head commands, and transferring his computer expertise to using a tablet computer, became as much his job as the actual research in which he excelled. Using a silver dot on his forehead, his tablet computer's camera responds to the movement of his forehead as it would moving the cursor to respond to a mouse or tracking device. With practice, Clark has become quite adept at using the tablet computer, not only using it for his own personal needs and for work, but also to facilitate the constant practical jokes he plays on his fellow workers, some of whom have come to fear his approach.

"Dr. Shepherd", the head Security officer says to Clark. "I need to check your computer to make sure that the network settings are correct. We have a rogue access point showing up on the network, and we've tracked it to this part of the building." "Sure", Clark replies, pausing every few words to wait for his lungs to fill. "I can't...imagine what the... problem might be", he says as he rotates his chair away from the officer, smiling slyly.

"There. I've returned the network settings to default. Let me know if you need any help with your tablet in the future. I'll have someone come work on it for you." "I sure will", responds Clark. "If that device continues to show up as a rogue access point, we'll need to send it back to be serviced", adds the Security officer. Clarke answers, "You know that... I cannot work..., or even... get around without... my computer. Check with... the General about it... I can't work... without it..., so you better... get authorization to... take the tablet... before you give... me a paid vacation. Oh, and with... a paid nurse, too."

"I'll take that under advisement", the Security officer says gruffly, as he turns on his heel and marches out of the lab. Laughing, Clark says to himself, but loudly enough for everyone to hear, "Don't mess with... the computer guy."

Dr. Zeke Williams was one of the first researchers to begin working on Henry's team at the Institute. While technically their boss, Henry and Clark see Zeke more as a mentor and friend, even though he runs a pretty tight ship in his labs. The two research participation programs that Zeke is in charge of are funded by the U.S. Army Telemedicine and Advanced Technology Research Center (USATATRC) and the U.S. Army Research Laboratory (USARL). The fields of research for the USATATRC are Computational Biology, Biomonitoring Technologies, Simulation and Training Technology, and Proteomics/Genomics. The mission statement of the USARL is "to provide the Army the key technologies and the analytical support necessary to assure supremacy in future land warfare."

Even though there is quite a bit of overlap in their job duties, Henry has been assigned primarily to two top secret projects, both involving ants. The Army has commissioned the study of the communication of ants via pheromones, with the objective of enabling battlefield communication without electronic devices. In modern warfare, electromagnetic pulse weapons can render all electronic communication useless, and no amount of shielding can completely protect losing the ability to communicate with the front line troops. The Army has made it clear that it is very interested in discovering a way to use chemical communication for the battlefield.

For this pheromone project, Henry is in charge of studying the genetic link, looking for common DNA between ants and humans. In addition to the Army, additional funding for this project has been provided by a large pharmaceutical conglomerate, UNIPHARM. Their interest is in securing the contract with the Army for any drug that might result from the project. Henry uploads data from the project each day, both to the Army and to UNIPHARM, with the pharmaceutical labs providing modified drugs for the next human trial.

Clark's primary role in this project is to run the simulation lab, which had involved using exclusively soldiers in the past, but now is increasingly using civilians, teenage and young adult men. The Army recently purchased a popular battlefield simulation role playing computer game, and assigned Clark to head up the modification of the program with specifications relayed down from the Pentagon. Players of the game are hooked up to an individual console, with a sophisticated headset that measures dozens of brain functions during game play. Clark's expertise in simulators is evident in the detailed monitoring stations in a control center, where technicians observe multiple players simultaneously. Game play data is recorded in real time on the massive server farm located within the facility, and is uploaded, also in real time, to a fiber network maintained by the Army. Clark often wonders where this data is uploaded, but he figures, "That's above my pay grade."

The other main project that Henry has been assigned to do research on is completely unknown to him. Zeke has let him know that it has been assigned even higher clearance than Henry has been granted. "The only thing I can tell you is that it involves asexual reproduction", said Zeke the only time Henry asked about it. Since then, Henry often has wondered to himself how asexual reproduction relates to battlefield communication, but "One less thing for me to worry about", he decides.

What Zeke knows, however, is that the study of ant reproduction has nothing to do with battlefield communication, and everything to do with the desire to manipulate human reproduction by other organizations that have also contributed financially to the Institute. He has observed his boss, General Green, in many meetings with Senators and the heads of organizations which have public mission statements of ending war by shifting power away from men and toward women. Until recently, he had just stored the meetings away as coincidence, but recent findings in his research that have resulted from very specific demands made from higher up the chain of command, have prompted Zeke to dig deeper into the project.

One day while comparing Henry Lee's DNA research from his ant subjects, to the DNA of human test subjects in the battlefield simulation game project, he discovers a link. "They are looking for a common chromosome." Zeke compares the charts, then reads the list of parties to be notified of the test results, and notices some odd entries. "What would the new Science for Optimal Learning Center, which is supposed to treat attention deficit disorders, have to do with asexual reproduction? And what is this UNIFEM outfit, and what do they have to do with a secret government project?"

The deeper Zeke looks, the more disturbed he becomes. "These people want to be able control human reproduction. They also seem to think they're very close to figuring out how to do it. They've taken Henry's research and appear to have narrowed it down to one specific chromosome, but there's a problem; not every male can be controlled. There is an immunity gene, and they know who has it. They are trying to round up people with this specific gene."

The speaker phone on Zeke's desk crackles, "Dr. Williams, come see me, please. Immediately." Zeke answers, "Yes sir, General Rogers." Zeke swallows hard and thinks, "This can't be good. He never wants to see me." He quickly searches for a spare storage drive, and copies the entire research file, then sticks the drive in his lab coat pocket. As he walks the hallway toward General Rogers' office, he swings by Henry's lab.

"Henry, I need you to keep this for me. It's very confidential. Please keep it to yourself It's very important that no one else knows about it." Henry cocks an eyebrow and looks at his friend, and answers, "Sure, Zeke. No problem. Let me know when you need it back." Zeke responds, "I don't think I'll need it back. You'll know what to do with it." Henry looks even more confused, and turns to ask what he means, as Zeke walks toward the General's office.

Chapter 2.

"Hear the story of The Ancestors", calls Santana, Chief of the unified Comanche tribes. A dying bonfire is struggling for breath in the center of the gathering, casting a reddish orange glow on the Chief. The tribes are gathered together at the sacred Spirit Song Rock, the night before they are to sign a treaty with the Texans on the banks of the San Saba River, a half day's travel away.

The Spirit Song Rock, called "Enchanted Rock" by the white men, has been considered a holy place by Comanches, the Apache and Kiowa before them, the Tonkawa before them, the Coahuiltican before them, and on and on, back to the beginning of man. This dome of one solid piece of pink granite, rising hundreds of feet in the air, has stood guard over countless generations. Among the legends told of Spirit Song Rock are that creaking and groaning noises coming from the rock are ghosts of ancestors; that anyone spending a night on the rock becomes invisible, and that bad fortune or death will come to anyone who climbs the rock with evil intent. The most important legend is the one that describes how the secrets of The Creator are passed to Man at this portal to The Ancestors.

"I hold the one copy of 'The Secret of The Ancestors', passed down to one man each generation for safekeeping. Hear the story." Santana lifts the delicate animal skin parchment up for all to see, taking care not to smudge the charcoal lettering that was rubbed from a stone tablet. "The Ancestors themselves are charged with keeping the original stone tablet safe.

We must never let this copy fall into the hands of our enemies."

Santana begins, "This copy of our ancestors' history was transcribed from The Creator's words. It tells of how Man first came up from the Earth, and how The Creator gave Man the Tablet of Creation to safeguard. But as Man disappointed The Creator, all were destroyed except the few who were obedient. Those who were obedient were saved by returning underground to live with their ant brothers."

"The First World was destroyed by fire.
The Second World was destroyed by ice.
The Third World was destroyed by flood.
We are now living in the Fourth World."

"Each time a new World was created, Man would emerge to live above ground, the previous tablet was destroyed and a new tablet was written, to provide instructions as the essence of that World. Each time, a corner was broken off of the original tablet, to ensure that Man could not create Man. This corner is the key, without which the tablet would be very difficult to understand. The Creator has commanded the Ancestors to keep the tablet and the corner in two separate colonies, so that Man could never know of its existence."

"Only one man of each generation is trusted to hold this copy, and only to reveal it in the case of the existence of the ancestors being threatened. Should Man ever find the entire code, he will be tempted to play Creator himself, endangering both Ancestors and Man. The secret is always kept in one who can see. The

Ancestors will know of the one who can see. They will protect him and help him hide the secrets. He must help them keep the original tablet and the key safe."

Santana rolls up the scroll and places it in a protective pouch, then continues speaking, "I do not know if we are at the end of The Fourth World, but it is almost certain that the world will change for our people. Our traditions, our history, must be protected."

He holds up the pouch again and continues, "This must be protected, at any cost. That cost may be our lives. Tomorrow we are to negotiate a treaty with the Texans. Such treaties have so far not been honored by the White Man, but we have no choice but to negotiate the best conditions possible. We took this land from those who took it from those before them, and the future has always been for someone to take it from us. The Creator allowed us to live on this land for a time, and The Creator has now given it to the Texans."

Santana looks through the crowd before him, his eyes stopping on the boy standing next to his wife, Lola Shaw, a young woman captured from a white settlement during a raiding party many years ago. The boy is his son, Jim Shaw. His voice steadily growing louder and louder, Santana proclaims, "We will never die, as long as there is at least one who continues to live in their world."

The shrill sounds of yelps and beating drums fill the air around the crowd, the warriors lifting their spears and bows and shields into the air as they yell. Santana blends into the crowd, as they begin to dance around the glowing fire.

Two Arrows, named for his ability to fire two

arrows before most warriors can fire one, is Santana's most trusted aid. "Two Arrows, walk with me", Santana motions to his friend. As they walk away from the group, Santana begins, "I do not trust the Texans." Two Arrows responds, "You should not; they have no honor." Santana continues, "I must go tomorrow and fulfill my promise to negotiate a treaty, even if no good comes from it. I must ask you to do a very important thing."

"I will go with you to fight. If there is a battle, you will need my arrows." Santana holds up his hand to stop him, "If I am successful, there will be no battle tomorrow. If I am not successful, we will all die. That is why I need you to promise me that you will do what I ask." Two Arrows looks directly into Santana's eyes and slowly nods, I will do what you ask."

Santana begins his instructions, "Jim Shaw is both Comanche and White Man. He will be accepted in the White World, but he will need a teacher. He will need one who is wise in the ways of our people, to instruct him and give him the history and teachings of our people, so that he can keep us alive. Most importantly, he must protect 'The Secret of The Ancestors' from harm, and be taught how it should be handed down to his son, and his son, and his son. Promise me that you will be the one to protect him and instruct him, Two Arrows." Two Arrows places his hand on Santana's shoulder and says, "I will protect Jim Shaw, and will instruct him in our ways." Santana places his hand on Two Arrows' shoulder, and smiling says, "Thank you, my friend."

The next morning, Santana and five other chiefs

lead the tribes toward the San Saba River on horseback. From the front, Santana looks almost European, wearing the blue suit coat he received in a trade with a German trapper years ago, but from the back, his long braided hair and leather leggings make him look like the others. Two Arrows rides next to Lola and Jim Shaw, a few hundred yards behind the procession.

As the chiefs and warriors dismount and lead their horses to the river to drink, gunfire explodes all around them. The warriors quickly gather their weapons to respond, but the Texans have positioned themselves behind trees and earth berms, having carefully prepared the ambush. Arrow after arrow finds its mark, taking one Texan after another down, but there are too many guns, and there is no cover for the warriors. Every Comanche falls.

Out of sight of the Texans, Two Arrows hears the gunfire. His instinct is to rush into the fight, but he remembers his promise to Santana, and steers Lola and Jim Shaw to a side trail and slaps their horses to make them gallop. The group does not slow until the horses begin to tire, and they then stop by a stream for a drink.

Young Jim Shaw asks his mother, "What happened to the others?" Lola Shaw's head drops as her voice lowers, "We are alone." Jim follows with the question, "Is father dead, too?" Two Arrows answers the question, "Chief Santana died in battle, as was his wish. Now it is our duty to follow his orders and move to the reservation."

Two Arrows has a singular purpose, to protect and teach young Jim Shaw. For days, as the group rides North toward the Clear Fork Comanche reservation, Two Arrows thinks about how he will teach young Jim

Shaw everything he needs to know. "There is so much for him to learn", Two Arrows thinks to himself. "I cannot wait until we arrive at the reservation. There is no guarantee that I will even be allowed to remain with him. He and his mother will be accepted by the white man, but I will not."

"Jim Shaw", Two Arrows commands, "Ride with me." Lola Shaw does not protest, knowing that Jim's instruction must begin immediately. She rides silently behind the two men. For the next three days, Two Arrows tells the stories of The Ancestors while they ride north. As they settle in to camp each night, the stories continue in song, and Jim Shaw sings along with Two Arrows and his mother, the stories working their way into his memory.

In camp the night before they are to ride to the reservation the next day, Two Arrows pulls out the pouch he was given by Jim's father Santana, which contains the parchment copy of "The Secret of The Ancestors", and reads it to the boy. As the two discuss how this secret has been passed down from father to son for generations, Two Arrows sees the light in Jim's eyes that reveal his understanding. He knows that Jim Shaw will understand and accept his responsibility to his people.

Jim Shaw and his mother and Two Arrows live at Clear Fork Reservation for a little over a year, learning to farm the land, despite the Comanche dislike for farming. By day, they sing stories of their fathers before them as they worked the fields, able to practice in song the tongue that they are forbidden to speak. By night, Two Arrows and Jim Shaw study "The Secret of the Ancestors" by candlelight, while Lola silently listens as she sews nearby.

The white settlers nearby have noticed how large the Comanche crops have grown, and how plentiful the deer and wild turkey were for hunting, and assuming that the Comanche were fortunate enough to have been given more fertile land, begin to lobby the Governor to relocate the Comanche and take over the land for themselves. They are successful, and one day, the entire collection of Comanche tribes are rounded up and informed they will be sent to the Kiowa-Comanche reservation in Oklahoma.

On the day Jim and his mother are to join the rest of the tribes and be transported to Oklahoma, Two Arrows asks Jim to walk with him. "Your father is proud of you, Jim Shaw. You have learned well. You are ready to carry on with our traditions and stories. You are ready to be the protector of the 'Secret of Ant and Man', and to teach these things to your son some day.

Jim grows concerned at the tone of Two Arrows' voice and the look in his eyes and asks, "Two Arrows, why are you telling me this? How can my father be proud of me if he is dead? I still have much to learn, and we will have time while we travel to our new home. Why do you sound as if you are leaving?"

Two Arrows looks into Jim's eyes and answers, "The Army soldiers here have told me that I will not be leaving with you. I am to remain with them as a scout and translator. I do not want to do this, but I will do as they command, until I find the opportunity to leave them and join you. I wanted to prepare you, in case I am unable to join you for a time."

Two Arrows pauses, and then continues as the two walk alongside the creek, "Your father will always be with you. When you need guidance, you will see a sign of his presence, a Spirit Helper, which will help you take the right path." Then Two Arrows takes out the pouch containing the parchment document, and gives it to Jim. "You are now the protector of the secret."

Jim notices something out of the corner of his eye, and turns to look at what appears to be a small tree standing in the middle of the creek. As Jim stops to get a better look, Two Arrows notices him looking and stops to look in the same direction. At that moment, a large, gray, Great Blue Heron leaps up out of the water, sweeping its wings in long, slow strokes, and flies slowly away. The two watch in silence as the large bird flies north until it is out of sight, and then Two Arrows finally is the first to speak. "That was your Spirit Helper. It is a sign that you are on the right path. You are ready, Jim Shaw."

That was the last time Jim ever saw Two Arrows. The story was passed on to those who lived on the Oklahoma reservation that Two Arrows escaped the soldiers while on a raiding party that was supposed to be on a mission to destroy a Comanche tribe that refused to submit to being relocated, and that he joined that tribe and fought against the soldiers. The Comanche tribe escaped that day, but eventually all but a handful were killed in battle. A few of the women and children joined the other Comanche in Oklahoma, and told of his story.

Jim Shaw has grown to become a highly respected leader among the Comanche, not only excelling in building the tribe's farming operations profitably, but becoming a successful rancher. Watching and learning the white man's ways, Jim leased Comanche land to white ranchers, and invested money in land in the towns surrounding the reservation.

Jim marries the daughter of a prominent rancher, and they move to property he has purchased, not too far from the reservation. He encourages fellow tribe members to leave the reservation whenever possible, and provides jobs and housing to anyone who wants to leave. Year after year, more and more people move off of the reservation and fade into the white communities. Even as they move into the white world, they keep their traditions and language, but only away from the eyes and ears of the white man.

Jim Shaw teaches his son, Preston Shaw, all of what he was taught. Some details are forgotten, some words of some songs are changed, and their manner of dress and how they live take on the style of the white world they live in, but the most important thing of all, "The Secret of Ant and Man" is passed down and kept in complete secrecy.

Preston goes off to fight in a war between countries, and uses his native tongue as an unbreakable code to help win the war. While in a foreign land, he receives word that his father has died in what is reported as a hunting accident, but those closest to the family suspect the local ranchers, who were envious of his success, staged it as an accident.

Preston returns from the war and marries a local girl he has known since he was a boy, not a Comanche. They have a son, Jim Shaw, named after the grandfather he never knew.

Preston waits for the opportunity to begin instructing Jim on the ways of his people and pass on the responsibility of being the protector of the secret, but Jim never shows any signs of being ready. He never draws the figures of the ancestors that Preston did as a boy, like his father before him, and his before him. Preston eventually comes to the awareness that his son will not be the next in line to be the protector. He decides to put all of the documents and instructions down on paper, and make sure that his grandson or great grandson are taught when the time is right for the one who is to be chosen.

Jim has a son, also named Jim. Preston keeps an eye on his grandson, constantly looking for any of the signs that he might be the next one to learn of the secret and become its protector. Jim Jr. is just like his father in every way, and like his father, shows no signs of being the next protector. He has no visions of the ancestors, never draws or paints them as he should if he could see them, and never reports having any odd interactions with animals that would point to having met his Spirit Helper. Preston decides that he will be patient and wait for the next opportunity, when Jim Jr. has a son.

When Solomon is born, Preston is certain he will be the one. As he grows, he shows all of the signs, constantly drawing the stick figures that show a child's understanding of having seen the ancestors. As he grows, anyone who sees old family photos is shocked to see the resemblance between Solomon and his great grandfather when he was younger. Preston takes a very special interest in Solomon, and they form a very special bond. They seem to think alike, and Solomon never wants to leave when visiting his great grandfather. The two go for long walks, Preston pointing out birds and plants as they walk along, and he sings old songs to his great grandson. Preston always smiles the biggest smile when Solomon comes to visit, and it is obvious to all that the two have a very close tie.

But the old man knows that he will not have enough time to teach Solomon everything he needs to know. One day, when the pain in his chest is more powerful than usual, he thinks to himself, "I must prepare everything for when I am gone. I must hide everything in a locked box that Solomon's father can use to teach him what he will need to know. No one can know what is in there until after I'm gone, but it has to be enough to teach Solomon. I haven't had enough time to give him the tools to carry this responsibility, but I have seen enough to know he is the one. It has to be enough. It has to."

Chapter 3.

"Henry, here's something you might find interesting. I've got one colony attacking another, probably to raid for workers or food. As long as they're here together, I might as well pick up samples from both colonies." Except for the grey ponytail, the man squatting next to the ant mound could easily be mistaken for a boy, studying the battle taking place at his feet.

Shelton Tarver has been studying Harvester ants, or Pogos as he would call them, for their genus Pogonomyrmex, for all of his thirty plus years at Van Ross University. The book signings, the speaking engagements, and lectures in front of bored college students, are all necessary evils he knows he has to tolerate to justify the time he spends out in the field.

Being out in the field, actually studying the Pogos, takes him back to when the ants first caught his eye as a boy. He would spend entire afternoons in the hot, West Texas sun, squatting over an ant mound, poking the opening with a stick and watching the ants defend their colony against the invader. He never could bear to harm any of them, even when he remained in one spot too long, providing the opening for the brave soldiers to begin their counterattack by creeping up his shoes and onto his socks. Sensing them just in time, he gently brushed them off before moving around to another part of the mound.

His mind slowly returning to the present, he softly mutters to himself, "Funny how I was never stung. Good thing, too. Pogo stings are one of the most painful of all ants." He looks down at his feet, just to make sure none of his current subjects had ambushed him. He quickly checks himself, from his boots to his jeans, to the pockets on his trademark khaki vest, the kind that you see photographers wear on African safaris. He takes off his straw hat with one hand and wipes his forehead with the other, dropping it back on his head as Henry Lee joins him

.

Henry thinks to himself that the older man could easily pass for a scrawny cowboy checking his fences. "Let's see what you have there, Professor", he says as he crouches down next to Shelton. "Lose the 'Professor', and just call me Shelton", protests Tarver. "OK. Sure. Shelton, it is. Looks like you've got some P. barbatus attacking some P. rugosus. We already have plenty of the barbatus at the lab, let's just dig up the rugosus colony and I'll take it back with me. Just make sure you get the Queen, and try to get as few of the red ones as possible."

While technically on the payroll of the Army, Shelton is only a consultant on this project, assigned to Henry Lee. All Tarver knows is that Henry's superiors in the Army seem to have a great interest in how ant communication might be useful in identifying friends and foes.

Henry looks up from the ant mound, over at Shelton, and thinks to himself that it might be fun to have a life like Shelton one of these days. "The Army said I would be involved in an exciting project that would change the world."

"Well, I guess they were right", thought Henry, still to himself. "They promised me a job, and I've got one, collecting ants. Not terribly glamorous, but at least it gets me out of the lab for a while." All Henry knows about this newest project is that it involves comparing ant and human DNA. For all he knows, some perfume company is looking for a new way to make human pheromones. "Hardly saving the world", Henry thinks to himself.

"Look at these two", says Shelton. "They're really going at it." He is holding a magnifying glass a few inches off the ground, watching two individuals locked in combat. "Here, take a look." Henry takes the magnifying glass, closes one eye, and watches the struggle between the two enemies. One is all red, a little smaller than the other, the larger being a very deep reddish brown, almost black.

"Who do you think will win, Shelton? My money's on the rugosus. It's a little bigger. Which one's more aggressive?" The older man squints and looks at the ants for a few seconds and counters, "Well, no species of Pogos are particularly aggressive in their natural state, but when they get riled up, they can all get pretty mean. It will probably come down to whichever one gets tired first, or who gets help from another colony mate. Not much telling. Come on, let's get to digging."

While Dr. Zeke Williams is the civilian head of the Y12 labs, General Clifton Rogers is his military equivalent. General Rogers started out as an Army doctor, remained in the Reserves after going into private practice as a neurosurgeon, but fairly rapidly returned back to the Army after finding that civilian life did not require the discipline that he finds so comfortable in military life. Having worked under General Green previously, when the opportunity to be a part of the new Battlefield Communications research project was offered, Rogers accepted immediately. The chance to expand his expertise with the human brain within the Army's Swarm Intelligence Theory project was too fascinating to miss.

Both Williams and Rogers report directly to General Helen Green, and while not exactly friends, the two lab researchers have a reasonably good working relationship. Always on both men's minds however, is the fact that this is a military research facility, and that the Army is clearly in charge. Zeke knows that between the two of them, he is the more dispensable one.

As Dr. Williams walks into General Rogers' office, and sees General Green standing to the side of his desk, a sinking feeling settles into his stomach. General Green, motioning to a chair in front of the desk, bluntly states, "We need to talk." Zeke swallows hard, thinking to himself, "Nothing good ever follows that." He steps over to the chair and slides into it, preparing for the worst.

General Green begins, "Dr. Williams, it has come to my attention that you have been copying large numbers of files from your research. What is the purpose for making copies, and where have these copies been saved?" A bead of sweat appearing on his forehead, Zeke starts to answer, "I, I was simply making backup copies of my files, for redundancy."

"You are aware, are you not, that all research files are backed up remotely in both real time and on an incremental basis?", General Green queries. "Why is it that you felt it necessary to make your own copy of the files?" Williams responds, his voice quivering slightly, "I have always saved all my own files. Just a habit, I guess."

"Where is the storage drive that contains the copied files?", General Green asks. Zeke nervously answers, "I'm not sure. I think it might be at my desk." The General narrows her eyes and asks, "You are saying that you regularly back up files, but you don't know where your backup files are located?" Williams is having difficulty making eye contact as he answers, "Not off hand. No, General."

General Green frowns at Zeke and tersely snaps, "Dr. Williams, I need you to hand over your lab coat to General Rogers. General, search his pockets for any storage devices." Rogers goes through all the pockets in Zeke's lab coat, and places the contents on her desk. "I don't see anything like a storage device, General Green."

Green then turns to Rogers and orders, "General, escort Dr. Williams to his office, have a security detail observe him as he packs his personal items, and ensure that he is safely placed on the transport that will take him to his new assignment." "Yes, General", answers Rogers.

As Zeke Williams carries the single box containing his personal effects, walking down the long hallway toward an exit he has never seen before, he asks General Rogers, "I don't suppose you are authorized to tell me where I am going?" "You are being reassigned to another facility, Doctor." answers Rogers. "It is for your own safety, and for the security of the mission. We cannot take any chances that our research might fall into the wrong hands."

While Zeke knows he is being punished for knowing too much, he thinks to himself, "I guess it could have been worse; I could have been arrested, or worse." The security detail accompanies him to the waiting van in back of the facility, and when they arrive at the air base, he is transferred to a waiting cargo plane, and handed off to a waiting new set of security officers. The plane takes off immediately. One of the first set of security officers speaks into his microphone, "Subject is in route, General."

Back in General Green's office, Green and Rogers look warily at each other. "Did you find anything?", General Green asks General Rogers. "How much does he know, and did he tell anyone else?" General Rogers looks straight at her and answers, "Based upon what files it appears that he copied, he knows quite a bit. He spent quite a lot of time looking through files related to UNIPHARM and the Y12 project. He also accessed files related to the research on asexual reproduction, and the connection to UNIFEM. It is impossible to know which files he only read, and which ones he actually copied, but we must assume that he copied all of them."

General Green pauses, obviously calculating the damage that has been done, and asks, "Does he know about the common link between the ant DNA and the gene on the male 12th chromosome?" General Rogers takes a moment to look through the logs and replies, "It appears that he has opened that file recently."

General Green, still staring intently at the computer screen, says, "We need to find those copied files. Interview the other lab personnel." General Rogers answers, "Yes, General. I'll start with Henry Lee."

General Green had been scrolling through the

research data logs during the discussion, but now looks up and asks, "Do you think Williams has said anything to Lee?" General Rogers replies, "I don't know, but I'll find out." General Green states sternly, "It is essential that Henry Lee remain unaware of the link between his specific genetic makeup and the research he is conducting, not only because of the classified nature of the research, but because he is one of the study subjects." Rogers replies, "I am aware of that, General."

"Henry, I need you to come with me to the lab." commands General Rogers. Still seated at his desk, with his hands on the arms of his chair, Henry looks up at the General as he slips the storage drive Zeke gave him into his lab coat pocket. "Yes, General", Henry says as he rises from his desk and walks into the hallway.

As the two men walk down the hallway, Henry turns and looks back to see three security officers walking in. "What's going on, General?" Henry asks General Rogers. "Just being thorough." answers the General.

"Have a seat", the General directs Henry with a wave of his hand toward the chair in front of his desk. Henry sits down, crosses one leg over the other, and places his hands on one knee, fingers laced together.

General Rogers begins, "Henry, you've got a very promising future ahead of you. I want to remind you that your security clearance is very valuable and that it opens a lot of doors for you here, as well as other government and contractor jobs in the future. It would be a shame for anything as small as a backup copy of some lab files to destroy that future."

"I don't understand, General", Henry responds, his eyebrows knit tightly together. "What is it that you are looking for?" General Rogers, eyes unblinking, stares at Henry and answers, "Henry, what we are looking for is whatever information Zeke gave you. What has Zeke Williams told you about the projects?"

Henry, never looking away from the General's eyes, answers firmly, "General, all Zeke told me was that the second phase of the project was above my pay grade. He said that it had something to do with asexual reproduction." The General frowns and asks, "Anything else about that subject? Is there anything else you need to tell me?"

Henry, still staring straight at the General, answers, "No, sir." The General stands up and says, "Well then Henry, you are free to go." As Henry reaches the door, the General has one last thing to say, "But Henry, I can count on you to report anything unusual, can't I?" Henry stops and answers, "Yes, General."

General Rogers stands in the doorway of his office as Henry walks back to the lab. The security officers have cleared Henry's office and look toward the General. The head officer looks at the General and shakes his head, indicating that they did not find anything in Henry's office.

"General Green", Rogers reports. "Williams has spoken to Henry Lee about the project, but Lee will only admit passing statements about the general nature of the research. It does not appear that Williams shared any details with Lee. I do not think Henry Lee is a security risk at this time."

General Green, a frown growing on her face,

asks, "How does this affect our timetable with the civilian center?" General Rogers answers without hesitation, "At this time, since there is no evidence that Dr. Williams has shared his knowledge with any other personnel, it is my opinion that the project should remain on schedule."

The public announcement of the opening of the civilian center is to take place in the United Nations' General Assembly building, where dignitaries from all over the world will be invited to see the unveiling of the new center and the new battlefield simulation computer game that the Army has purchased and incorporated into the Y12 project. The sponsoring organization for the event is the United Nations Development Fund for Women (UNIFEM), the group that includes Vice President Rebecca Anthony, Geraldine Zoecker, CEO of Universal Pharmaceuticals, as well as General Green, among many of the world's business and government leaders.

"General Green, your plane is waiting", announces an aide who is accompanied by two security officers. She answers without looking up, "Very well. What time are we scheduled to arrive?" The aide looks at the itinerary and says, "You are scheduled to arrive at O one hundred hours." The aide holds the itinerary out for the General to take, but she walks past him without taking the papers. "Your hotel is only two blocks from the U.N., General". "Very good", replies General Green.

"Ladies and gentlemen", the presenter begins. "One World Warrior is the most popular online game in the world today. With over 50 million units sold through last quarter, it has replaced all other hardware and software gaming combinations ever produced, and is on track to double in sales each year for the foreseeable future."

On the screen behind the presenter is a wall sized screen, with video scenes from actual One World Warrior game play. Audience members, from pharmaceutical corporate executives, military brass, and academia, stare wide-eyed at the video being projected, only looking away to nudge the person next to them to comment on its realistic portrayal of battlefield situations.

The presenter continues, with the video behind her changing to scenes of what appear to be computer labs or classrooms, with rows of young men seated at special multi-screen computers, and with what appear to be helmets on their heads.

"And with the introduction of the new biofeedback equipment developed for use in the upcoming Systems for Optimum Learning education center, One World Warrior will become the most important field research tool for diagnosing and treating attention disorders, ever implemented."

After a strategic pause to wait for the applause to die down, she continues, "As is often the case, technology developed for military use finds a peaceful purpose in the civilian world. With the new One World Warrior Biofeedback system, not only will the free countries of the world be able to train soldiers faster and more safely, but both military personnel and civilians will receive the most technologically advanced assessment and treatments for what has become the number one mental health issue for young men;

attention deficit disorders."

After another round of applause dies down, the presenter adds, "We would like to thank the generous support of UNIPHARM, the world wide consortium of pharmaceutical companies and academic institutions, in conjunction with the U.S. Army, which has made it possible to place these new systems in the hands of all young people who can benefit from them. UNIPHARM has pledged to provide a system to each patient of the SOL Center at no cost."

Wrapping up the presentation, she adds, "The Systems for Optimal Learning Center will be opening in a very short time for new patients, and will immediately make these gaming systems available for patients in their homes when their residencies at the SOL Center are completed. This will not only present the opportunity to extend the benefits experienced while at the Center to the home, but will help make the entire system safer for all patients by monitoring compliance and continued effectiveness of the treatment, from uploaded game play results. Home use game play results of the One World Warrior system will be uploaded to the central servers, and will be analyzed to further refine treatment for future patients, as well as to make military training more effective and realistic."

As applause slowly dies down, the presenter finishes with, "We hope you have enjoyed the story of One World Warrior and the Systems for Optimal Learning Center. Thank you all for your support in making this dream become a reality."

General Green had been sitting next to Geraldine Zoecker, CEO of Universal Pharmaceuticals, and as the two of them stood to leave, they smiled at each other and shook hands. "The Vice President will be pleased." commented General Green. The UNIPHARM head smiled and replied, "We have taken a big step toward out goal."

Chapter 4.

The brighter red P. barbatus and the almost black P. rugosus are locked together, rolling around in the middle of the battlefield, each totally intent upon destroying the other, seemingly unconcerned with anything else around him. P. barbatus' jaws are firmly clamped on the other's front leg, while P. rugosus snaps at the other's antennae. They wrestle for position, each trying to gain enough leverage to be able to use his most dangerous weapon, his powerful stinger.

Their hard exoskeletons protect them against the sharp jaws of their enemy, but in a weak moment, if one lets down his guard, a weaker joint might be exposed to the efficient slicing action of the other. The loss of a leg, while itself not life-threatening, would almost certainly spell defeat and subsequent death in such a duel. Neither exposes any weakness, each being battle hardened and determined to defend his colony with his life. The fight drags on and on, through the hot afternoon. So single-minded in their purpose are the fighters, neither notice that the other members of their respective colonies have abandoned the battlefield.

Both are tiring. Their energy almost spent, each having been damaged by the other ant's fierce jaws, they take longer and longer pauses in the action between periods of frenzied fighting. The red ant knows that if he doesn't think of something, he will tire before his opponent. His darker, larger adversary has strong jaws and is beginning to find holes in his defense. Having been forced onto his back, Barbatus notices that the sun is nearing the horizon, and calculates his one opportunity.

Barbatus frees his two back legs and begins to push both of their bodies in a circular motion. When the rotation places the sun directly facing their heads, Barbatus strikes a violent blow to the black ant, forcing his head up, temporarily blinding him in the direct sunlight. In the split second that the other ant is distracted, Barbatus works his stinger into a gap not defended by his opponent's legs, and plunges it into the crease.

As the stinger pierces his abdomen, the black ant feels the searing pain of the venom entering his body. He fights back as hard as he can, causing the two of them to roll around faster and faster. The damage is done. the stricken fighter begins to feel weak. He loses his grip on Barbatus, and rolls over on his back. He feels sleepy, and it seems as if night is coming much faster than it should. He feels his legs curling up uncontrollably, and everything goes black.

Barbatus knows he should finish off his enemy. His instinct is to cut the other ant into pieces, first cutting off his legs and then cutting him in half with his powerful jaws. For some reason, one he can't explain, he knows he cannot execute this ant. Out of respect for the valor and strength of the fighter, or some other reason beyond his understanding, Barbatus leaves the paralyzed ant there on the open dirt of his now vacant colony and turns to go home.

The sun is sinking below the horizon. Barbatus is not able to move as quickly as he should, feeling the effects of the day-long battle. Still a long way from his colony, the familiar scent of the Queen's pheromone is very faint and difficult to distinguish from the confusing trail of the defeated colony. The Queen's pheromones tell the ants of his colony what type of food to gather, where to travel, who is a member of the colony, and as today, when to attack a foreign colony. He slowly traces the path, but the sun has set and night is coming.

The Queen controls the entire colony, and Barbatus knows this all too well. Barbatus is one of the few members of the Queen's Consort Council, which means that he was selected to mate with the Queen. It is quite an honor, for which he is proud to have been chosen. The honor subsequently became a dangerous obligation. Those males who mate with the Queen are soon not to be heard from again. Many die in battles or raids ordered by the Queen. Others just disappear. The unspoken story among the males is that if you are selected by the Queen, your time is short.

Barbatus has seen many of his contemporaries sent out on such missions, and not return. It seems that he is being sent out more frequently to more and more dangerous situations, almost as if the Queen intends for him not to return. Today appears to be one of those.

Earlier in the day, in the briefing meeting for today's mission, the Queen relayed her plan of attack. Maricopa, her formal title, Queen's Defender, began the briefing. "The Queen has ordered that we attack at sundown from the West, so that the sun will be at our backs and in our enemies' eyes". Barbatus thought to himself, "At our backs? Easy for her to say, since she will be nowhere near the battlefield." Attacking with the sun behind you is one of the most basic of tactics, but Barbatus noticed a problem on the large map of the enemy colony Maricopa had displayed at the front of the room.

He waited for an invitation for questions, and spoke out, "Sister Queen's Defender, the map indicates that our enemy's colony entrance faces the West. Will we not lose the element of surprise by attacking at their strength? Would it not be better to begin at sunrise, attacking from the East? We would then have the same advantage of coming in with the sun, while maintaining the element of surprise by coming in on the opposite side from their entrance."

Maricopa dismissed his idea, "The Queen has spoken. There will be no discussion. Prepare for battle." Barbatus, knowing his place and respecting the Queen, dutifully accepted the Queen's wishes for the timing and direction of the attack. He couldn't help but feel that something was wrong, and somehow knew that he would not come away unscathed.

As the attack party prepared to leave the colony, Meridiona, another of the Queen's trusted council of Sisters, asked Maricopa, "What about the objections raised by Barbatus? I think his argument has merit. We may be sending them to their death." Maricopa turned to Meridiona, smiled glaringly, and answered, "We can always make more."

The scent of the Queen's pheromone trail grows stronger as Barbatus nears the nest. The sun has completely set, and he knows that if he doesn't get inside soon, he may have to spend the night outside. "I know it is here", as the desperate warrior tries to reassure himself, but no opening can be found.

The entrance has already been closed for the night. Barbatus knows that he will have to face the dangers of the night alone. Quickly thinking to himself, "The colony we defeated today is no longer in their nest. I can spend the night there, and come back and report in the morning." Barbatus gathers his remaining strength, and returns to the abandoned nest he will use as his shelter for the night. He finds it empty, as expected, and climbs down into an open tunnel, collapsing in complete exhaustion, immediately falling into a sound sleep.

Slowly, the defeated black ant awakens from the empty battlefield. His head swimming, he tries to comprehend what has taken place. It is dark, and he knows he should be inside the colony nest. The once familiar scent that should lead him to the colony seems to be very faint, but he is able to find the trail. Weak from the battle, he limps his way inside the nest, finds a protected area, and curls up to rest.

The morning sun is now high enough to warm the nest entrance, and Barbatus starts to stretch his legs to stand. "Don't move", booms a loud voice from above. Barbatus tries to spin around and get up, but the large black ant standing over him has pinned him to the ground, open jaws ready to clamp down around his neck. "I said, don't move, or you are finished." Barbatus, realizing that this is the same adversary he spared the day before, angrily responds, "I knew I should have finished you yesterday."

"You are the one who defeated me?", growls the black ant. "Why did you spare me?" Barbatus responds, "Yes. I do not know why. In that moment, it seemed the right thing to do, but now it seems to have been a very bad decision. I let my respect for your strength and courage cloud my judgment, and now I must pay the price."

"Consider my debt to you repaid", the black ant barks grudgingly as he slowly backs away, releasing Barbatus from his hold. "I don't know if I would have done the same for you yesterday, had I been in your position. Whatever the reason, thank you."

As the red ant quickly jumps to his feet, he acknowledges his former enemy with a quick bow of the head, and turns to begin the trip back to his colony.

Chapter 5.

The television set in the hospital emergency room holds the attention of the handful of people waiting. The early morning sun creates just enough glare to make it difficult to see the screen clearly.

One man is holding a bloody shirt against his head, while his wife nervously glances back and forth from the reception desk to the televised news report. Another group, a family waiting for word about their grandfather who had collapsed earlier the previous evening, all sit in a row directly opposite the television monitor mounted high on the wall.

"Quiet, something's happened to the President", the father commands, slightly cocking his head from side to side, trying to get a better look, despite the glare. The family falls silent as their attention turns to the events unfolding to the world. The news reporter recounts the details known so far, "President Cole was taken to George Washington University Hospital Trauma Center early this morning, after having suffered an apparent heart attack. Hospital spokesmen have not released any details, other than that the President is in critical condition. We will continue to monitor the situation and will bring you updates when available."

The news reports had been repeating this same information all day, and rumors were building that the President might already be dead. The news reporter continues, "Vice President Anthony has been with the White House Staff since the first announcement, and has scheduled a press conference for 12:00 Noon, Eastern Standard Time."

"Shaw family?", the emergency room physician

asks quietly, scanning the room and stopping at the group assembled near the television set. "Here", answers the father, "I'm James Shaw, the grandson. Jim. This is my wife Diane, and my son Solomon. May we go in and see my grandfather?"

"I'm Dr. Harrison" the doctor replies in a practiced, hushed volume, designed to get a difficult message across quickly, while not attracting the attention of others nearby. "Your grandfather is comfortable, but I'm sure you know that his time is very close at hand. I think it is time for you all to be with him. The group walks quickly and quietly through the hallway leading to the room. "I will be in the next room, watching the monitors. Take your time, and let me know if you need anything."

The family circles the bed as the old man gazes through the hospital room window overlooking the empty field next to it. He turns back to face his family and smiles at them as they hold his hand. He looks at each one in turn, smiling even more deeply at Solomon.

He treasures the special weekends, holidays, and summers they had spent together, and wishes now that he had shared more about his family history with his family, but especially with his great-grandson. When he knew that his time was at hand, he had tried to tell all the stories about how his family had settled in the area, and the wild frontier times of his journey by wagon train.

He knew he was out of time now. There was one last story to tell. He gestures to his grandson to come near, and tries to speak. Jim, recognizing that he will need to come much closer to be able to hear, turns his head to place his ear next to his grandfather's lips.

For a few moments, he listens intently to his grandfather's words, then nods and steps back, placing his arm around his son's shoulders.

The tired, old man closes his eyes, and breathes in a long, deep breath, as if his lungs know it is the last time they will taste the sweet air. Holding his last breath for a moment, unwilling to give up this final possession of a long life, he finally allows an even longer exhale. Beginning almost as forcefully as the breath in, the sound gradually grows softer and softer, and eventually merges into the silence of the room.

Not yet fully understanding, Solomon asks his father, "May I go outside to see what Grandpa had smiled about?" His father smiles and nods his head. As the boy walks across the dusty field, he sees what appears to be a small sapling tree standing in the middle of the empty field. As Solomon walks closer, he can see that it is not a tree, but a living thing, standing straight and still, as tall as a man.

A dark, staring eye locks onto his eyes, and for what seems to be hours, nothing else exists, only the two of them. Suddenly, a great, gray bird leaps into the air, and with great sweeping strokes of its wings, creates a wind that forces him to take a half step forward, to keep from being pushed back. Solomon watches it fly into the distance, seemingly in slow motion, until it is just a tiny speck on the horizon. He remains frozen in that same spot, unable to move, trying to get one last glimpse.

"Solomon, it's time to go," his father says, standing next to the boy. "You've been out here a long time, what have you been looking at? There are ants crawling on you, for crying out loud". The father quickly brushes the large, harvester ants off of Solomon's pant legs, and quickly pulls them up to check for any on his socks. "Dad, I saw this huge bird, right here. It was standing so still, I thought it was a little tree. It looked at me. I could see its eyes, and he looked at me. It was almost like a person looking at me. As I walked up to it, it jumped up into the air and flew off. It was huge!"

"It sounds like you saw a crane or something like that", the father offers. "It was bigger than any pictures of any cranes I've seen, Dad", protests Solomon. "We'll go look it up later and see what it was", the father says as he guides his son back to the car.

As they walk, Jim Shaw turns to look back to the spot where his son had seen the bird, thinking about his grandfather's last words, telling him of a special chest, asking him to care for it, and to pass it on to his son. He wonders what is in that chest. "I'll go through the chest tomorrow, when we sort out everything in his house", he thinks to himself.

Chapter 6.

As Barbatus finds his way back to the colony, he notices that he doesn't feel as eager to join with them as he should. Something has changed within him. While he can still sense the Queen's pheromone trail, he is not drawn to follow it the way he was only yesterday.

Nearing the opening to the nest, he greets the guard posted there. The guard waves her antennae, challenging Barbatus as a member of the colony. He responds in the same fashion as always, in a hurry to get back and report yesterday's success to the Queen's Council.

Instead of welcoming him and moving aside to let him pass, the guard raises its abdomen and sprays the alarm signal. "Intruder!" she calls out, and immediately clamps down with her jaws on his front leg. Barbatus pulls free and quickly moves backward. Dozens of workers move in and snap at his legs. Instinctively, he keeps as many legs free as possible, moving farther away from the nest as he uses his jaws to free his trapped legs.

Barbatus turns and sprints away from the nest opening, chased by now up to fifty of his own colony members, all intent upon ripping him apart. In turn, one, two, or three ants at a time grab a leg or clamp down around his waist, trying to hold him back so that others could join in to destroy what they believe to be an invader. Fear begins to creep in, as he begins to understand how the colony's main weapon, sheer numbers, can be so deadly. He almost feels like a spectator, watching the process as he had done so many times before as an active participant.

A fast shadow of black flashes over him, and suddenly his legs are able to move. The jaws, and the heads that control them, are still firmly grasping him, but they are no longer connected to their corresponding attackers' bodies. Something had cut their heads from their bodies.

Without looking to see what had freed him, Barbatus slides and slings off the loosening sets of jaws, and turns and runs at full speed toward the tall grass, trying to put as much distance as possible between him and the now hostile colony. Only when he reaches the safety of the grass does he understand what has happened.

He sees a large, black ant, wildly swinging some sort of slashing weapon, fending off dozens of red ants, cutting them into pieces. As they die, the red ants release the chemical that sends the danger signal, sending their fellow defenders into a frenzy of attack. There is no organization or order, and the individuals run around attacking everything, plant and animal, without knowing exactly where the danger is. This gives the black ant the chance to slip away unnoticed, and he turns to take the same path Barbatus had just used to escape.

"Are you injured?", the black ant asks Barbatus. "No, not seriously" answered the confused former member of the red colony. "You're the one who spared me in your colony's nest. What happened, and why did you help me?" asked Barbatus. "I don't like red ants", said the black ant. "My name is Rugosus", he said as he bowed slightly and extended his antennae.

"I am Barbatus. Thank you for coming to my side. I doubt I would have survived alone. What is that you used to fight the attackers?" "I observed other animals fashioning weapons, and have found items that can be used to equalize the enemy's numerical advantage. With such weapons, I can defeat a much larger force. I had to do the same with my old colony. They tried to kill me, exactly the same way yours did to you."

"It appears that it is now I who owes you a debt", admits Barbatus to Rugosus. "Will you teach me to use such weapons?" "Yes, and we will likely need to use them often, now that we have no colony to protect us", says Rugosus, clenching his jaws.

"I am very hungry", complains Rugosus. "In the colony, we had to but only ask, and food was immediately provided. How will we find food?" Barbatus responds, "There is plenty of food in the colony, but it is too dangerous to return to either of our homes. Your weapons would help, but the colonies' numbers are just too great."

"I think I have an answer", says an ant who had been hiding and listening to the discussion, as he steps from the cover of tall grass into the opening where Barbatus and Rugosus are standing. The newcomer has a red head and thorax, and black abdomen, and speaks in terms the other two do not quite understand. "I am a member of Pogonomyrmex bicolor, but you can call me 'Bike' for short. I have discovered something that might be useful for getting food from the colonies you described. I had the same problem with my old colony, but I observed that if I roll around and rub myself on the fresh trail left by colony scouts, I am able to fool the colony guards and make them think I belong there. I have successfully been back into my own colony, and think that I can do it with others, but would like to have some friends go along with me to test it."

"So your colony rejected you, too?", asked Rugosus. "Yes", replied Bike. "It appears that if you are away from the colony for more than one or two nights, the colony's scent disappears, and you are no longer welcome." "That's what must have happened to me", says Barbatus. "It looks like we are stuck together for now. I think I know how we can use Bike's discovery to get a steady supply of food."

"How? Unless we find a fresh trail, we can't rub off enough to wear a strong enough scent to fool the guards", complains Bike. Barbatus observes, "The scent comes from the scouts' stingers. They constantly touch it to the ground when going to and from food and the nest. Can we extract the needed scent directly from the stinger, instead of the trail?"

"Yes, that would work, even better than rolling around in the grass", says Bike. "But how are we going to get an ant to agree to let us have the scent?", challenges Rugosus. "I think that's where you and your weapons come in.", answers Barbatus. "We capture individual scouts from the trail, and force them to provide us with the scent. We then apply it to ourselves and simply walk in and get whatever we need."

"But won't the individual ant then have the same problem as we do? Won't they be prevented from returning to their colony?", asks Bike. "That is possible. And if so, then they will have to choose to join us or go out on their own", Barbatus replies.

And so formed the group of rogue ants, each separated from their former colonies, sometimes by accident, sometimes being captured by the rogues.

When the occasional "liberated" ant tried to rejoin his colony, they were usually torn apart by their former family members. Some joined the band of outcasts voluntarily, some reluctantly, but all who remained vowed never to return, and to free as many others as possible.

As they joined the group, each ant was given a new name, either from their colony name or reflecting some unique individual characteristic. No one could remember exactly why the next to join, a brownish red ant with a quiet disposition, was named Patch. It could have been his colony name of P. Apache, or from the patchwork quilt design of the armor he had pieced together from seed husks. The armor is quickly adopted by all the members of the group, and its lightweight yet hard surface offers great protection during colony nest raids.

These first four use their new technologies to secretly enter colonies, avoiding detection, gathering food and adding to their group. With Bike's chemical expertise, Patch's armor, Rugosus' weapons, and Barbatus' battle training, the group gains in skill and daring, able to enter colonies almost at will. Barbatus admires the ferocity and warrior state of mind in Rugosus, and the latter respects the discipline and strategic thinking of Barbatus. This mutual respect will serve the group well.

Chapter 7.

Randy Runnels and his parents walk up the steps of the main Entrance of Greenwood Hills Middle School. The sun is setting, and the three shadows walking up the steps in front of them remind Turner Runnels, Randy's father, of some sort of dream-like creatures, stretched exaggerations of insects. Turner, a computer game company executive, was very athletic in his younger years, and his stride is still the long, loping one of an athlete conserving his energy for the big moment.

"One World Warrior", Turner Runnels' runaway success computer role-playing game, became so popular with not only the usual gaming crowd, but with active members of the military, that he recently sold it to the U.S. Army for use as a training simulator. He still runs the nationwide OWW tournaments, and is on retainer with the Army as a consultant.

Lane Runnels, a corporate attorney representing several major pharmaceutical manufacturers, assumes her correct place, deliberately several steps behind her husband and son, assuring she will never be seen as unfeminine by taking the lead, or as a simple housewife by walking with them, always confident that Turner will always look back and check to make sure she's not left behind. She wears the typical uniform of a female lawyer, a matching navy skirt and blazer, with just the right size and quantity of jewelry. She knows exactly when to smile, and at whom, without ever appearing to be playing any favorites.

Lane is first to extend her hand and greet Ms. Evans, Randy's Art teacher. "Hello, Ms. Evans. It's so nice to see you. Thank you for meeting with us at the Open House." Turner follows his wife's greeting with a smile and a firm, but gentle handshake, and they move into the classroom to discuss Randy's schoolwork. Randy, lingering in the background, looking through the windows facing the playground, seems to be searching for something in particular. He squints into the quickly dimming sunlight.

"Thank you for coming tonight", Ms. Evans offers, in a genuine, but cautious tone. "Randy is a great kid. He seems to really want to do well. It's just that he seems to have difficulty concentrating in class. He is always off in some other world when he should be paying attention to class lectures or completing an assignment. I'm worried that he may be falling behind, and don't want him to fall between the cracks."

"Randy has always had a little difficulty with sitting still", Lane offers, apologetically. "He's better than he used to be, but we really have to stay on him when he does his homework, or his mind will wander far away." Turner jumps in and adds, "As long as I sit right there with him, and make him stay focused, he can get his work done, but as soon as I leave him for a moment, when I come back, he's drawing some bizarre creature."

"Speaking of that", Ms. Evans says as she stands and moves toward the wall of student artwork, done in class specifically to show parents during the open house, "I wanted to talk to you about Randy's work. He seems to have a fascination with bizarre animals, dragons, monsters, and such. Does he draw these kinds of pictures at home?"

On the wall, about a third of the way down from

the top, near the right side of the class drawings, is one of a group of tall creatures. They appear to be exaggerated, elongated versions of some kind of insect, with a warrior-like appearance, similar to an insect version of ancient tribal warriors. There are about a dozen of these armor-clad warriors, standing on a mound of dirt rising out of the grass. They are all standing at attention, with grim faces and what appear to be spears and various weapons at their sides, and a teardrop is visible on the cheek of the apparent leader, in the center of the group.

Turner and Lane Runnels look at the drawing, then each other, and then the drawing again. "I like it", says Turner. "They look kind of like ants, but almost human. I've never seen him draw a group of them like this before." Lane doesn't say anything, but continues to study the drawing, as if trying to find something positive to say about it. She has never understood Randy's drawings, but has always humored him and praised him as a creative boy.

"Look at this", Turner says, almost laughingly, as he motions toward a blue ribbon, with "12" printed on it, tacked to the upper right corner of Randy's drawing of the warrior ants, "What is this for?" Ms. Evans answers immediately, in a quiet, stern way, "That is something the Principal has asked to meet with the two of you about. I've scheduled a meeting tomorrow afternoon. I hope the both of you can make it."

As the parents leave the classroom, the teacher returns to her desk, and looks through the stack of folders. Each folder contains documentation she has been collecting on students; students who have been exhibiting behaviors that she believes indicate they are candidates for a new program that her Principal recently discussed in a staff meeting.

She opens the top folder, and slowly looks through the detailed reports she has constructed; whole days of classroom observations, noting minute characteristics listed as among those being helped by the program's unique procedures. As she organizes the folder's contents, she grimaces as she sees the stack of dozens of drawings of what she has started to call "Ant People".

The teacher hurriedly walks down the long hall to the Principal's office, the folder under her arm. "Ms. Willingham?", Ms. Evans asks, hesitating at the door to the office. The Principal, raising her head from the mass of documents on her desk, replies "Yes, Ms. Evans?" The teacher walks in, extending her arm and offering the folder with the blue ribbon attached to the cover, "I have another one. His name is Solomon Shaw."

"It's all here. I've thoroughly documented the behaviors. Three full day chronological studies, six Anthony Scale reports, and these", Ms. Evans says in a disappointed but eager tone of voice, as she shows the Principal the drawings that have become the common thread with the boys. Ms. Willingham takes the drawings, and as she slowly shakes her head, says, "More of these ants. I'll contact the parents. Thank you, Ms. Evans. Good work."

"Hello?", Diane Shaw answers the phone, in the middle of a flurry of household chores. "Ms. Shaw, this is Principal Willingham at Solomon's school", announces the voice on the other end of the line. The busy mom thinks to herself, "Not again. I thought we were finished with trouble at school."

"Yes Ms. Willingham, what can I do for you?", she answers as pleasantly as possible. The Principal answers, "I would like to have you and Solomon's father meet with me here at school to talk about the details, but it seems that the problem is not getting better, and may be worsening." "Problem?" the mother asks.

In a slightly annoyed, yet practiced tone, the Principal replies, "Yes, the same problems with paying attention in class, his grades are still below his capability, he's still missing a lot of homework, and there are more of the..." "Drawings?", Ms. Shaw interrupts. "Yes. That. It indicates a problem that we have identified with other boys at school, and I would like to talk with you and your husband about a program that I think would really help Solomon. Do you think you both could come to my office tomorrow, just after school is out?"

"I'll need to confirm with Jim, but I'm sure that we can both be there", Diane answers confidently. "That's great", responds the Principal. "I know Jim has been reluctant to label Solomon in any way," the administrator says cautiously, as she thinks to herself, "I think he is the main problem, resisting the treatment that would help his son, despite all the evidence we have found and suggestions we have offered." She continues to the mother, "I look forward to seeing the two of you tomorrow afternoon then."

"Jim's not going to like this at all", Diane thinks to herself, as she hangs up the phone. "He was so angry at the school staff after the last meeting, when they had placed notes in Solomon's file, recommending he be treated for his attention problems. He actually made them close the folder and quit referring to the old notes. The teachers and the Principal were so angry with him afterward, they asked me if I would prefer a separate meeting with them, without Jim. I'm glad I refused, but they're not going to let this drop. I don't know how he's going to take it this time. He admitted that he feels like we are losing control of the situation, and that we may not have much of a say as to what happens with Solomon. I hope he's wrong."

Principal Willingham hangs up the telephone, and turns to her computer to log on to a website. The welcome screen of the site displays a brilliant sun logo, an artistic depiction in an American Indian style, with rays radiating up and out. The initials SOL are prominently featured in the logo.

As she types on the keyboard, Solomon Shaw's information is entered into their database. She has no way of knowing that this one boy, who she assumes will simply be another of the many she has referred for routine treatment, will actually be the key to ending the entire program.

Chapter 8.

Underneath where the heron had been standing, a three feet wide disc of earth, with the grass completely cleared away, is busy with the activity of the colony of harvester ants living below. The ants quickly travel in and out of the opening in the center of the circle, gently touching their antennae, reassuring each other that they are friends, and not enemies.

As the ants move away from the nest, they follow the trail left by the returning ants, leading them to the seeds that need to be brought back to the storerooms, deep in the cool caverns of the colony.

The returning ants tap the ground as they walk, releasing chemical markers from their stingers. Instinctively, they recognize their Queen's unique marker signature, following it back to the nest, and leaving a fresh trail for their fellow workers to navigate their way.

Holding a seed larger than her head, a returning worker wriggles past the crowd at the entrance, and begins the path down to the food storage cells. Down long, narrow, winding tunnels, slowly she makes her way to the protected main court of the colony.

The narrow tunnels make the colony easier to defend against invaders, but this far down, there is a greater need for room, and less danger from above. Leaving the tunnels, and moving into the cavernous interior of the main court, the entire city comes into view. Shiny columns of rock contrast with the concrete-like hardened earth, creating the Queen's city, Optera, a city rivaling Athens or Rome.

Optera is designed as a wheel, with the Queen's

main court at the very center of the wheel. Food storage areas and living quarters are at the ends of the spokes of the wheel. Between the walkways that form the spokes, are the areas that are the most important part of the colony, the nurseries.

The Queen does not need to move to manage her colony. Her Court Sisters bring her anything she needs and take any action she demands. All her energy is needed to produce the food for the young, and to produce the large number of eggs needed to keep the colony population stable.

To all outward appearances, the city seems to run itself. Every aspect, every task, seems to take place automatically, with each citizen of the colony instinctively knowing their exact role. But, it does not run itself. The Queen controls every action, even though she almost never leaves her court.

The Queen produces her own unique pheromone, made up of a combination of chemicals, known only to her and her closest Sisters. The exact ratio of chemicals in the colony's pheromone, or marker signature, is controlled by a combination of the foods that are chosen. The Queen decides what types of foods are to be gathered by worker ants, to replenish specific chemicals needed to manufacture and adjust the colony's marker.

Under normal circumstances, the marker signature should remain the same. An important aspect of the Queen's pheromone formula is that it is the determining factor in whether young will develop into female or male adults. Maintaining the precise ratio of female to male adults in the colony is essential. Deviating from the ideal ratio can be fatal to the survival of the colony. The Queen and her Sisters constantly monitor this ratio, and when the need to adjust the marker signature appears, the call goes out for the appropriate food source.

"Quickly, quickly, come on", instructs the storeroom supervisor. Theresiae, who has moved up from the lower position of storeroom food stacker to supervisor, knows that time is running out for the day. Nighttime is coming, and the storeroom is not adequately stocked as her Spoke Sister will expect. She knows that she will need to keep her Sister happy, if she wants to get the promotion to Nurse that she has been working toward.

All storerooms are divided into two sections, the majority of which are labeled as "F" foods, and a much smaller amount, labeled as "M" foods. While she is not quite sure of the significance of the two ratios, she knows that her Sister monitors the amounts of each throughout the day, and reports the levels daily in meetings of the Queen's Court.

"There seems to be an unusually high amount of "M" foods building up", thought Theresiae. "I wonder if I should say anything to Sister Seven?" She realized that would be a bad idea, and decided to keep it to her self.

"Call the meeting to order", announces the elder Sister, Meridiona, the Queen's most trusted advisor. Meridiona, her formal title being Supreme Queen's Sister, has been a citizen of the colony since the Queen began her reign, and she always makes a point of getting down to business as quickly as possible. "I would like today's Spoke Report. As usual, begin with percentages of total capacity, and then ratios, please. Around the table, beginning with Sister One."

The Sisters are dressed in very colorful robes dyed with extracts from the unique plants each Spoke is charged with collecting. As the Supreme Sister, Meridiona has her pick of any colors, and has selected a brilliant blue one for this Spoke Report session.

One by one, the Spoke Sisters report, "Spoke One is at 82% capacity, with a ratio of 8.9 to 1. Spoke Two is at 84% capacity, and a ratio of 8.7 to 1." Similar reports came from all eight Spokes, with most reporting in the range of 80-90% capacity, and ratios of just below 9 to 1.

The one exception is from Sister Seven. Her face is flush, almost matching the red cloth she wears, made from the seeds collected by her Spoke workers. As she prepares to report, she quickly checks the report a second, and then a third time, and softly begins, "My apologies to the Queen's Sister and the Queen's Court. I seem to have been given incorrect information for the Spoke Seven storeroom ratios. Send in my messenger to retrieve the correct information."

The messenger, a captured male from another colony, is dispatched to the Spoke Seven storeroom, to relay the message that corrected information is needed immediately. The Court continues with other business. "To speed things along, we will hold Spoke Seven's report until all other business is completed", says Meridiona, unsuccessfully concealing her frown.

The messenger tries to report to Theresiae, gasping for air between phrases, "The Court…", panting, "Sister Seven… ", huffing, "They say they need the correct figures for the Spoke Report. The whole Court is waiting for the numbers from our Spoke."

Theresiae looks at the report the messenger is carrying, and sounding a little annoyed, says, "These are the right numbers. I counted them myself. What is the problem? What are they looking for?" "I have no idea", whimpered the messenger, knowing that he would have difficulty escaping some of the blame for this apparent error, despite his innocence. "Wish me luck." The messenger turns to run back to the Main Court.

Chapter 9.

Shelton Tarver and Henry Lee near the end of their long drive across the miles of dry, flat lands between the research center where Henry works and the rest of civilization. Shelton knows only that this is a secret government project, and since he doesn't have a security clearance, he can only go as far as the circular drive of the front entrance, where he drops off Henry each time they complete their specimen collecting. Even then, the "Ant Man", as the guards have named him, has to show his credentials, and sign a log book, each time he delivers Henry Lee and their specimens.

The public face of this center is called "Systems for Optimal Learning" or "SOL" as it is more commonly known. The SOL Center has grown to be the largest, and considered to be the most effective treatment center for adolescent attention disorders.

Entirely subsidized by a consortium of the Department of Education, the Pentagon, and UNIPHARM, a public corporation whose sole function is to provide low cost or free drugs manufactured by its member pharmaceutical manufacturers, the SOL Center's free treatment program has quickly taken over as the leader in the treatment of young people with attention disorders. The vast majority of their patients are teenage boys, and almost all are referred by their public school teachers and administrators.

Combining the products provided by UNIPHARM's member manufacturers, with "One World Warrior", a battle simulation, massive, multi-player, online role playing game, or "MMORPG" as its players call it, the SOL Center claims a success rate of greater than 99% for those who complete their program. In addition to receiving treatment at the center, participants are given a free game system to take home.

The Pentagon has agreed to fund this part of the program for two reasons; one is that it provides them with ongoing data uploaded from each game played, valuable data in fine-tuning the simulators they use in actual military training, but an even more powerful justification is that they have found that players of the game are significantly more likely to enlist in the military than the general population. It is the most successful recruitment tool the military has ever used. The Army is the title sponsor for the game tournaments, and long lines of potential recruits are seen at each weekend's events.

"What exactly do you do with the ants?" Shelton asks Henry. "I know you're studying pheromones and ant communication, but what interest does the military have with ants?" "You know I can't tell you that", Henry replied with an annoyed tone of voice. He was just as annoyed with the secrecy involved as he was with Tarver's question.

Henry knows that Shelton would be fascinated with the results he has seen from the Army's use of his ant pheromone research, when used in the computer games used at the Center. The Army is particularly interested in how to use this technology on the battlefield. Ants can communicate their location, direction, and speed with only the neurotransmitters they produce. The Army is really pushing the technology as a way to defeat electromagnetic pulse weapons in the battlefield. But all of this is top secret, and even though he would really like to share it with one of the few people who would really understand and appreciate its significance, he cannot.

The SOL Center is closed to the public, except for the Visitor Center, which is in the front of the main building. Parents and other family members are allowed to visit once per week, Sundays only, and only after the patients have been through their first week of treatment.

Parents are led to a viewing area with special one-way glass walls during their visits, where they are able to observe their children playing the computer game, and interacting with other patients. By the time the parents are able to see their children in person, they are convinced that the center is helping in ways that could not be achieved anywhere else.

Watching her son for the first time today, Heather Davis, a single mom whose son Colton has already been here for two weeks, feels only a little better about how things turned out. She was absolutely against any kind of medical treatment for the behavior that her son's teachers and school Principal had tried to persuade her needed action.

She still thinks that they were wrong when they recommended treatment for such trivial behaviors, such as tapping his pencil, moving his feet at his desk, and squirming in his chair. "He's just a boy", she thinks to herself, still feeling as if she has failed her son, not being able to prevent him from being committed to this place.

"Ms. Davis", starts the white coat-clad Parent Relations advisor, who has quietly walked up next to Colton's mother. "Here are some documents and informational brochures for you to take home and read.

They will help you understand about the drugs Colton will be taking, as well as details about the game and computer we will be sending home with Colton when he is released in a few weeks."

"He already has a computer. He doesn't need another one. I can't afford that", she protests. The PR person replies in a well-rehearsed and comforting manner, "Don't worry. The entire treatment process, including the computer, the game, the internet access, and the ongoing medication Colton will take during his ongoing treatment follow-up, are all provided at no charge to you."

"How can you give all that away free?", she asked, incredulously. "It's simple", responded the advisor. "Treatment at and after the SOL Center is paid by your tax dollars, along with funding by UNIPHARM, a consortium of pharmaceutical companies. They consider the cost of the computers and medications as well worth the patient data they gather from the online gaming results."

"That's why it is very important for Colton to continue playing the game at home. He'll want to play twenty four hours per day, but you will want to limit his playing to the standard two to three hours per day weekday, and four to six hours per day on weekends, for a weekly total of eighteen to twenty-seven hours." "Twenty-seven hours?", objects the mother. "I'm not going to let him be on the computer for that long. That's like a part-time job"

The advisor gently counters, "Let me remind you Ms. Davis, that you signed a contract when you authorized Colton's treatment. In that contract, you agreed to follow the treatment protocols that the SOL

Center prescribed. We will be monitoring his use of the computer and game at home, and if he does not spend adequate time in his treatment, we will be required to reinstitutionalize him as a patient here at the center."

Heather Davis stands still, stunned into silence. "I have lost control over my son's well-being", she processes this danger in her head. "What can I do? I have to go along with this, or Colton will have to come back to this place. I can't let that happen. I'll just have to make sure that he does the minimum required to let him stay at home with me."

To the Parent Relations advisor, Heather forces a smile and says, "I understand. When can Colton come home?" The advisor looks at the chart and reports, "It looks like Colton is progressing nicely, but we have noticed a couple of things that will require a little extra time to address."

"What do you mean?", asks the mother. "It appears that he is exhibiting some self-destructive behavior at this time", the advisor replies with a look of disapproval. "Self destructive behavior? Like what?", asks Heather. The white-coat clad representative reads from the chart, "Colton is exhibiting self-destructive behavior, damaging the skin of his arms by picking at them with his fingernails. He appears to be doing this during his time on the computer, as a way of diverting his attention away from the game. Colton does not exhibit this behavior during actual game play, but only during cut scenes and inactive periods. Medication has been adjusted to address this issue."

"What medication is he taking, and how much?", asks his mother. "That is addressed in the materials you have now, but basically, they are combinations of NDRIs, or norepinephrine-dopamine reuptake inhibitors, and SSRIs, or selective serotonin reuptake inhibitors. We adjust the ratios of the two, based upon the data collected during treatments. We will continue to monitor and adjust the drugs after Colton goes home. This is why it so important that he participates in game play for the minimum amount each day."

"For example, when Colton was observed to be picking at his arms, the amount of SSRI to NDRI was increased. That seems to have helped, but will be something that will be closely watched over the rest of his stay here."

Heather looks at the clock at the same time as the advisor, and both realize that her visitation time is nearly over. Thinking to herself, "I don't feel any better about this than when I got here, but I have to put on a good face for Colton."

To the official, she smiles and says, "Thank you very much for showing me around and helping me understand what my son is going through." "You're very welcome", replies the advisor with a tight smile. "I guess we'll see you next week?" "Yes, and hopefully I will be able to take Colton home with me then", the mother said, half question, and half promise. "We'll see", comes the adversarial response.

Shelton watches as Henry gets out of the truck, an uneasy feeling growing in his stomach, as he wonders what purpose the government has for Henry's and his research. "I know Henry's a good guy, but I don't trust the government. I don't like the thought of my research going to a military use, but then how could anything they learn from ants harm people?"

"See you next week", calls Tarver as Lee closes the door with a shift of his hip, both hands occupied with the samples they collected today. "Yeah, see you then", answers Henry, and he turns and walks up the main promenade to the SOL Center entrance. As he enters the building through the public entrance, Henry passes the main security desk, which is invisible, hidden behind a dark glass wall, opposite the two-way glass that parents use to view their children. He turns to look at the wall as he passes, allowing retinal scan verification, while radio frequency receivers simultaneously read the chip in the identification card clipped to his lab coat, and a hidden door opens at the end of the hall.

Henry walks the corridor to the research lab, gently places the ant containers on a table, and sits down at his computer to go over the data collected so far. "Where's Williams?", Lee asks himself. "I haven't seen him for a few days. The last I heard about him was that he had been called into General Rogers' office. I wonder what happened in that meeting? I need to give him this storage drive that he gave me before he left the lab. I wonder what he meant when he said that I should make sure that no one else in the lab knew I had it?"

General Rogers, the head of the military communication research project, technically his boss, comes in at his usual time, coffee thermos in hand, to make an appearance and see if his main researcher has anything new to report.

General Clifton Rogers, one of the first medical doctors to make General, is a no-nonsense career Army man. He does not like the path the military has taken, being run by politicians with no combat experience, and by women who seem determined to take away any remaining power from men like him. But, he does not have the luxury of allowing such thoughts to get in the way of his duty. He is more than anything else, a soldier, and follows orders.

"General", Henry addresses his boss. "Morning, Dr. Lee", answers the General, straight-faced and expressionless. "Where is Williams?", asks Lee. "I haven't seen him in a few days, and we were supposed to go over my research and prepare the presentation for the committee's review next week. Do you know when he will be back?"

"Williams has been reassigned", relies the General, matter-of-factly. "You will be working on the remainder of the project solo. Now, you'll get all the credit, or all the blame", as he smiles in a dangerous way. "Did you talk with Williams any that day? Anything to report?", the General directs toward Henry. "No, sir", Henry answers, feeling a little dishonest about not mentioning the storage drive, but getting a bad feeling about what had taken place with Williams.

"I trust that you will have the report ready in time for the committee meeting", commands the General. Lee responds, "Yes sir, but I will need access to Williams' data. Where was he reassigned? I may need to ask him about a couple of things."

"That's classified", snaps the General. "You will be provided all the data you need for your report. The data is being vetted by the committee. This report is important; some big contracts hinge upon the success of this project. Make sure you verify the results from the game logs, so that we have good data for the committee meeting."

"Yes sir", Henry replies subordinately, then, to himself, "Something's not right." Williams had said that he had found some odd things in the research that didn't make sense, and that he was looking into it on his own time. "I wonder what he found, and if that got him into trouble. I think I need to be especially careful with whatever's in that data."

Chapter 10.

From ten feet off the ground, the long lines of ants going to and from the newly discovered food source in the forest move like blood vessels. Closer, the lines almost look like cars during rush hour on the freeway, end to end, no gaps between them. As the ants pass each other, they touch antennae, passing to each other the Queen's marker signature that identifies the members of the colony. In one quick touch, friends and enemies are identified.

A fork in the trail causes a break in the train of ants. Most are able to backtrack and find their way back. One male ant continues in the wrong direction, and is unable to find his way back to the trail. He circles, trying to recapture the marker "scent".

On the food trail, every few steps, his fellow ants touch their stingers to the ground, leaving the neurotransmitter roadmap to the food and back to the colony. Now, having wandered from the chemical trail, the lost ant casts back and forth, waving his antennae in a vain attempt to smell for some sign of the correct path.

From somewhere, a very small hint of something familiar tingles the base of his antennae. "Maybe this is the way", he thinks out loud. He quickly moves toward the scent. His pace quickens as he nears the opening in the grass. The tall grass makes it almost impossible to see more than a few steps ahead, but he moves steadily toward what he hopes will be the trail.

As he leaps from the grass into the opening, he realizes it is not the trail, but a small area of cleared grass. Disappointed, he drops his head and wonders how long it will take to get back. Something rustles in the grass around him, and he lifts his head. A single ant steps through slowly and stands just inside the clearing, directly in front of him. One by one, a dozen ants step into the clearing, and surround him completely. He anxiously studies these silent strangers, unable to detect any scent that would identify them as friend or foe. They do not seem to have any recognizable scent at all. He waves his antennae aimlessly, frozen in indecision.

The strangers do not look like members of his Queen's colony. In fact, they don't look like they are all from a single colony. They aren't even the same color. Some have rounded heads, while others have more square shaped heads. Some have eyes more to the front, and some were more to the side.

This group of ants seems to be a combination of representatives from many colonies, but they are all dressed in similar style, and all have weapons that appear to have been made in the same fashion, from similar materials. They wear body armor which accents and augments their natural exoskeletons. Their headgear appear to be helmet-like, while leaving considerable room for jaw movement. Each carries what appears to be a spear or lance or similar sharpened weapon, fabricated from one of two materials; some are made of crystal or glass, and others are shaped from salvaged metal shavings.

One ant steps forward. "You are no longer a member of your colony", he commands. "I am Barbatus." He slowly turns in a circle, gesturing with his arm for the lost ant to notice the group. "We were all once members of different colonies, but no more. You may join us, or you may leave. It is your choice."

The lost ant cocks his head, confused. "Why do you say I am no longer a member of my colony, if I am free to go?" Barbatus responds, "You will be free to leave, after we have collected specimens of your colony's chemical keys. We need the keys to be able to safely avoid being detected and attacked by your former colony. You will not be harmed, but you will no longer be recognized by your colony. If you decide not to remain with our group, I suggest that you not try to return to your colony. If you do, you will not be recognized as a colony member, and I'm sure you know what happens when your colony finds a stranger in its midst."

The stranger gulps, having seen the Queen's soldiers tear apart invading ants from other colonies. "Yes, but surely they will recognize me. All I have to do is find the trail. Will you help me find it?"

"We will take you to the trail, after we have collected the necessary keys from you. You will be free to return to your colony, but I strongly suggest that you reconsider. After a couple of days away from our colonies, we all began to notice that we didn't want to return. You will learn how to find your own food, and when you do not need the Queen's food, you will find that you want to leave the colony forever."

"I don't think so", protests the lost ant. "I want to get back to the colony, as fast as possible. Just hurry up and take what you need, and help me get back to the trail."

Bike, the group's chemist, approaches the lost ant. The ant with a red head and black body moves closer to collect the chemical keys from this latest donor. He takes a specially shaped metal sliver that has one side sharpened to a fine edge, and gently scrapes the stinger of the lost ant. Slowly, the liquid emerges and is collected in Bike's pouch.

"All finished", Bike says, flatly. Barbatus adds, "It's getting dark. We'll return to camp for the night and take you to the trail in the morning. Thank you for your help. I hope you'll reconsider and stay with us. There won't be much of a future for you with your old colony. Rugosus, please watch over our guest until morning." Rugosus, usually called upon as the enforcer of the group, firmly grasps the newcomer. "Come with me."

As he is escorted away, the lost ant thinks to himself, "There's a lot more of a future there than here. Ants belong with the colony and the Queen, not out here." The group moves quickly and quietly to their camp, only a few minutes away, near the base of a cedar tree, and settles in for the night.

The lost ant reluctantly settles in for the night under the tree, and asks Rugosus, "How did the others become members of your group?" Rugosus looked around the group and began to tell their individual stories.

"See that black guy over there? That's Schmitty, a member of a P. Schmitti colony, from the Dominican Republic. He came over on a boat in a shipment of lumber, and wandered on to a trail we were working one day. He and I don't get along. He thinks I'm lazy and dumb, and I think he's arrogant. He's a good fighter though, and I trust him completely."

Rugosus looks next at a dark brown ant from a P. Wheeleri colony. "Wheels, came from an isolated colony that arrived in a truck bringing produce from Mexico. When his colony was raided and destroyed by a P. Barbatos colony, we were watching and brought him in when he escaped the battle. We named him 'Wheels' because he's our fastest runner."

He then turned to a bright orange-red colored ant. "Naming Tex was easy. Even though he looks just like Barbatus except for the color, he came from a colony of P. Texanus. Tex is the most stubborn guy I've met, but he's a dependable fighter who can always be counted on to be first into tough situations."

"Banshee picked up his name as much for his fighting style as for his colony name, P. Comanche", Rugosus says, pointing to the reddish-brown ant next to Tex. "Comanche ants have a reputation as fierce fighters, and when we found Banshee, he was fighting off what looked like his entire colony with his scythe, swinging it in a wild frenzy. He was the most difficult so far to capture and bring in; he seems to have only an on/off switch. It's truly a thing of beauty to watch him remove opponents' limbs in single strokes."

Next, Rugosus looks over at a dark red ant named BA. "BA's short for BadAss. He came from a colony of P. Badius from Florida. BA ended up in a load of sand delivered to a school playground, and his colony was quickly destroyed by a P. Barbatus colony. He considers himself to be the best fighter in the group, but he is the only one. You'll usually see him finishing off already wounded enemies, but I can't remember ever seeing him attack alone."

Looking to the next ant, Rugosus continues. "See that dark brown one over there? That's Z, short for Zzzzz. He came from a P. Desertorum colony. He's our smallest and least aggressive fighter, and someone always has to wake him up from a nap. I think he's spent too much time in the sun."

"Then there's surfer boy, Cal.", Rugosus says with a smirk, pointing to a reddish brown ant, a P. Californicus that even looks like he has a dark tan. "Seems like every other word he says is 'dude'. He's a good kid, but he needs a lot of supervision."

Then Rugosus turns to Axe, a deep red, almost brown ant. "Last, but not least, Axe doesn't particularly like his name; he got it as a result of his being the most accident-prone of the group, and because it sounds a little like the name of his old colony, P. Occidentalis. When it came time for choosing weapons, it seemed natural that Axe picked an axe.. Everyone has learned to stay away from Axe when he carries his weapon."

Finished with the introductions, Rugosus now turns his attention to the lost ant. "Time for you to go to sleep. You've got a big day tomorrow." Rugosus sits with his back against the tree and watches as the guarded ant dozes off. As Barbatus trusted he would, Rugosus does not sleep at all, vigilantly keeping watch over their guest until morning.

Chapter 11.

Jim Shaw's grandfather's attic is caked with dust. Jim finds the chest his grandfather asked him to open. It has not been touched in decades, but opens easily. Gently removing each layer of its contents, he reverently lifts and sets aside each item; birth, marriage, and death certificates, old war rations books, ragged and faded photographs, assorted pen knives, and watches. Finally reaching the bottom, he uncovers a leather pouch decorated with beads. Jim examines the pouch and thinks to himself, "This looks like some kind of Indian artifact. Kind of cool."

He carefully opens the weathered pouch. Inside are dozens of drawings and handwritten documents on either old parchment or tooled into leather sheets. Most are drawings of what appear to be stick figure people; long and tall, with elongated limbs and what look to be armor and weapons. "They look kind of like ant-people", Jim thinks to himself." With them, are several drawings of large birds. "These look like what Solomon was describing that he saw earlier", he thinks to himself.

Then at the bottom of the stack of documents, is an old sheet of what feels like dried animal skin, but as thin as paper. Some kind of writing has been copied on to this skin, by scraping charcoal across its surface. "Looks like someone rubbed an old tombstone or something", he thinks, having watched people use this technique to record the names and dates from the old cemetery.

Beneath the papers, there is a stack of parchments, bound together by string. Jim unwraps the strings, and begins to look through the pages. Each page draws him more and more deeply into the story his grandfather wanted him to know. He reads the pages, one by one.

"My grandfather's name was Santana. He was chief over all the Comanche, when they were being pursued and pushed southwest by the U.S. Army. Their camps constantly moved, and the herds of buffalo were growing smaller. He knew that his people would not survive this fight, and decided to capture as many white people as possible, both as hostages, and to add to their numbers, to help preserve their heritage in any way he could."

"My father's name was Jim Shaw, the only child of Santana's marriage with one of these captive white women, named Lola Shaw. She had been young when abducted, and knew no other life. He and his mother escaped an ambush by U.S. Soldiers in which Santana and the rest of the tribe died, and joined the other remaining Comanche on reservations."

"Before Santana was killed, he asked one of his trusted warriors to make sure that his son was never harmed, and to teach him the ways of their people, including keeping the sacred records that had been passed down through generations of Chiefs. The most important of all, a copy of 'The Secret of The Ancestors' that had been copied by placing a thin sheet of animal skin on top of the original stone tablet, and rubbing it with the black coal from a fire. This is the only copy remaining of the tablet that remains with our ancestor, the ants."

Jim Shaw looks over at the document, and as

the reality of the age and importance of it begins to sink in, his hands begin to tremble. "This document could be hundreds of years old", his thoughts racing. "What did he mean by our ancestor, the ants?"

He returns to read from his grandfather's papers.

"This copy of our ancestors' history must be preserved, not only as a historical record, but because of the secrets it contains. The tablet was transcribed from The Creator's words, describing how Man first came out of the ground, then as they disappointed The Creator; all were destroyed except the ones who were obedient, who were saved by returning underground to live with their ant brothers."

"Each time Man would emerge to live above ground, the previous tablet was destroyed and a new tablet was written, to provide instructions as the essence of that generation. Each time, a corner was broken off of the original tablet, to ensure that no one person could ever know the entire code and recreate Man on his own. This corner contained the keys to the code, without which the remainder would be very difficult to understand. The main tablet and the broken piece were always held by two trusted ancestors, in two separate colonies, so that Man could never know of its existence. Only one man of each generation is trusted to hold a copy, and only to reveal it in the case of the existence of the ancestors is threatened."

"Should Man ever find the entire code, he will be tempted to play Creator himself, endangering both Ant and Man. There are few men who know of the ancestors; many knowing of them when they are young, but losing their faith and vision. For this reason, the secret is always kept in one who can see."

"The ancestors will know of the one who holds this copy. They will protect him and help him hide the secrets. He must help them keep the original tablet and the key safe, too. I do not know which of my descendants will be the one to read this and assume the responsibility of guarding the ancestors' secret. You will be reading this after I am no longer a part of this world, so I must assume it will be my son, grandson, or even great-grandson who will become the new human key."

"You will know if you are the next one, if you can still see the ancestors around you. Look at the drawings I made of the ones I have seen throughout my life. If you do not recognize them, if you do not dream of them, are not compelled to draw them yourself, then you must pass down this information to your son or grandson who still can see. You will know if he sees them, because he will not be able to stop seeing them."

"You will know I am with you, as my grandfather was with me, and his before him, by the appearance of a Spirit Helper, a Great Blue Heron. The Spirit Helper will appear on the day of my death, and will carry my spirit with him, for as long as we are needed. The ancestors will appear with this Spirit Helper, and you will know they are there to protect the secret and its holder. If you are not able to see the ancestors as anything but ants, you will know it is them by their appearance with the Spirit Helper. The holder of the key will always be able to see the ancestors, and will not understand about the Spirit Helper. Tell the story of the Spirit Helper, that it is one of your forefathers, sent to guide and protect the key."

Jim stops for a moment and thinks, "That was

the big bird that Solomon saw in the field. And the ants that were crawling on him, but did not sting him, must have been what this is talking about."

Jim reads the last sheet.

"Do not tell anyone other than the boy himself, not even his mother. The fewer who know of the existence of the code and its key, the safer the key will be. The safer the whole world will be."

"You have an awesome responsibility. Your son, and his son, and his son, will have this same responsibility. Much depends upon you, and them. I have faith that you will do what is required. Live long and well."

Jim Shaw sits in front of the chest, staring at the pile of documents for hours, wondering what to do next. As the sun begins to set, he slowly places all the documents and items back into the chest in the order he removed them. He carries it down to his car and places it in the trunk. As he starts the car, he thinks to himself, "I can't tell anyone about this. Solomon. He's the one. That is why he draws those figures."

Chapter 12.

The messenger quickly enters the Main Court and hands a piece of paper to Sister Seven. Her voice cracks slightly as she slowly addresses the Court. "I am certain a mistake has been made, and that it will be corrected immediately." Meridiona presses, "Sister, read us your report now, and we can hear your explanation tomorrow".

"Again, I am certain these figures are incorrect", says Sister Seven apologetically. "Just read the report, and we will make that determination, Sister", demands a now visibly angry Queen's Sister. "You are taking up valuable time that could be spent getting our storerooms up to maximum capacity. Get on with it."

"Sisters, I apologize for taking so much of your time. I am sure that this will all be easily straightened out by tomorrow. Here are the figures that we will be double-checking for Spoke Seven. I am happy to announce that we are up to 92 percent of capacity. Our workers have been doing an extraordinary job and I am very pleased with their efforts."

The Queen, obviously growing impatient, takes the highly unusual step of intervening in the Court meeting, "What about the ratios?" Sister Seven turns and softly says, "The ratio is 7 to 1. But I am sure that...", she begins apologetically. Gasps and comments among the other Sisters drown out the rest of her attempt to reassure the group. The Queen shouts, "Stop everything and recount Spoke Seven's stores immediately. I want a full report in one hour. If these numbers are correct, you know what we will have to do."

Meridiona quietly slips out of the Main Court, unseen by the Queen or the other Sisters. She moves quickly to Spoke Seven's storeroom, where a visibly shaken Theresiae is trying to find anything she might have missed in earlier counts. "Theresiae", she calls, "I need to have a word with you."

"Queen Sister", Theresiae replies mournfully. "I am terribly sorry, but I counted the storeroom contents carefully several times. I can't find anything that was missed. I feel terrible. I have worked so hard to be accurate and make the Sisters all see that I am a good worker and deserve to be promoted to Nurse. Now I might never be promoted. What will I do?"

"Theresiae, you do not need to worry", says Meridiona, attempting to comfort the shaken storeroom supervisor. "I need to let you in on a little secret. Can I trust you to keep it just between the two of us?" Theresiae nods with some uncertainty. "I can assure you that if you do what I ask of you, then you will not only be promoted to Nurse, but you will be given a special assignment and will be answerable only to me. If you successfully perform this assignment, I will be in your debt."

"Of course, Queen Sister", Theresiae responds reflexively. "Anything you ask of me, I will do." Meridiona begins her explanation, "Your numbers are correct. The ratios of M and F supplies have been different lately, haven't they?" "Yes, I noticed that we have much higher M supplies than normal", Theresiae replies, beginning to feel better about her inventory skills.

"I knew of the change in your supplies ratio",

the Queen Sister further explains. "In fact, I was involved in the change. There is a reason why the ratios are controlled so carefully. The survival of the colony depends upon it. Lately, however, there have been some elements of the colony leadership that have decided that we might be better off by lessening our dependence upon males born to the colony, by replacing them with captives from raids on other colonies. I know this to be a dangerous way of thinking, one which might threaten the very existence of the colony."

"What can I do, Queen Sister? I am just a storeroom supervisor", Theresiae questions cautiously. "You will be a good nurse, won't you?", asks Meridiona. "I think I will. I will try to be the best Nurse I can be", promises Theresiae. Meridiona steps closer and becomes more serious, "I will need the best. Now that the whole Court knows about the ratios in Spoke Seven, big changes will take place. You need to be ready. The task I have for you is a dangerous one, for yourself, for me, and for one other. Will I be able to count on you?" Theresiae nods and says, "I am your servant, Queen Sister."

"Sister Seven," the Queen Sister asks at the next day's Court meeting, "do you have your revised report?" "Yes, Queen Sister", Sister Seven replies shakily. "The numbers we were given yesterday were actually correct. The ratio in Spoke Seven is in fact, seven to one." Murmurs around the table rise and then fall, and the Queen herself speaks, "We all know what this means. Beginning at daylight tomorrow, all male nursery residents two weeks of age and younger will be removed from the colony." Even quieter murmurings fade to silence as the Sisters let the action to be taken sink in. "Any questions?" asks the Queen. All around the table, each Court member shakes her head, knowing what is to take place.

"Queen Sister", Theresiae greets Meridiona as she enters her residence quarters. "What will you have me do?" Meridiona slowly seats herself and begins, "The ratios of M to F foods has been altered for some time now. I knew this was taking place, and was a part of the decision to allow it to happen." She continues to explain to the confused Theresiae, "Because of this change in the ratio, the Queen's eggs have been assigned a greater proportion of males being born than usual. As I will explain to you later, this is not the problem it would seem, as our male population has been dwindling to abnormally low levels, and some of us think that this step is necessary for the survival of the colony. The Queen and most of the Court disagree, and have decided that all the young males born in the past two weeks must be cast out of the colony."

"What do you mean, 'cast out', Queen Sister?" asks Theresiae. "They will be killed", replies Meridiona solemnly. Theresiae sits silently for a moment, weighing the thought of what will occur. "I have brought your assignment with me", and Meridiona gently unwraps a two week old male ant larvae. "I can only save one, and I need you to watch over him and make sure he is well cared for. This is your first nursing assignment."

Meridiona pulls something else out to give to Theresiae. It is a corner, broken off of a stone tablet, with ancient text carved into it. "Keep this with the young one, at all costs. It is the key to our existence. No matter what happens to me, or to you, the young one, and the key must remain safe. Do I make myself clear?"

"Yes, Queen Sister" replies Theresiae, the weight of her responsibility beginning to take hold. "I will not let anything happen to either of them."

"The Queen demands your presence", booms the voice of the guards that have accompanied Maricopa. "Come with me now." Meridiona knows full well what is about to happen, and quickly shoves Theresiae out a secret exit she has prepared for this inevitable outcome. "Go, now. Quickly, you must find a safe place for the young one and the key. You will not have much time."

As the guards take Meridiona to the Queen, Theresiae frantically searches for a safe place to hide the young one and the stone tablet corner piece. She does not know why the piece is important, but knows that it must be if the Queen Sister charged her with keeping it safe.

She can sense the guards approaching near. Quickly, she fashions a basket of dried grasses, and places its precious cargo in a swiftly moving stream, heading downwind from the colony, so that its scent will not be as easily detected. She watches it float downstream for a few moments, and then hurriedly heads back toward the colony. Before she reaches the entrance, she is met by her arrest party.

Theresiae joins Meridiona, already standing in the Queen's Court. Meridiona is in the center of the Court, and Theresiae stands behind her, in a back section. The Council has been debating their fate, and has reached a verdict.

Maricopa addresses the Queen's Court, "The Queen has reached a decision. The Supreme Queen's Sister, and the Spoke 7 Supervisor are to be executed, immediately."

Meridiona turns to look at Theresiae, asking with her eyes for assurance. Theresiae nods her head, and the doomed former trusted advisor to the Queen breathes a sigh of relief.

"Let this sentence serve as an example to anyone who would consider other treasonous acts against the Queen", warned Maricopa, with a sneering smile on her face. "Remove these traitors from Optera, and eliminate them."

The two were treated as any common trespassers, and were swiftly dispatched and left outside the colony. Neither said a word, and no one in the colony knew about the young male that was saved, or the key that accompanied him.

Chapter 13.

"Madame Vice President", calls the Chief of Staff, "I think it is time that we formulate our message to the Press, and the American People, as to what has happened, and what will take place next."

Rebecca Anthony had not calculated this exact path to the Presidency. As Lawrence Cole's personal physician for many years before he ran for President, Vice-President Anthony had the White House in mind, but not quite this way. As she prepares to address the American public with a national television and radio address, her main concern is how to protect the former President's reputation, but even more importantly, to make sure the real cause of his death is never revealed. If the facts were to become known, not only would she be suspected of some personal involvement in a medical "coup", everything she had worked for her entire professional life would be jeopardized.

"The first thing that must be done is that the President's medical records must immediately be moved to secure storage at the Y12 complex. His treatment history must be protected at all costs. Absolutely nothing can ever be shown to link his death to his treatment. I will not allow the media or our administration's critics to defame our honorable President by publicly changing his legacy from hero to psycho."

As she prepares for the most important speech of her life, and possibly the most important one in the history of the country, she weighs each word intended to calm the American people, reassure business leaders, and dissuade enemies and potential enemies across the world from taking advantage of this brief moment of chaos. She vows to herself not to let the remaining testosterone-filled dictators and religious opportunists turn back the clock on everything she and her coalition have built. "The world is forever different", she thinks to herself, "and I won't let them screw it up again."

Had anyone else other than Lawrence Cole been President for the past six years, Rebecca Anthony knows that she never would have been able to accomplish all the work she has completed. Her life's ambition has been to further the goals of her youth, of reducing violence and war and hatred in the world. She has always known that if she could find a way to get more women in positions of power, that the world could avoid repeating the errors that caused so much pain and suffering throughout history.

As a prominent physician, then Governor Cole had selected her to be his personal physician. Her research into the relationship between childhood attention deficit disorders and adult aggression had made her a polarizing figure, but in this particular situation, a little known secret catapulted her into the circles she so desperately needed to be a part of to accomplish her dream.

With the help of the heads of several international pharmaceutical corporations, influential academics, and now with her well-placed contacts in government, she has been instrumental in the formation of a coalition of the three into the SOL Center, chartered to provide medical and psychiatric care, behavior modification, and biofeedback training to children suffering from learning disorders.

The SOL Center is only a small part of a much larger, secret government research facility, known only as Y12. No one outside of the President and her staff, and top military and National Security Agency (NSA) brass knows exactly what all takes place there, but what is known among those with proper security clearances is that the military is the primary benefactor and beneficiary of the research conducted at Y12. Unlike most other secret government buildings, Y12 has never been photographed. Even satellite photos have the facility removed before public release. The SOL is now a great public face to put on a very elaborate and secret operation being undertaken, hidden deep underground in the Y12 research labs.

Before being asked to run as Lawrence Cole's running mate, Rebecca Anthony had worked her way to the very top of education research and reform. First as a Psychiatrist, and then as a PhD in classroom structure and gender bias in education, she authored several definitive textbooks used by university education degree programs, and was highly sought after as a speaker to groups on education.

Her "Anthony Rating Scale" has become the most frequently used tool for identifying potential attention deficit disorders. The fact that over fifty percent of all boys given the test show signs of attention deficits severe enough to warrant psychological or psychiatric treatment, only serves to strengthen her arguments about the male condition.

President Anthony owes a considerable amount of her current power to national and international women's rights organizations. Her first exposure on the national scene had been as a spokesperson for world health issues for women for both the National Organization for Women (NOW), and for the United Nations Development Fund for Women (UNIFEM). In this role, in addition to meeting other women who felt as she did, that most of the world's problems had been caused by men, the groundwork had been laid for a basis of power, without which, none of this would have been possible.

"We are so close now. I can't let anything stop the work that has been done so far." She fears that she might not be able to reach her goals, while balancing them with running the country.

What very few people know, and what must continue to be kept secret, is why President Cole had turned over so much control of his administration's work on education and health care. Not only did he trust her with his personal health, he needed her for his political survival.

Governor Cole might never have become President Cole, had it not been for Rebecca Anthony's recognition of his depression and attention problems. All his life, he felt lucky not to have been discovered, but constantly feared that his condition would be made public. By asking Dr. Anthony to become his personal physician, not only did he have the best medical treatment available, but he also insured that she would help to protect his secret.

When Vice President Anthony was placed in charge of a proposed national education reform plan, she excitedly set out to initiate her plan. Her efforts were severely attacked by the President's critics, and every proposal was destroyed in the media and in back room meetings. She knows she can never trust the male dominated legislative branch of government to do the right thing. She was determined to find another way.

A chance meeting at a UNIFEM conference with the U.S. division head of an international pharmaceutical conglomerate, set in motion what would eventually be Universal Pharmaceuticals, or UNIPHARM, a Swiss-based corporation, fully funded by the major international pharmaceutical corporations. UNIPHARM's mission statement is "Universal access to health through universal access to medicine". The unstated goal of UNIPHARM is to monopolize the world market, by securing legislation in as many countries as possible, promising free medication for participants in its sponsored programs. The cost to end users is free, but its member manufacturers are compensated by insurance companies, subsidized by government health systems, and partially funded by the military in several major countries. In exchange for the free drugs, UNIPHARM receives automatic fast track approval by any regulatory bodies. UNIPHARM conducts its own safety trials, providing results to these regulatory agencies. Questions have risen in the past about the accuracy of the results provided, but the public acceptance of the program has outweighed any concern over potential harm.

As more meetings took place, and more professional women were brought in, Vice President Anthony began to see the way to accomplish her goal, not by forcing people to submit to treatment, but by offering a way to get exactly what they want, without having to pay for it.

She received assurances from pharmaceutical companies that necessary drugs could be provided, at no cost to patients, in exchange for the research value their medical histories offered. Streamlining approvals of new drugs would not only help offset the drug companies' costs, but would help more people, faster.

That was the arrangement that ended up costing President Cole his life. As a patient of Dr. Anthony and the SOL Center, Lawrence Cole received drugs that might not otherwise have been approved. The Vice President had confidence in the pharmaceutical companies to provide safe, effective drugs, and the President trusted his physician. Everything was working well, until the President began experiencing chest pain.

It was chalked up to a genetic defect, even though there had been no history of such a defect in his family. SOL researchers knew of the risks associated with the new drug, but had downplayed the risk to the President.

The delicate balance among scientists, educators, physicians, and military planners all hinges on the safety and mass adoption of SOL Center's programs. Now the President is dead, and everything is at stake.

The new President barks out to her Chief of Staff, "Get me the Y12 people on the secure line. We need to move up the schedule. It has to go live, ASAP." "Yes Madam President. Already on it", she quickly replies.

The Chief quickly goes through the courtesies of weather and family with the General in charge at the Y12 Center, and then in a deliberate tone and cadence, orders "We are going live with the tournament this weekend." "Yes Ma'am. We'll be ready", was her immediate answer.

As the Presidential motorcade enters the side entrance of the Y12 complex, General Helen Green, recently appointed by the President herself as the new director of the research arm of Y12, walks down the corridor to greet President Anthony.

"Welcome Madam President", the General says, saluting her superior. "Hello, Helen", replied President Anthony, extending her hand. The two women shake hands, and turn to walk down the corridor to the main research center.

"Do you have any news for me?", the President asks. "Yes ma'am. We are ready to go live, pending your approval", replied the General. A slight smile creeping over her previously stern face, the President sets the agenda, "Let's see what we've got."

Entering the research center, Secret Service detail flanking the two and entering first, General Rogers is standing at attention, awaiting their arrival. "Welcome Madam President", the General offered stiffly. General Green introduces her second in command, "Madam President, this is General Clifton Rogers, head of our Battlefield Communication Project." "Good to finally meet you, General", the President offers politely. General Rogers replies, "All of us at Y12 are eager to get started with the project. Come, let me show you the research center and explain what we are doing."

"Let me introduce Dr. Henry Lee. He is our top research scientist. Dr. Lee was brought in for his expertise in ant communication, which is the core of the project." "Good to meet you, Dr. Lee", President

Anthony says, looking at the scientist only briefly before looking behind him at the activity at the back of the room.

"Let's begin the demonstration, shall we?", asks General Rogers. "Dr. Lee, please give us a brief description of what we will be seeing." Henry Lee takes a deep breath, smiles, and even though he has been eager to see the results of the all his research, he wishes he didn't have to be the one to present it to the President of the United States.

Henry begins, "Madam President, the entire Y12 team has been working hard on the Battlefield Communication Project, and even though there is still work to be done to finalize it, I am happy to announce that the system is ready for beta testing." Henry thinks to himself, "If it were up to me, I wouldn't allow it to be tested yet, but I don't call the shots."

"Dr. Williams, who is no longer at Y12, was instrumental in the development of the 'Ant Colony Algorithm'." Henry still wonders to himself, "Williams should be here presenting this. Not only is he more comfortable speaking to dignitaries, it's his research. I don't know why I'm presenting this stuff. I haven't even finished reading through all the material he left me on that storage drive. I've still got to figure out what to do with that."

"This 'Algorithm' is further described as a 'solution for combinatorial optimization problems'. Henry sees the slight look of confusion and disapproval on the President's face and adds, "In other words, how ants organize themselves for defense and finding food."

Seeing her face soften a bit, evidently grasping this concept, he continues, "We have learned how to combine modified ant pheromones with behavior modification techniques in battlefield simulation computer games to develop a virtual 'Swarm Intelligence' technology, which is nearing readiness for deployment in real time. With adequate training, and pharmacological neurotransmitter modification, soldiers in the field exhibit 'microbehaviors', which are recognized and communicated to and from each other, without the need for the previous implanted microchip technology, which was subject to EMP, or electromagnetic pulse weapons."

The President interrupts, "So what you're saying is, soldiers can think and know where the other soldiers are." General Green steps in at this point, "Exactly, but even more, they know where the enemy is, and can relay this command and control information back and forth between a command center and the field. Dr. Lee, from this point forward, the content of the conversation is classified. Will you excuse us please?" Henry leaves the room and enters the network operations center, on his way to the game observation room.

"Do you have any questions, Rebecca?", asks General Green. "Only one, Helen", the President replies. "How far away from each other can players of the game communicate?" The General replies, "So far, we have seen results of up to 100 yards distance between players, with a high degree of accuracy. With appropriate troop deployment patterns, and adequate numbers, there is no reason why we will not be able to receive communication from the entire grid on a continual basis, in real time."

"OK. That's what I was waiting to hear. It's time to put the program into effect", commands the

President. "Yes, Madam President", answers the General. "Are we a go for the tournament this weekend?" President Anthony smiles and answers, "Yes. We are go for this weekend."

Chapter 14.

The chemical keys taken from their most recent visitor, a member of a nearby P. Barbatus colony, has allowed Bike to formulate a pheromone that will allow the group to quickly get in and out of the colony, and collect some food. Barbatus has an additional goal in mind for this raid, one which he will soon share with the others.

"You are free to go", announces Barbatus, to his distant relative. Being from another colony of P. Barbatus himself, he knows both the desire to rejoin the colony, and the desperate feeling of abandonment this newly freed member is destined to feel when he tries to return to his colony.

"We will accompany you to your colony. I suggest that you stay with us at first, until we see whether or not you are accepted by them. We will try to rescue you if they do not." The newly freed colony member silently tells himself that he will run as fast as he can, as soon as he gets back with his fellow colony members.

Bike lays out the plan for using the chemical markers, "Apply this generously, all over yourselves. This one is the identifying pheromone for the colony we will be entering. This will allow us to go in undetected, being treated as any other member of their colony." The group's chemist then holds up two other batches he has concocted, "This one is of from a neighboring colony..."

Barbatus interrupts, "I need two volunteers to take it to the back entrance to the colony, and break it open inside, to distract and confuse them. This will buy us time to get in and accomplish our mission, and escape."

Tex steps up "I'm in." "Sounds like fun", chimes in Banshee. Barbatus smiles approvingly and adds, "Make sure you see Patch to secure your armor, and check with Bike about the details on the chemical keys. You don't want to mix them up..."

Before Barbatus finishes his warning, "Dude, what's in the other one?", asks Cal in his usual laid-back manner. Bike answers with, "That's a little something I came up with to give the Queen. It will alter her food gathering instructions for the colony, so that they will gather more of the foods that stimulate a higher percentage of male eggs."

Barbatus follows this explanation with further instructions, "Rugosus and I will take this batch to the Queen. This is the primary objective for the mission." "What about the food gathering part?", asks Z, apparently waking up from a quick nap. Obviously a little annoyed, Barbatus returns with the rest of the plan, "Z and Cal, as our more 'reserved' members, you will remain here, just out of sight, and be ready to help us as we exit the colony. Take out any colony members that might return."

"Axe and BA, you will remain at the entrance as the rest of us go into the colony. Make sure no one follows us in, and be ready to take out any defenders that follow us out." "Finally, I get some action", says Axe, thinking to himself that he needs this opportunity to prove to the others that he is not nearly as accident-prone as they think he is. BA has to add, "Just stay out of my way, Axe. I'm going to be busy." Despite his outward bravado, BA secretly hopes that he doesn't have to fight off any colony defenders.

"Enough, you two", Barbatus chastises. "Wheels, Schmitty, don't leave Bike and Patch behind. You four go straight to the food storage rooms and grab as much as you can carry. There are fewer of us available to carry food this time, so you faster ones need to really load up to make up the difference."

"Most importantly, leave no one standing on the way out, so you will not be followed. The injured colony members' alarm pheromone will cause the others to come to their aid. You will need to act quickly to avoid capture or..." Barbatus lets those words sink in to the group.

Minutes later, the group of outcasts is marching toward the colony of their visitor. They approach the back entrance from the East, using the bright light of the rising sun to avoid being seen by scouts. Barbatus announces the plan, "Tex, Banshee, give us five minutes to circle around to the main entrance. We'll wait until the enemy pheromones have their effect, and then we'll go in."

The raiding party stands just beyond the view of the main entrance's guards, waiting for the reaction that they hope will come from Bike's chemical cocktail. At that moment, the ant who had given them the chemical keys, the member of the colony they are watching, the one who is moments away from finding out if he will be accepted back in or be forever banished, can wait no longer. "Not yet!", yells Barbatus, but it is too late. The escaped colony member is already in the clearing and nearing the main opening.

He approaches the guards confidently, touching antennae with each one. For a moment, it appears that he is safe, home. As he passes the main guards, someone sprays the call, "Intruder!", and soldiers immediately swarm the entrance. In seconds, mandibles rip legs from thorax, and stingers plunge into what is considered an enemy. The group watches from the tall grass, as he is cut into pieces and carried away from the entrance.

"Told him" said Rugosus, muttering. Barbatus responds, "That may have jeopardized the mission. Too much attention at the front entrance. We'll have to wait and see if Tex and Banshee can create enough of a distraction to draw everyone to them at the back. It will be dangerous for them, but they can handle themselves."

Tex is slightly in front of Banshee as they walk up to the guards at the back entrance. The two approach slowly but confidently, acting as if they belong there, touching antennae and quickly moving toward the entrance. The guards seem unsure about them, with their odd coloring, and their body shapes altered by their armor, but they sense no danger. Tex and Banshee continue inside the colony's back entrance, where no one is around.

As Tex opens up the package containing the pheromone of the enemy colony, Banshee takes his scythe out of its sheath, and holds it head-high, ready to swing. Tex breaks the container, releasing the pungent odor of the enemy colony's pheromone, and the two raiders run for the entrance.

Dozens of guards run in from the back entrance, reacting to the intruder signal. Most ignore the two raiders, but as Banshee and Tex near the opening to the outside, guards begin to focus on them as the problem.

Quickly, efficiently, Banshee swings his scythe in circular motions, slicing ants in two, lopping off legs, and decapitating the rest. Tex lunges at the rest with his forearm-length knife and, spinning like some sort of Texas twister, finishes off those who remain in the entrance with his hatchet.

The two are outside the colony now, and they run full speed toward the designated rendezvous location. One last guard grabs at Tex, and with a whoosh, Banshee's scythe ends the threat. They wait for the rest of their tribe, catching their breath, and nursing a few minor wounds.

The front entrance appears empty now. "Tex and Banshee must have either done their job, or they're dead by now. I don't see any guards at the front", Barbatus says grimly. "It's time." The six main marauders leave their two friends in the taller grass, and quickly move across the clearing to the main entrance.

"Give us two minutes, and then return to the rendezvous point", Barbatus says to Axe and BA, now positioned at the entrance to the colony. "Here is where we split up. Wheels, Schmitty, Bike, and Patch, get all the food you can and get out. Rugosus and I will plant the package with the Queen, and we'll meet up at the stream. Don't wait for us."

Barbatus and Rugosus turn to go down toward the Queen's chamber, while the four food gatherers head hurriedly toward the food cache. The food is close to the surface, and they quickly load up with as much as they can carry, and return to the opening. Two minutes have come and gone, and as Axe and BA see their four friends carrying food emerge, but not seeing the other two, BA says excitedly, "Barbatus said two minutes.

We should go." Axe angrily responds, "I'm not leaving without Barbatus and Rugosus. You go ahead with these four to the stream." BA immediately answers, "I'm not leaving you here by yourself. I don't want to miss the chance to knock heads with these guys", even though he feels a little shiver go through him at the thought of it.

Rugosus is in front as he and Barbatus go down the tunnel to the Queen. They encounter no guards, until they reach the main chamber. Even then, Bike's masking pheromone seems to be working, and the guards seem to pay no attention to them. Barbatus pulls out the payload and places it in front of the Queen. She notices the new item in front of her and hungrily eats it without pausing between courses.

The two quickly turn and retrace their path to the entrance. By the time they reach the main fork in the tunnel, colony guards have noticed that food is missing. "Protect the Queen! Kill the intruders!", goes out the call among the guards. Dozens swarm toward the main entrance, just as the two can see sunlight from the opening. "Here we go", warns Rugosus, as he shifts his weapon in his hands for a better grip. It is as long as he is tall, with a sword-length blade atop a long pole handle. Barbatus remembers how he first saw Rugosus swinging his hand-fashioned weapon, saving his life. He had since asked Rugosus to make him a similar weapon, and also tightens his grip on his own.

Both sprint toward the light, spearing guards blocking the entrance. When those behind them do not fall, stopping momentum, the two warriors face opposite directions, slashing, tripping, and stabbing everything that moves in front of them. They move closer to the entrance, tripping and stumbling over fallen guards, stepping out of the grip of dead defenders' jaws.

As they reach the outside air, Rugosus has to duck to avoid Axe's wild swinging of his weapon. The guard behind him does not duck, and his head falls to the side. BA stabs the headless corpse, and backs away. Several more guards fall prey to the swinging axe, and BA darts in and out, cutting off limbs and stabbing those fallen.

"Move!", yells Barbatus, running full speed with Rugosus. BA needs no prompting, already running alongside. Axe, chest heaving from his effort, takes a moment to let it register, and then joins them. The four quickly move across the clearing into the taller grass, and realizing all are accounted for, head toward the stream where the others are hopefully all waiting.

As Barbatus steps from the grass onto the sandy beach of the stream where the others are waiting, he does a quick count in his head, "one, two, three,...twelve." "Everyone made it. Good." Rugosus adds, "All except that guy who decided he wanted to rejoin his colony. I guess he joined them after all." "We can't afford to lose anyone", Barbatus griped, narrowing his eyes.

There are a few minor nicks and cuts, but for the most part, the group's armor and weapons did the job. Everyone who went in came back out, and they now have enough to eat for a while. Time for a much deserved rest; the group settles down for a brief nap in the sun.

Just as the last one of the group begins to doze

off, a great bird silently glides in and lands on the bank of the stream. The breeze from its wings awaken the ant closest to the stream, causing him to look up after noticing the movement out of the corner of his eye. "Dude, check that out!", calls Cal from the beach, looking up from his sun tanning session, and noticing something floating down the stream at the now ignored bird's feet. It appears to be a small basket or container, made of dried grass. "Come on. Give me a hand, so I can grab it." A few others reluctantly link together to make a ladder for Cal, and he pulls the basket in to shore.

As he gets to the beach and looks inside, he blurts, "Whoa, there's a little dude in there, and some kind of piece of stone." The group surrounds the basket, fascinated by this unexpected discovery. "You're a daddy, Cal", jokes Z. "Cut it out", asserts Barbatus. "Someone put that kid in there for a reason. He must be pretty important, to go to all that trouble. Cal, you and Z take care of the kid. We'll come up with a name for him later."

"What is this stone? It looks like a corner, broken off of something bigger. Bike, can you make anything of this?" Bike examines the piece of stone, with what looks to be carved designs in it, "I recognize some of this. It looks like ancient text, and I can tell that it is a part of a bigger piece. I'll have to look up the text in some old manuscripts I have. It may take me a little while, but I'll figure it out."

As Cal picks up and holds the young male ant, Z notices a note that was underneath him. "Look at this. It's a note." "Let me see", says Barbatus. He reads the note to the group.

"To the one who finds this basket, thank you for rescuing the young one. His name is 'Thesaurus', because he is our treasure. Our Queen ordered all the young males killed, and we were able to save only one, Thesaurus. Please protect him."

"He is important, almost as important as the key that was sent with him. The key, a corner broken from the 'The Secret of The Ancestors', a stone tablet detailing the history and genetic makeup of the first men as they came up from under the ground, as told by ancient ancestors of ants and men, holds the key information needed to read the larger tablet. The Queen possesses this tablet, and will stop at nothing to obtain the key."

"With the key, the Queen could read the tablet she now holds, and would learn how to produce heirs without males. This would spell the end of all males, both ant and human. This key must never be found by a Queen. There is only one safe place for it. You must find the safe place and take it there. You are the only hope for both Ant and Man."

The bird quietly jumps into the air and with whispering wings, flies into the distance. The group of renegades look at each other, beginning to understand that their mission is about to change from one of simple survival, to saving entire races of beings.

Chapter 15.

The Runnels family waits impatiently outside Ms. Willingham's office. Dierdra Willingham is in her second year as the Principal of Greenwood Hills Middle School, after teaching for twenty years, beginning in First Grade and ending in High School. Married, but with no children of her own, she feels almost as if all of the students she had taught through the years were her children.

She had struggled for years to work her way up through the school system, believing that she had to work harder than anyone else to get her shot at joining the administrative ranks. She feels strongly that classroom structure, gender roles, and outdated textbooks and other curriculum materials have hindered the progress of many students in the past, especially girls. All the students know is that boys don't like having to go to Ms. Willingham's office.

"Welcome, Mr. and Ms. Runnels, Randy. I'm glad you were all able to be here. I think it's important that both parents be involved in these issues, and all too often, we are lucky to be able to talk to even one. Thank you for coming. Randy, would you like to tell us what you were thinking when you drew this?"

Randy shrugs his shoulders, "I don't know. I thought of it while playing out in the field after lunch the other day. I saw them standing out there, and drew them."

"What do you mean you 'saw them', Randy?", his mother asks. "Saw what?", shooting a sideways glance at her husband. Randy replies without hesitation, "The ants. I saw them standing there on the ground."

Lane and Turner Runnels look worriedly at each other, as if they know a troubling secret.

"Randy", Ms. Willingham says, "Would you please wait outside for us? We'll be finished soon. It was nice to see you." Randy stands up, walks outside the office, and sits on the bench in the hallway, slowly swinging his feet back and forth, so that the bottom of his shoes lightly scuff the polished floor.

"I'm concerned about Randy's behavior in class", Ms. Willingham starts, "His teachers report that he has difficulty sitting still. He fidgets and taps his pencil. He whistles during class, and sometimes makes odd noises. He forgets to turn in his homework, and well, his drawings are troubling. Have either of you noticed these types of behaviors at home?"

Turner jumps in, "Of course we have. We've been dealing with this since day one. It's difficult to deal with, and we have to work with his teachers a lot, but, believe it or not, he actually seems to be better now. He's a regular boy, though, and he likes to move around and do things." Lane adds, "He doesn't like to sit for long, and he draws constantly. It's hard to get him to concentrate at home, too. We've tried all the suggestions that have been offered by teachers over the years. It's been very hard to find things that reward him enough to make him change his behavior. We don't know what else to do."

"Well, Mr. and Ms. Runnels, I think I have another option for you to consider", Ms. Willingham states tentatively. "We have had great success with a new treatment center for children Randy's age. They have a very high success rate." She shows them brochures for the SOL (Systems for Optimal Learning)

Center, a government subsidized medical facility, specifically designed to treat children, primarily boys, with learning difficulties caused by attention disorders. "The beauty of this program, and this facility in particular, is that there is no cost to you. It is a public facility, with one hundred percent of the cost paid by government subsidies and private contributions. In a matter of days or weeks, your son will be back in school, with remarkable improvement in his ability to focus and learn. Does this sound like something you would like to look into?"

Turner and Lane Runnels take their time looking over the brochure, with photos of smiling children in front of the center's welcoming entrance sign, with its glowing sun-inspired logo.

"Do we really have a choice?", asks Lane, alluding to the case of the boy who was recently taken from school, against his mother's wishes. "Of course, you always have the choice," says Ms. Willingham, "but if you send Randy voluntarily, you will have more control over what treatments he receives". "Control?", Turner protests, "I don't feel very much in control of any of this."

"You know that my hands are tied in such cases", the Principal complains. "I think you will be doing Randy a great service by taking advantage of this fine program, and by doing it voluntarily, you will be able to get him back home and in his regular school as quickly as possible."

As they carefully pass the application back and forth, the concerned parents nod in agreement as they murmur and discuss how wonderful it would be for Randy to be able to perform better in school, and how great it is that it would be cost free.

Turner thinks to himself, "This is a battle I can't win. Lane is not going to help me if I fight this. I've already been labeled as a 'problem father' in too many other situations like this, when teachers have decided that Randy needs some kind of treatment. The only way to prove them wrong is to go along with this, at least for a while. If it doesn't work, they'll finally drop the issue. And if I'm wrong, at least he'll receive the best treatment possible."

A black SUV pulls up in front of the school. Three men, dressed in black suits, with black sunglasses, walk up the steps, turn down the hallway toward the Principal's office, and stop in front of Randy.

"Randy Runnels?", one of the men asks. Randy nods yes, frozen in terror at the sight of these mysterious, dark men. "Come with us." Two of the men each take one of Randy's arms, and all four begin walking to the front entrance of the school at such a fast pace that Randy barely manages to keep from dragging his feet.

The group quickly reaches the SUV. One gets in the driver's seat, one opens the rear door and gets in before Randy, and one after Randy. The fourth man, already standing by the open front passenger door, scans the area while speaking into a micro-headset in his ear, then ducks inside as the SUV begins to move. They hurriedly drive off, leaving behind a swirling cloud of dust.

"Don't worry, we'll handle everything. You won't even need to drive him there. Transportation is also provided free of charge. We'll get this going right away, so that he can get back even sooner. We'll keep you fully informed as to the progress of the treatment and when you can expect Randy to come home. You're doing the right thing." Ms. Willingham pats them on the shoulders as the three of them walk to the front door.

The big black vehicle, now covered in dust, rapidly pulls into the main entry of the SOL Center, never slowing at the main guard station. The guards, dressed exactly like the men who picked up Randy Runnels at the school, stand as it goes by, and one speaks into his headset as they close the gate.

Before reaching the public entrance in front, the SUV turns into a drive that is partially hidden behind a thick row of hedges next to the guard station. As they pull around behind the building, the wall of hedges swings open to reveal the side drive way, and closes behind them.

The drive leads to an underground entrance, and the SUV pulls into the well lit tunnel. Guards are positioned at the entrance, and at the doors at the end of the hundred yards long tunnel. The men get out first, and Randy follows, terrified. No one has said a word during the entire trip here from the school. Randy wonders if this is what happened to the others who just disappeared from school. At the time, he thought they were just stories, but this is real.

"Hello, Randy", a gentle looking nurse says to the wide-eyed boy. He does not answer. "Your parents know where you are. Don't worry. This is a safe place. You will be treated as a guest and you'll be home in no time. I'm Ms. Minard, and I'll be showing you around today. Let's go see your room first. OK?" Randy nods tentatively, "Where am I?"

"You are at the SOL Center; Systems for Optimal Learning. Your parents and teachers decided that you would be helped in school by coming here and going through our program. I think you'll have fun here. We use computer games to train your brain to do better in school." Randy's face softens a little bit at the idea of playing on a computer.

"I think you'll make a few friends while you're here, too. There are quite a few boys here just like you. You'll even be able to play with them online after you finish here and return home. Let's go see your room and then meet a few of the other guys."

On the way to the dormitory rooms, Randy and the nurse walk down a glass corridor to a dimly lit room full of computers. Inside, dozens of boys are playing a game that looks like the one from his father's company. "Is that OWW?", asks Randy. "Yes, it is", replies Ms. Minard, totally unaware of Randy's knowledge of the game or its origin. Still wary, but a little more comfortable, Randy thinks to himself, "Maybe this won't be too bad."

"We'll get you started on the computers right away, but we need to get you settled in your room, have you meet a few of your roommates, and meet the Director. There are a few rules that you will need to know about, but the main one is that you have to play on the computer at least eight hours per day while you are here." "I get to play OWW for eight hours per day?", Randy asks suspiciously. The nurse answers, smiling, "Yes, and that's not even the best part. When you get home, your parents have to let you play at least two hours per day during the week, and at least four hours per day on the weekends." "Sweet", quips the Runnels boy, feeling a little better about the situation.

"You'll be sharing a room with another boy. His name is Colton Davis. Hi, Colton." Ms. Minard greets the sandy haired boy, who is lying on his bed, one leg propped on the other knee, reading a book titled "One World Warrior, Oblivion". There is a bookcase of similar paperback books, with an empty space where his selection normally sits.

The boy on the bed moves the book below his chin and answers, "Hey, Ms. Minard. Who's the new geek?" The nurse half frowns, half smiles, "This is Randy. He just arrived, and I want you to make him feel at home. He's going to need someone to show him around and introduce him to some of the other guys. You'll do that, won't you?" "Yeah, sure", he replies, reluctantly.

"Nice to meet you, Randy." "Nice to meet you, too, Colton", Randy says, not fully meaning it yet. "You two can get better acquainted later, but Randy needs to meet the Director, and then we'll get him set up for the game" the nurse said, indicating that it was time to go. "Set up for the game?", Randy thinks to himself. "I've played this game more than any of these dorks. I don't need to be set up for it."

The two leave the boys' room and walk back past the glass walled corridor again, to a large office at the front of the building. It is just behind the main reception desk, with one wall being the curved glass exterior of the building front, overlooking the pond that the entrance road circles. The fountain in the center of the pond pulses as if a heartbeat.

At the desk in the center of the office, with nothing on it, no computer, not even a phone, sits a silver-haired woman in a navy blue suit, her hands clasped together in front of her, gently resting on the table top. As Randy and the nurse enter the office, she smiles at him. Randy thinks to himself, "She looks like a Principal." "Hello, Randy", she offers. "Sounds like a Principal, too", he thinks again. Cutting off his thought, she follows with, "My name is Rosalind Burlington. I am the Director of the SOL Center. I want to welcome you here, and to hope that you have a very nice stay with us."

"Your time with us will be fun and productive, if you follow a few very simple rules. Most of it will be very easy, but there are a few things that are very important. I'm sure you've already heard that you'll be playing on the computer a lot." Randy nods that he has. "I suspect that is most of the boys' favorite part of being here, and that leads me to some of the specific things we are going to ask you to do."

"The game and the computers have been set up so that we can monitor what is taking place in your brain as you play. The process we go through here is to watch how your brain behaves during game play, adjusting medications to optimize the training, and using feedback from your brainwaves to adjust the game for you and everyone else. Do you have any questions so far?"

Randy shakes his head no, but is wondering to himself, "Medications? I wonder what she means, and I wonder how they monitor my brain?" His face evidently betraying his concern, the Director replies in a way meant to allay common fears of new arrivals, "Don't worry. You'll be given one or two pills per day. No shots or anything, and you'll be wearing a special headset while you play the game. You won't even notice it after a short while."

"The most important part of your treatment here is after you leave and go home. Did Ms. Minard tell you the part about getting to play at home?" Randy nods again. "Not only do you get to play, your parents have to let you play. How's that?" the Director asks, smiling knowingly. Randy grins slightly, still not sure how much he can trust her or this whole process.

"OK. Let's get you started. Ms. Minard, take Randy to the observation center and get him set up with his headgear and other equipment." The nurse smiles and nods in agreement, and turns to leave. "Enjoy your stay, Randy", Ms. Burlington adds, as Randy turns to follow the nurse out into the main lobby. He follows her back down the corridor once more, but this time, they turn down a hallway that ends with a wall. The nurse looks at the wall on her right, and the wall at the end opens to reveal a room with banks of dozens of computer monitors on the walls.

A half dozen men in white coats sit at computers, each monitoring ten to twelve of the monitors, each monitor showing a boy playing the game. The observers glance at one screen after another, clicking on their keyboards to make notes of the readings being recorded for each player. Behind one wall of the observation room is a huge room with racks of computer servers, the green LED lights blinking, some in unison, some randomly.

"That's the main computer room for the SOL

Center", volunteered Ms. Minard. "That is where all the game play results are stored, not only for players here at the SOL Center, but also for everyone playing at home, and even for all the tournaments played around the world. Every game that is played is stored here; the individual player actions, as well as the way the brain reacts to the game. The game is modified and improved, based upon these results. The goal here is not only to hopefully help you in school, but to help soldiers perform better in real combat. How does it feel to know that when you play a game, you will be helping real soldiers?" "Good, I guess", Randy answers, with a little shrug of his shoulders.

"All right. Let's get you suited up", the nurse says, as one of the observers turns from his console, rotating toward the couple in his motorized wheelchair. Randy notices that the man controls the chair with a tablet computer mounted on a bracket in front of him. He has no use of his arms or legs, and controls the computer and chair with voice commands, and by using a special dot on his forehead tracked by the built-in camera on the computer. His voice is pleasant, but halting, having to pause every few words to let the mechanized breather push air into his lungs.

"Come in this room...Randy... I'm Dr. Shepherd... You can call me...Clark...I'll be assigned...to monitor your...game play...I'll be here...at this console...while you...are playing...You won't really...notice me much...but if you ever...have a question...about the game...you can talk to...me on your headset...or you can chat...with me on-screen...I'll show you...how to do all that."

Clark rotates his chair in the direction of a

group of cabinets that contain banks of headsets, game controllers, and other assorted computer parts. As he moves his head toward the cabinets, Clark activates a laser pointer attached to his own head-mounted equipment, and he uses the light to direct Randy to the part of the cabinet where his equipment is located. Each set of equipment is labeled with a resident's name, and Randy finds the set with his name.

"There's your...headset...You just put it...on like headphones...Be sure and...have both earpieces...in while you play...for the best sound...There's a built in...microphone, so...you talk to me...if you need to...You can also talk...to the other...players here...as well as...anyone, anywhere...in the world who...is playing...at the same time."

The headset, while different from anything he has used before, fits comfortably and makes him feel less and less hesitant. Randy trembles just a little as he adjusts the headset and moves the microphone toward his mouth. The top of the headset is shaped like a small beanie that fits directly on top of his head. Randy thinks out loud as he adjusts the fit, "Feels a little weird at first, but it's not as heavy as it looks."

"OK?...Let's get all...the equipment...calibrated...Sit down here at...this computer." Randy sits down in front of one of a bank of state-of-the-art gaming computers, each with a two-row, six monitor setup. "Cool" is all that Randy can say. "Yeah...pretty cool", says Clark, smiling. "And you'll get...a computer pretty...much like this...when you go home...It will have...only two...monitors, but...that's still...not too bad." "Yeah, not bad", thought Randy to himself, as he sits at the computer.

"Are you...familiar with the...One World Warrior game?", asks Shepherd. "Yeah, I play all the time. My Dad invented it", Randy says, as he thinks about how he will show all these guys how the game is played. Clark responds, "The game is...probably a little...different than the...one you have...played on...but I'm sure...you'll pick it...up quickly...Start the game...and I'll go...to my console...and start...calibrating...some set points."

Eight hours later, Randy hears the crackle of Clark Shepherd's voice in his headset, "OK, Randy...Game over...for today...Good job...I got lots...of data." "I just started playing", argued Randy. Clark smiled to himself and answered over the headset, "Newbies lose...track of time...You've been playing...for eight hours...You'll get more...tomorrow." Randy stops for a moment and thinks he should be worried that he cannot remember anything from the past eight hours. It seems like he just sat down to start playing minutes ago. "This won't be so bad" he thinks to himself.

"So how was it?", Colton asks Randy, as he returns from the gaming center to their dorm room. "Went fast, huh?", as he smiles knowingly. "Wow, yeah. It seems like I was only there for a few minutes", agreed Randy. "After a while, you'll get tired of playing, and will want to take some time off. They won't let you, so you'll need to divert your attention some way", Colton advises, as he picks at his arm.

"I wont' get tired of playing", counters Randy. "As I get really good at it, I'll want to play even more." Colton smiles and offers, "They'll tell you to relax and not think about the game, just play and follow your instincts. They say you will eventually be able to control your player without even using your computer controls. I don't believe it, but some of the guys claim they can "smell" where the other players are. I think they're nuts. But then, that's why we're here, isn't it?"

"Not me. I'm here because they're trying to help me in school", answers Randy, now irritated. "Yeah, that's what they told me, too", says Colton. "Now they think I'm a little off, because I pick my arms, but I only do it to keep from getting sucked into that game. I'm not going to let happen to me what I see happening to the other guys." "What do you mean?", asks Randy. Colton looks around and lowers his voice, as if trying to avoid being overheard, "Look at the guys who have been here a while. Take a look at their eyes; they're like blank, gone. I'm not going out that way."

Randy is thinking about all this as Ms. Minard returns to their room with another boy. "Colton, Randy, this is Solomon. Be sure and make him feel at home."

Chapter 16.

As Bike compares the tablet key to his ancient manuscripts, he begins to understand the inscription on the stone piece. He begins to tell the group, "The back is newer, a map of a colony named Optera, that contains the actual stone tablet. On the front, the very old text, says that this is the key to the 'Fourth World' tablet. It says that there have been three worlds of men, and tablets, before this one."

"The First World was destroyed by fire, the Second World by ice, and the Third World by flood. Each time, The Creator allowed a chosen few to go below to live with the ancestors." "Us", Bike interjects. "Each time, the old tablet. along with its key, was destroyed, and a new one written. Each time, the key and tablet were hidden apart from each other, so that no one could possess them both."

"Then, there is a string of what looks like genetic code, which I can only guess is the human genome that is described in the old text. It is referred to as the human key."

Bike turns to Barbatus and asks, "So what do we do now?" Barbatus, quietly responds, "We have to go get that tablet." "Then what?", asks Rugosus, almost as an objection. Barbatus thinks for a moment, and then adds, "Then, we'll figure out what to do with the two pieces. In the meantime, let's get to camp and get this little one fed. Rugosus, you will be in charge of training Thesaurus. Let's call the young one Theo for short." "Why me?", objects Rugosus. Barbatus answers calmly, "Because no one else can protect him better than you."

Schmitty turns and smiles at Rugosus, "Happy babysitting, Rugosus", who returns the comment with a glare and the retort, "You should be the one watching the kid. You're the nanny of the bunch."

Barbatus cuts in, "Enough. We are going to need the chemical keys to the colony where the tablet is being held. Schmitty, go with Bike and help him get the chemical key from one of the members of Optera. As you look for the individual member you will use to collect the keys, make note of the main entrance and all other possible points of entry. Speed is of the essence, however. Don't bother bringing the captive back with you."

As Bike and Schmitty leave to carry out their reconnaissance, Barbatus details the plan to recover the ancient tablet. "As soon as Bike comes back with the colony's keys, we will go in and get the tablet. We need to make this a fast one, so only three of us will go. Tex and Banshee, prepare yourselves. See Patch to shore up your armor and see Rugosus to check your weapons."

"I should be going", argues Rugosus. "You need me with you." Barbatus considers this for a moment, and concludes, "You're right Rugosus. I do need you there. Things could get sticky in there, and we will need speed and skill. Tex, sit this one out."

"Should I see Patch about an armored skirt?", Tex complains. Barbatus smiles and answers, "Don't worry, Tex. There will be plenty of action for you later. Theo needs your protection, and your patience."

Bike and Schmitty return more quickly than expected, and Schmitty reports, "There are two main entrances, front and back, and two smaller ones on each side. There is not much traffic in and out of the smaller ones. They seem to be the better option."

Barbatus congratulates the two, "Good work, Bike. Do we have enough of the colony's keys to hide ourselves, and confuse the members inside?" Bike replies, "Yes. I can have a small batch ready in a matter of minutes. I hope that will be enough." Barbatus quickly answers, "It will have to be."

Banshee, Rugosus, and Barbatus suit up for their mission into the unfriendly colony. As Bike applies the keys which will make them invisible to the colony, he also hands over the batch of altered chemicals which will be opened to make the defenders of the colony think there is a massive attack from another colony. This distraction has proven to be an effective tactic for raids, and Barbatus hopes Bike's invention will work again.

"OK, here's the plan", starts Barbatus. "Banshee, you'll be working alone this time, taking the diversionary chemical into the main entrance. Go inside, past the first wave of guards, and find an unoccupied place to release it. Then, get out of there as quickly as possible."

"Rugosus, you and I will go in the side entrance, and travel down to the Queen's chamber. The Queen will have the tablet stored in a special room next to her main chamber." Rugosus interrupts, "How do you know that?"

"Because Optera is my old colony", responds Barbatus, grimly.

The three check the map once more, and head toward the colony. As they watch the main entrance from behind tall grass, Banshee states, "I hope Bike didn't rush this batch. I don't want to have to fight my way both in and out today." "Hopefully, you won't have to do either", answers Barbatus. Banshee complains with a smile, "Where's the fun in that?"

"Just make sure you have a clear exit path before you open up that stuff", says Rugosus. "I don't want to have to rescue you." "You just take care of yourself", answers Banshee. "I'll see you guys back here when it's over."

Barbatus orders the other two, "OK. Time to go, Banshee. Rugosus and I will wait until you get inside and release the chemical, and when the colony reacts, we'll go in the side entrance." "Good luck."

Banshee walks steadily to the main entrance, and is approached by the guards. They touch antennae, and move aside, allowing him to pass. "He's in", reports Rugosus. "Let's move", replies Barbatus.

The colony entrance is at the center of the clearing. The two keep it in view on their right as they circle around, staying in the taller grass, on their way to the side entrance. As they circle, they can see clusters of defending ants writhing in scrums at the main entrance, attacking each other, unable to discern friend from foe. Barbatus thinks to himself, "It works exactly the way it's supposed to."

"Show time", Rugosus says, nervously. "Follow me closely, and remember the way back out, in case we get separated", Barbatus warns. Rugosus replies, "I'm not leaving you alone. You need me to get out of here." The two smile at each other knowingly, and they walk up to the unoccupied side entrance.

"That's a good sign", Barbatus observes. "So far, so good. Let's move." Barbatus leads Rugosus downward through the maze of tunnels toward the

Queen's chamber. The path has not changed since he was last here, and they soon are within sight of the chamber.

"Two guards at the door", advises Rugosus. Barbatus replies, "That's OK. We're going to the room next to it, and there's only one guard. Bike's concoction won't do us any good at this point. Even colony members aren't allowed past here without permission. We have to quickly take that guard out, and find the tablet and go before the others sense the guard's signal."

"Let me handle him", says Rugosus confidently. As the guard turns to challenge them, the flash of Rugosus' blade separates the target's head from his body. Silently, they enter the side chamber. Barbatus walks straight to the row and the shelf that contains the tablet, having long known its location, but not its importance. He picks up the tablet, and places it in a special carrying sling, that leaves all limbs free to battle their way out of the colony, and the two hurriedly turn to retrace their steps.

"Halt!", shouts one of the Queen's guards. "What are you doing near the Queen's chamber", demands Maricopa, emerging from the Queen's quarters. "The Queen's Defender demands an explanation. Detain them." As one of the guards nears, Rugosus quickly swings his blade, and cuts off two legs with one stroke. Before the other guard can even move into an attack position, he is met with the down stroke of Rugosus' blade. He readies another swing, but the guard falls to the side. The Queen's Defender retreats behind the fallen guards, toward the Queen's chamber entrance, where additional guards would normally have already leapt to her defense. She wonders where all the guards could be.

"Don't move, or you will meet his fate", warns Barbatus. "I know you", says Maricopa, a look of angry recognition creeping across her face. "You were sent into battle, and should not have survived." Barbatus replies, "I was sent on a suicide mission, and you knew it. It is only because of your position that you will be spared the fate you intended for me."

Maricopa asks, "Why are you here?" "We are here to save Ant and Man", answers Barbatus. "What have you done?", asks a now panicking Queen's Defender. She notices the satchel, with the corner of the tablet protruding. "What is that you have there? You have no right to that. Return it immediately. That is the Queen's property." "We will find a safe place for this important document", says Barbatus. Maricopa vows, "I will pursue you to the ends of the earth to recover that. You don't know what you've done."

"I think we do", responds Barbatus, as he and Rugosus turn to make their escape. "If you follow us, you will die. I will not spare your life again." "Nor I yours", warns Maricopa.

As Barbatus and Rugosus run across the clearing to the tall grass, they find Banshee waiting impatiently. "What took you so long?", he asks the two. "Things are more complicated than I first thought", says Barbatus. "We need to get out of here, now."

Chapter 17.

"Mr. Runnels", Henry Lee calls across the convention center main ballroom, to the game designer, Turner Runnels. Runnels, who recently completed the last round of negotiations for the sale of his game, One World Warrior, to the Army, Dr. Lee's employer, answers, "Nice to see you again, Dr. Lee." "Please, call me Henry. We're going to be spending a lot of time together, and I think we should be on a friendly basis" the researcher suggests. "OK Henry, only if you call me Turner", Runnels counters, smiling.

Henry begins, "Turner, it's an honor to work with you on this game project." "I'm enjoying it", answers Turner. "It's tough to let go of my baby, but I guess it is a little easier knowing that the military will be using it to improve soldier training, and I get to stay on board as a consultant." Henry adds, "And don't forget that you'll be heavily involved in these weekly tournaments. I'll be at almost all of them with you. I'll be recording all the game play data, for use in my studies at the lab."

Turner looks around the ballroom, where the sponsor booths and team stations are being constructed for the upcoming weekend's tournament. He thinks to himself that they look a lot like ants swarming across the floor. "Are you a gamer?" asks Turner of Henry. Henry laughs and replies, "Well, I do play the game, but not at the level of the real players. "I'm using the data from the players to suggest modifications to the game, for use in some special projects I have designed for the Army. We're using technology developed from the game for battlefield situations. Right now, that's about as much detail as I can provide."

"Sounds interesting", Turner says. "I don't know if I can help at all, but since I wrote the original code, if you need any information from me, I'll be happy to do what I can." Henry responds, "It's not surprising that you were retained as a consultant. We know that there are bound to be situations that we will need your expertise in how the programs were originally written. I'm sure I'll need to ask a lot of questions as we get farther into the game. Let's go look at the new equipment that has been designed for the tournaments, and you can take a look for yourself at some of the changes in the game. I hear your son will be playing this weekend."

"That's right", answers Turner. "I'm excited to see him. It's his first weekend back home after being at the SOL Center for a while." Henry reports, "I had the pleasure of observing quite a bit of Randy's game play results. He's quite proficient at the game. I think he'll do very well in the tournament." Turner replies laughingly, "Well, he had a bit of an advantage, having played the game, as I designed it, from the very beginning. He was playing it before he could ride a bike. Sometimes I wish he had ridden the bike more." Both men laugh, as they sit down at the newly designed game consoles.

What Henry did not tell Randy's father, but that has continued to trouble him for several weeks, is that while Randy is exceeding all expectations in the game, his friend Solomon's treatment indicators are far different than expected. The Center's medical and psychiatric staff seem concerned that he is not responding to the treatment at the rate of other patients.

Henry has been asked to go over Solomon's results with a fine tooth comb, looking for any further unusual game results during this tournament. Solomon might be asked to return for further treatment, depending upon what Henry finds. He wants to share this with the boy's father, but is torn between wanting to help the boy and his loyalty to his employer.

Henry has noticed that Solomon's brainwave patterns don't seem to match those of the other boys. He quickly runs through all the levels of the game, finishing much faster than the others. He is progressing faster than the game designers are able to modify the game. While he waits for new levels to be loaded, he doodles on a pad next to his computer station. Henry has looked at the pad after Solomon's game sessions, and saw the intricate drawings that Solomon had made of tall, thin ant-like creatures. They remind him of drawings he made himself as a boy, and similar to drawings that most boys draw when they first arrive for treatment.

Most boys stop drawing after a short time in treatment, but Henry has noticed that a very small number do not, despite the medication and brainwave feedback treatments. Solomon is one of the few who seem not to "take" to the treatments. He also doesn't seem to get caught up in the game like the other boys do. Most interesting to Henry, is one particular response that Solomon has recorded during game play; the frequency of brainwaves that has been isolated for pheromone receptivity is completely off the charts. It's as if Solomon is controlling the game, and not the other way around.

Henry is not the only one who has noticed this

about Solomon. His unusual pheromone numbers and resistance to the treatment protocols has attracted the attention of the higher-ups in the Y12 organization. General Green herself has asked Henry about Solomon, inquiring about specific DNA characteristics and his family history.

It is generally known around the lab that there seems to be a relationship between resistance to the SSRI and NDRI drugs, resistance to the brainwave manipulation programming of the game, and a family history that includes Native American or Pacific Rim ancestry. Henry has been asked to shift some of his research into finding the specific gene that might be responsible for this "abnormality".

Henry, like all the other male researchers in the Y12 labs, has been added to the treatment protocols, and has become a test subject himself, receiving the same pharmaceutical drugs as the younger patients, and being asked to participate in game play. The male staff are not subjected to the longer periods of game play that the younger patients are, but the game center has been opened up during break periods for staff members to be able to get their minimum time in for the game.

Henry has noticed that he has been scrutinized a little more heavily than other staff members. He thinks it is because he doesn't seem to be responding to the treatment as other staff members have. The thought occurs to him, "Now that I think about it, I remember Williams telling me he had some Cherokee in him. He didn't seem to respond to the treatment, either. I wish he was still here; I sure would like to compare notes with him about that. I wonder what happened to him. It's weird that he just suddenly was 'reassigned'. I wonder if his failure to respond to the treatment was the reason he is no longer here. If that's the case, I have to be careful not to be obvious with my insensitivity to the treatment. Maybe I should act a little more like the other staff members; pretend that it is changing me. Maybe I should also start helping Solomon try to act more like the other boys too, so that he can stay home."

Henry opens up to Turner, "You know, I've noticed that Randy's friend Solomon doesn't seem to be affected by the game in the same way as most of the other boys who come through the Center; like your son" Turner inquires, "What do you mean?" Henry explains, "Have you seen the eyes of most of the boys when they finish a marathon game session? That look in their eye; vacant? Solomon doesn't have that look. He seems as normal now as he did when he first arrived at the SOL Center. I'm sure you've seen that look in Randy's eyes."

His father answers, "Yes, I've noticed it. Quite honestly, I'm quite a bit concerned about it. Why do you bring that up? What does it mean? Why is Randy affected this way, and Solomon is not?" Henry continues, "I've noticed other staff members having the same reaction, while I did not. The problem is that the medical staff see that look in the eyes as a good sign, and as the absence of it as a bad sign; a sign that the treatments are not working. It concerns them enough that they begin to look deeper into why it doesn't appear to be working. In a strange way, Randy is lucky that he is considered to be reacting normally. I am a little worried about boys like Solomon, and what might happen to them if they are considered to be 'untreatable'."

Henry follows up, "Have you noticed Randy drawing the same pictures as before?" "Come to think of it, no. Is that significant?" his father asks. Henry answers, "It seems to be one of the signs the staff looks for to see if treatments need to be modified. When they see a boy drawing what they call the 'ants', it is a sign that they need to adjust medications or make modifications to the game for that boy.

Turner thinks back to the school conference, where Randy's drawings were discussed. He thinks to himself, "That's why the teacher was so focused on those drawings. Randy had drawn ants." Turner, still thinking to himself, but now speaking loud enough for Henry to hear, "That's why they picked him. He was drawing ants at school. That's why the teacher, and then the Principal, forced us to put Randy into treatment. They set him up, because he was drawing ants."

Henry continues, "I've noticed that Solomon still draws them, after Randy and all the other boys stopped. For some reason, Solomon seems to be unaffected by the treatment, and he seems to have attracted some negative attention because of that."

"I know his father, Jim Shaw", replies Turner. Henry narrows his eyes and asks, "Do you think you can introduce us at the next tournament? I would very much like to talk with him about Solomon." "Sure", agrees Turner. "In the meantime, do you think Randy is going to be OK? That look in the eye really troubles me." "It troubles me, too", says Henry. "I'll do everything I can to make sure that your son is safe, but I think the best thing we can all do is to try to keep the boys out of the Center. Now that Randy is home, let's try to keep him there. Let me know if you see anything unusual with Randy, inside or outside of the game."

Turner Runnels arrives home before his wife, as is usually the case, and has dinner ready for the threesome. "Hey, Lane", he greets her as she walks into the kitchen. "I had an interesting meeting with Dr. Lee today at the game tournament. I'd like to talk with you about it after dinner, when Randy hops on the computer to get his game time in." Lane volunteers, "OK. I have some things I would like to talk with you about, too; also related to the SOL Center. I had some meetings with the UNIPHARM people over the past few days, and I need to share what I learned with you."

As the table is cleared and Randy logs on to the computer for his mandatory minimum game time, the two parents sit on bar stools at the kitchen counter, and Turner pours coffee into two cups. Turner says, "You first." Lane begins, "I don't know exactly where to begin. I guess the first thing is that I have an ethical dilemma." "What do you mean?", asks her husband. "I have learned about negative side effects caused by one of the drugs used in treatment protocols at the SOL Center."

"What kind of side effects?", asks Turner. She continues, "There aren't many studies for boys and young people yet, but it seems that some rather dangerous heart conditions are either exacerbated or maybe even caused by the drugs that are being used. Because of its preferential status granted as a part of the SOL agreement, UNIPHARM's drugs are exempt from the usual drug approval process. They are automatically granted safe status, and their studies are used in place of more extensive trials. Normally, this isn't a problem, and everything turns out OK."

She continues, "This same process was used with the latest combination of drugs used at the SOL Center, including the one Randy takes; Aggrepax. That's the same drug that President Cole was taking when he died of a previously undiscovered heart condition. It turns out that there are some lawsuits popping up from people who have had family members die after taking Aggrepax, and I have been assigned to defend those cases. As part of the discovery process, I have had to dig into UNIPHARM's clinical trials for the drugs. I am becoming quite concerned with what I am finding."

Turner narrows his eyes and asks, "What do you mean? What have you found?" Lane answers, "In all cases, patients who switch from other medications to Aggrepax, even those screened for no previous heart conditions, no family history of cardiovascular events at all, are turning up with heart attacks and strokes at an alarming rate. The rate of heart trouble in previously healthy people who begin this drug protocol is at least three times that of the drugs they replaced. "

Lane, now looking directly at Turner, continues, "And while it may not seem as dangerous a side effect as death, it appears that patients on Aggrepax have a huge increase in sterility and impotence. If patients are then taking more drugs to counteract these side effects, the risk to health is extreme. Nowhere in any of the approval submission documents were there any trials combining any other drugs."

Lane pauses for a moment, as the two stare at the table between them. Lane then grimly adds, "This drug is killing people. I think that might have been why the President died. And even worse, President Anthony, who was President Cole's physician at the time and prescribed it to him. She was instrumental in forming UNIPHARM, and in securing approval of their streamlining status. I think she must have known of the drug's dangers, and prescribed it anyway. I'm not sure what I should do. I can't represent the drug as safe, but I can't reveal what I know."

Turner sets his jaw, and answers, "We have to protect Randy. We also have to stop this. I am working on something from the game end of things. In the meantime, we have to start weaning Randy off of that drug."

Chapter 18.

Banshee, Barbatus, and Rugosus return with the tablet, and Bike immediately begins to decipher the ancient text. "It may take me a little while, but I'll figure this out. At first glance, it seems to detail how to identify the human key, which has a common ancestor with us, and tells us we must protect him."

"Protect him?", asks Barbatus. "That's what it says", replies Bike. "It says that a Spirit Helper, in the form of a great blue-grey bird, Brother Heron, will show us the one we are to protect."

Barbatus thinks back to the boy that had earlier been standing at the entrance to Optera, and the large bird that had stood there until he arrived. He and his former colony members had been so drawn to the boy that they had found themselves climbing on his clothing, but none knew why.

"Remember all those drawings we saw on the walls inside the school?" Barbatus asks the group. "Those boys can see us. I know who we're looking for. I saw him, and I saw his Spirit Helper. We have to go to the school and find him."

The rogue group quickly packs up and heads for Greenwood Hills Middle School. As the group nears the playground full of boys playing tag football after lunch, a black SUV pulls up to the front of the school. A group of men in suits escort one boy from the main office. They get into the SUV and it roars off in a cloud of dust, as the boys on playground stop their play to watch. Brief seconds pass, and the boys return to their game.

A tear collects underneath Barbatus' eye as the

rogue baker's dozen stand together, watching as the boy is taken. "What now?", asks Rugosus. Barbatus answers quickly, "We have to hide the tablet nearby, but in a different place. We can't allow ants or humans to find it and use the code to reproduce without males. If one is able to use it, both will." "How will we find him?", asks Z, tired from the quick march to the school, and hoping the answer will be that they will start tomorrow. "We follow him", Bike announces, as a Great Blue Heron flies across the field.

A small group of boys stand watching the ants as they walk away from the school. Each smiling face holds a look of wonder, even as the bell rings, and their fellow students return to class. The heron, the Spirit Helper, slowly flies back and forth between the rogue ants and the boy's house, until the group finally arrives with their payload. "Hide the tablet under the house", commands Barbatus. Together, the ants hoist the piece overhead and quickly run under the house, finding an obscure nook near the center, hiding it where it would be almost impossible to find, even if someone knew exactly where it is hidden.

The Spirit Helper stands quietly, tall and still, in the middle of the back yard. The group of ants circle at his feet. Barbatus orders Bike, "Leave the corner key right here at the feet of the Spirit Helper. That's the boy's father. He will know what to do with it." Bike lays the corner on the ground, and the ants line up, wait for a moment, and then turn to leave.

"Now we must plan how to destroy Optera", Barbatus says, ominously. "Take on a whole colony?", asks BA, incredulously. He thinks to himself, "Now I know he's gone crazy; trying to save humans, and now trying to take out an entire colony. I hope he knows what he's doing."

Barbatus answers, "I remember seeing a copy of the tablet that the Queen keeps in a separate archive room. I can only assume that other copies were made. There is no way to know how many of the Queen's Council or their assistants have seen it. The only way to make sure that no one finds it is to destroy the colony itself."

"Bike, can you make enough of one colony's chemical, to lay a trail all the way to another one? Enough to bring another colony into Optera and attack it?" Bike thinks for a moment, "Yes, but it will take a little more time." Barbatus warns, "We don't have much time. I need a couple of volunteers to capture a nearby P. rugosus colony ant for its chemical keys. Rugosus, you should be one of the two." Rugosus nods in acknowledgment "I'll go", volunteers Axe.

"No offense, but I would rather go alone", argues Rugosus. "He'll just slow me down." Axe lowers his head in disappointment, and looks to Barbatus, who overrules Rugosus. "You may need backup, and you'll need help carrying the captive. "Just as long as I don't have to carry them both", protests Rugosus. "You won't", promises Axe.

"Axe, Rugosus is in charge of this mission, and you will follow his every exact command. Is that understood?", Barbatus asks insistently. "Yes sir, understood", Axe says, straightening to attention, with a smile. Barbatus follows in a somber tone, "The colony's key is the aim of this mission. Should either of you fall in battle with the colony, the other must leave him and return with the captive. Is that understood?"

Rugosus and Axe look at each other, and then to Barbatus, and both answer, "Understood."

The two head out toward Rugosus' old colony, which has been repopulated by the original Queen that had survived the attack by Barbatus' colony. As they near the mound, Rugosus warns, "I will leave you, if it comes down to a choice between you and the captive." "I know. I was there", responds Axe, with a sideways glance. "Love you, too."

Positioning themselves next to one of the lesser traveled trails, they wait for a lone colony member to come near. "I'll grab him, and you tie his legs", commands Rugosus. "Got it", answers Axe. As the target approaches, Rugosus moves to a point slightly behind the colony member, and Axe remains at a point directly in front of the target. They look at each other, Rugosus nods, and both jump into the trail. The surprised ant immediately tries to turn and run back from where he came, and runs into Rugosus, who has his weapon at the ready. Axe pulls a cord from his waist, and deftly ties the ant's legs together. "Who are you? What are you doing?", screams the victim. "Keep quiet, and you will not be harmed", warns Rugosus. Axe has his axe over his head, ready to swing it down on the captive, but Rugosus commands, "Put that down. He's tied up."

As the captive ant struggles against his bindings, Axe has difficulty pulling the bag over his abdomen. "Hurry up", bellows Rugosus. Other colony members are almost to their location. The ant reflexively sprays his alarm pheromone. "We've got company", says Rugosus, as other members of the colony begin to react to the alarm. "Behind you!", yells

Axe, as he leaps past Rugosus, swinging his axe as he flies past, cutting off the head of a colony member that had just pinched his mandibles around Rugosus' leg.

Rugosus clamps on to the cord holding the prisoner, and carrying him at full speed, looks back to see Axe wildly swinging his weapon at the ants that surround him. Having no time for indecision, Rugosus does not return to help, realizing that Axe must sacrifice himself, to buy time for his escape. "I guess I misjudged him", Rugosus thinks to himself, as he races along. "He ended up being a warrior, after all."

"Where is Axe?" asks Barbatus, as Rugosus arrives at camp with his prisoner. Rugosus drops his load, and quietly answers, "I had to leave him. He was surrounded by the colony members, and I could not help him and risk not returning with the prisoner." "I know how you hate to leave anyone Rugosus, but you made the correct choice", says Barbatus, attempting to comfort Rugosus in some small way.

"He fought valiantly", reports Rugosus. "We all have made fun of his wild style and boastful talk of his fighting ability, but he turned out to be a true warrior. He fought with honor and allowed me to get away with the prisoner. I owe him a great debt. We all do."

"Oh, really?", calls Axe as he emerges from the thick grass, into the clearing. He is covered in blood, both his own, as well as that of the several colony members he dispatched, and he is obviously wounded, though not too severely. "Axe!" shouts Rugosus, as he sprints to help Axe walk into the group. Barbatus barks, "Bike, take care of his wounds. Axe, we thought you were lost. Rugosus was telling us of your bravery, and how you saved the mission."

"He would have done it for me", responds Axe, as he limps to a place where he can lie down for Bike to dress his wounds. "No, I wouldn't have", replies Rugosus, knowing full well he would have. They smile at each other in the way two fighters do, who have earned each other's respect after battling to a draw.

"Rest up", Barbatus warns, "We've got an almost impossible task ahead. We'll need every bit of strength, skill, and luck, to come out of this and achieve our objective. Bike, we'll need as much of each colony's chemical key as possible. We're going to have to cover the trail between the two colonies with both keys, and then we're going to ask our guest here to walk from his colony to Optera."

"I'll do what I can", says Bike. "We'll have to spread it as thin as we can, and still have both colonies able to pick up the scent." "Do your best", says Barbatus. "Take care of our guest. He'll need his energy, too. We've got a lot of marching, and then a lot of fighting to do. What we don't have, however, is a lot of time. We must do all of this today, before the chemical keys are modified, and before our guest loses his ability to recognize and be recognized." "So soon?", each of the rogue ants thinks to himself. The members look at each other, and quietly prepare themselves for the challenge.

Barbatus speaks to the group. "This is a very difficult mission. What we do today will decide the future of both ants and men. If we succeed, our fate is not assured. If we fail, it most certainly is. Look around you. One or more of those you see will not be with us after today. Remember each one, so that you can tell the stories of those who do not return. Fight today as if it is your last, for it may well be. Know that if you do not return, the story of your sacrifice will be told by those who survive you. Your story will join the stories told by elders to children, passed along from generation to generation, when they describe how you helped save the world. Now, prepare yourselves."

"Here are your assignments. Rugosus and Schmitty, you will be accompanying our guest along the trail from his colony, depositing his keys to draw his colony members toward Optera. Wheels and Cal, you will take the Optera keys and beginning at Optera, spread it out along a parallel trail, toward the target P. rugosus colony. Speed is of the essence; it is crucial that as many members as possible of each colony are spread out along the trails, to reduce the number of defenders there when we enter Optera. By using separate trails, each colony will have the maximum number of members attacking the other colony."

Each member of the group quietly arranges his gear, sharpens his weapons, and has Patch check his armor fittings, while mentally preparing for the fact that this might be his last day. Even under such circumstances, or maybe to help relieve the pressure, backhanded compliments and good natured jokes are passed around.

"Wheels, you're going to have to run backward to keep from leaving Cal behind", quips BA. "Dude, not cool", Cal says, annoyed but never looking up from his preparation. Z opens one eye, and says, "BA, wake me up when we're ready to roll." BA answers, "Sure thing Z. Just try not to fall asleep when the action hits." BA has prepared all of his equipment, but he wonders silently if he will be able to avoid being in the main action. "I hope that stuff Bike is making works. The fewer in that colony, the better."

"What are we going to do with Theo?", asks Patch. "I've fitted him with armor, but he's still too small to see any action." Theo swings his spear at Patch, striking him in the shoulder, causing him to take a step to catch himself. "I can take care of myself." "We know you can, Theo", Barbatus replies, "It's just that it is going to be extremely dangerous on this mission, and we need every team member to watch out for himself. We can't spare anyone to protect you."

"Why don't you cover our escape with BA?", says Barbatus, half asking, half commanding. "BA, your job will be to make sure nothing happens to Theo, and the two of you will be there to help any of us who remain to get out of here." Theo glares at BA, and responds, "Yes, sir." Barbatus adds, "If none of us return, it is absolutely essential that Theo makes it out of here, and that the two of you go to protect the human key. Is that understood, BA?" BA thinks about that for a moment, and answers, "Yes, sir."

Chapter 19.

Jim Shaw walks out the back door with a bag of trash, and stops when he sees a large bird, standing in the middle of his back yard. "That's the Spirit Helper that Grandfather's papers talked about", he says loudly enough to hear himself speak.

"What dear?", his wife asks. "Nothing", he replies. Jim slowly places the bag in the trash can, and moving slowly to avoid scaring off the bird, walks toward the center of the yard.

The father walks up to the bird, and stands within feet of it for a moment, each eyeing the other. His hand moves slightly toward the bird, and it leaps into the air, the force of its wings puffing Jim's hair in gusts. He watches the bird fly toward the horizon, and then looks to the ground where it had been standing. He sees the group of ants in a straight line, and in front of them, a piece of stone, that looks to be a corner of a larger piece of stone.

Jim Shaw picks up the corner piece, and recognizing the writing as being identical to those he saw on the ancient papers in his grandfather's chest, realizes that he must hide it in a place where no one will find it. He looks back to the ground, as the ants walk single file into the taller grass.

"What were you doing out there?", Diane asks her husband. He answers with a smile, "Nothing. Just saw another one of those big birds that Solomon saw the other day. I figured out it is called a Great Blue Heron. Pretty cool." He pockets the stone piece, and heads up to the attic, where he has stored his grandfather's chest. He places the corner inside the leather pouch and pushes it to the very edge of the attic on the opposite side of the house from the chest, where no one else will ever look.

"Solomon's Principal called", Diane says to Jim, now sitting at the kitchen table. He looks up and asks, "What now?" Still stirring the pot on the stove, she adds, "She said that she wants to talk with us about sending Solomon back to the SOL Center. He's still drawing those ants, and she says that is a sign that either the game or the medications need to be adjusted."

Jim considers the wisdom of telling his wife about what he has seen. He thinks to himself, "If I tell her about the ants, she'll think I'm crazy. She already thinks I'm being unreasonable by pushing for Solomon to come home as early as possible. I can't say anything about this, or they'll all think I'm nuts, and then assume that's also Solomon's problem."

He finally answers, "You know how I feel about Solomon having to go to that place, and it doesn't seem to have had much of an effect on him. To be honest with you, I think that's a good thing. I don't think anything's wrong with him, anyway. But whenever I tell them that, they give me that look that tells me it doesn't matter what I think."

"You're being oversensitive, Jim", objects Diane. "They're just trying to help Solomon." Jim quickly argues the point, "Then why do they keep taking him out of school? His grades are fine, and he's a normal boy. I wish they would just leave him alone. What's so bad about drawing ants, anyway? Something's not right. I don't trust them."

Solomon's mother considers these objections for a moment, and answers, "Let's just go hear them out, and we can make a decision then. Maybe they see something we don't. We can ask more questions then." Jim concedes the point, "You're right. I'll wait to hear what they have to say", and then thinks to himself, "I have some thinking to do over the weekend. I don't want Solomon to come back looking like those other zombie boys. I can see the emptiness in their eyes, and I can't let that happen to my son. For whatever reason, Solomon doesn't look like them when he comes home. I can't help but think that's a good thing. Maybe I can figure out something while we're at the OWW tournament this weekend."

"Remember that we're going into town for Solomon's tournament this weekend." Diane sighs and answers, "Yes, I remember. You'd think that he would have had enough of that game, having to play it every day. I don't understand how something he wants to play 24 hours a day can be good for him." Jim replies sarcastically, "Your wonderful SOL Center says he has to play every day, so we're just following doctor's orders. Besides, all his friends are there, and he doesn't have much of a social life outside these tournaments." Diane glares a laser beam stare through Jim for what seems like hours, and the subject is dropped for the rest of the evening.

The next morning, the father calls out as they are walking out the door, "We're leaving now." "Have fun", the mother says, not really caring if they do. She is still thinking about the meeting with the Principal next week, and is worried that she will have to referee between Jim and the Principal about Solomon's treatment at the center.

Jim tries to initiate a conversation with his son,

"Are any of your friends going to be there this weekend?" "Yeah." He tries again, "Is Randy going to be there?" Solomon answers, "Dad, we're on the same team, and his dad runs the tournament, remember?" Jim nods, remembering this fact, and says, "Maybe I'll get a chance to meet Randy's father. I'd like to find out more about the game."

The black "Y12" markings that had been painted on sidewalks and streets, indicating the high speed fiber optic cable that had been buried over the past year, running from the SOL Center network operations center to each major metropolitan area in the country, were almost completely faded now. The network is larger and faster than any private enterprise, and is completely independent of any other telecommunication network. The only access to this network is through terminals inside SOL, by patients on their home systems, or through OWW tournament servers directly connected to the SOL Center. This closed system does not have any access to or from the old internet, but all terminals are also connected to a secured, parallel network that does access the internet.

Each weekend, the half dozen trucks and semi-trailers of the One World Warrior fleet pull away from underneath the SOL Center, and drive to the city where the tournament is scheduled. Painted black, with the intensely designed OWW logo and image of the futuristic game character splashed along the sides of the trailers, the trucks arrive the day before the tournaments begin, and the crews jump into action, setting up the equivalent of an entire city's telecommunication system overnight. Security rivals that of a Presidential protection detail; Y12's private security force having been selected from the most elite candidates from military and private security forces. Teams of fully armed guards are assigned to each trailer, and a perimeter is established around the fleet from the moment they arrive.

Each trailer is a completely self-contained data center, each with the computing power of a whole room of racks of servers in an ordinary corporate setting. Each is capable of handling the simple game traffic and commands, but this is no ordinary game, nor ordinary communication center. The volume of data that is processed through these six trailers of servers is far greater than could have been handled by any existing private or public system, but even these powerful centers pale in comparison to what exists back at the Y12 Center. The volume of one hour of data transfer handled by the composite Y12 system, exceeds the global traffic for all the known search engines combined, for a 24 hour period. There exists no other computer system that would not instantly crash if subjected to a fraction of this volume.

There are over forty million known players of One World Warrior in North America, and another ten million scattered over the rest of the world. Of these players, one thousand of the top scorers during home play are selected to play in weekly tournaments in each of the twenty major metropolitan areas where games are held.

Players are grouped in squads of ten players, generally selected based on geographic proximity or having been through the SOL Center at the same time, or a combination of the two. All equipment is provided, so players only need to bring their custom fitted headsets, which provide the live data feed to the main data center in real time.

Jim and Solomon show their credentials at the sign-in desk, and are issued a tournament wrist band. They are handed a bag with promotional items, including Army, Navy, Air Force, and Marines recruiting brochures, informational flyers about medications, and a brochure for SOL, along with the usual ads from computer manufacturers and game makers.

The convention hall is dimly lit, with the blue tinted light from thousands of computer monitors creating an eerie glow on the faces of those seated in front of them. "Cool", breathes Solomon, as his father squints at the tournament map, trying to find the team's assigned area. "We're over there on the right", says the elder Shaw, and the two pick a path among the preoccupied players.

There are no team uniforms, but there is a sort of uniform that gamers wear; torn jeans hanging low and too long and frayed from walking on the hem, hooded sweatshirt pulled up over knit cap, t-shirt underneath with gratuitous gaming equipment manufacturer logos, and the ubiquitous skateboarding sneakers. There are various methods used to show individuality; unusual hair, sunglasses, wristbands, pins, and for the more extreme individualists, tattoos and piercings. Of course, there are players dressed more conservatively, but they are more often than not an employee of one of the event exhibitors, just keeping fluent with the game, so that they won't look "lame" when approached by real gamers.

Not a single player looks up or acknowledges

them as they walk by. The servers are open for the next hour and a half for practice, and the top players take full advantage of the opportunity to familiarize themselves with the new landscapes they will need to negotiate during the tournament.

"Hey, Solomon", announces Randy Runnels, cheerfully. "Hey, Randy", answers Solomon. "Check out the consoles", says Randy. "They're just like the ones at the SOL Center. Six monitors! Awesome!" "Yeah, pretty cool", Solomon says, looking past Randy, at the console setup. The screensavers are a video clip of the newest version of the OWW game that they will be playing this weekend. Solomon has not seen this version before.

"Hello, Jim", Turner extends his hand to shake with Jim Shaw. "Good to see you again, Turner", Jim responds. "The tournaments just keep getting bigger and better. I can't wait to see what you've got planned for the Championships." "Thanks. We've got something special planned that weekend", replies Turner.

"How's Solomon doing with the game at home?", asks the game designer. "Is he making progress? I'm not sure I'm happy with the amount of time the boys have to play. I know that may sound strange, coming from the guy who designed the game." Jim answers, "Solomon really enjoys playing the game, but the Center personnel seem to think that he's not doing well there. They keep suggesting that he come back, but I see nothing wrong with him at all. I wish we could just be done with it."

"I know what you mean", responds Turner. "Randy can't stop playing the game, and we literally have to drag him off of it. I don't like the look in his eyes he gets after playing all weekend. Quite honestly, I'm concerned with this process of monitoring their brains during play. How do we know what they're collecting, or for that matter, putting in?"

"I know what you mean about the look in the boys' eyes. I've seen it in a lot of the players here", explains Jim. "I don't know if it's good or bad, but I've also noticed that Solomon doesn't seem to have that same blank look. I guess that's why the people at the SOL Center want him to come back, saying that 'adjustments have to be made'. No offense, but I'm glad Solomon doesn't seem to be changing like the other boys are."

Turner replies, "Randy does seem to be different than when he started, like the other boys I see, but I have noticed that your son doesn't seem to be affected in the same way. Honestly, I think I agree with you that it is good he hasn't changed. I wish I could get Randy out of the program, but we both know what happens when parents push to end the treatments." The two each consider the situations they have heard about in the past, where parents were forced to relinquish parental rights, when the Center filed charges of neglect when the parents tried to end the treatments before the boys were released. Their sons have a teammate whose mother faced just such a choice. Colton's mother decided she would rather have her son part time, rather than not at all.

"Hey, Colton", says Randy, greeting his former roommate. Colton Davis is wearing his usual long sleeved jacket with rolled up sleeves, just covering the sores on his arms, and a wool cap pulled down over his ears, letting just a little hair peek out in front. "Hey,

Randy. Hey, Solomon", answers Colton. "Practice has already started. Check out the new landscapes. They're a little tricky."

Colton's mother has been standing just out of sight, making sure he gets situated and settled, before turning and leaving. She has no interest in the games, but knows that once he's playing, he'll be there until she drags him away. She makes eye contact with the two fathers, smiles, and leaves.

Henry Lee has been attending the One World Warrior tournaments for the past six months, after he started noticing some unusual results showing up in the Y12 computer database, coming from players' brainwave data. The logs clearly show communication taking place between players, but the volume of communication far exceeds input recorded from player keystrokes and trackball actions recorded.

When he first noticed this discrepancy, he thought the equipment was faulty, simply failing to record players' hand movements, but after months of observations, and cross checking the player data with the game data, he has come to the conclusion that his research into chemical battlefield communication is paying dividends.

Henry has been fascinated with how the game play data lines up almost perfectly with Dr. Williams' Ant Colony Algorithm; a direct result of the collaboration between Dr. Williams and himself, using the ant data gathered from his trips into the field with Shelton Tarver. He is especially interested in the scores and brain activity generated by Solomon Shaw. Solomon's numbers make Henry very hopeful that he will be able to present his new theory on Swarm

Intelligence to his bosses at the lab. Henry quickly moves toward the team's section.

"I'm Henry Lee", offers the young man with credentials that indicate he has a very high security clearance. You must be Solomon Shaw's father", talking to Jim Shaw. "Hello, Henry", replies Turner Runnels. "Jim, Dr. Lee works at the SOL Center." Henry counters, "Well, a lab that works with the Center. I do research on the findings that we gather from all the game play, and report it to be used to modify the game. I met your sons at the Center, and I expect them to do very well in the tournament this weekend."

Turner chimes in, "Henry and I have worked together at several of these tournaments, and we've had some interesting discussions about what he has observed at the SOL Center. He has some interesting ideas that I think you'll want to hear."

Jim Shaw answers, "Good to meet you, Dr. Lee." "Please, Henry", insists Henry. Jim continues, "OK, Henry it is. Henry, I have so many questions I would like to ask you. You saw Solomon's treatment at the Center, and I am curious about why you think he is not responding."

Henry smiles cautiously, looks into Jim Shaw's eyes, then turns to Turner and asks, "Turner, are we able to speak frankly?" Turner replies, "Absolutely. Jim has expressed some serious concerns about the SOL Center and his son's treatment there, as well as the effects of the game upon his son and other boys. He has as much at stake here as I do."

"Have you been able to find out any more about what we talked about last time?", asks Turner. "Jim,

Henry is looking for the specific changes in code that were added to the game to interact with players' brainwaves, both to improve the game, and to change the players' brain chemistry. That capability is something that I never imagined when I designed the game. Had I known what the military had in mind for the game, I really don't know if I would have sold it to them."

Henry replies, "I don't have the exact code changes, but I'm working on it. I have to be very careful; there are numerous safeguards protecting both the game and the computer system. I want to talk with you about your sons, and to share some of the data that I have observed being generated by game play. While the boys are practicing, why don't we go have some coffee in the cafeteria."

As the three men walk to a corner table with their coffee and are seated, Turner begins, "Henry, I recently became aware of some serious issues with the medications the boys are given as part of their treatment. I've also noticed something unusual about differences in the way boys respond to treatment, that I hope you can shed some light on". Jim jumps in, "I know this may sound odd, but Solomon doesn't seem to be affected by the medication and game programming the way the other boys are, including Randy."

"No offense Turner, but I've also noticed that Solomon doesn't look like Randy when they come back from treatment or a tournament", Solomon's father adds. Randy isn't nearly as bad as a lot of the boys, but they all seem to come back with blank looks in their eyes. I've even heard some of the boys call them 'zombies'. That's a pretty accurate description, I think."

"Why is that Henry?", Turner asks. "Why is it that some boys come back looking like they did when they left home, while most of them are clearly changed?" Randy's dad, now appearing a little more agitated, follows up, "Clearly, the medications the boys are given, in combination with the game's ability to alter the boys' brain waves, is what is causing the majority of the boys to look and act this way. It turns out that the drugs are not nearly as safe as UNIPHARM has said they are. I think we should get the boys off of them, but why does Solomon seem the same as he always was?"

Henry, shifting in his seat, knows he is on dangerous ground here. This is all highly classified information, and he wonders if he should even be meeting with fathers of test subjects. "If anyone, anyone, discovers that I have been discussing my research with people with no clearances, especially parents of test subjects, I will not only be fired, but will likely be brought up on charges, or maybe worse, 'reassigned'?"

He continues with the two men, "For a long time now, I have been noticing that there are amazing similarities between the chemical research I have been doing with ant pheromones, and how they communicate with each other, and the brain wave patterns that are produced by players in the OWW game." Henry looks up at a few of the countless cameras positioned throughout the building. Turner sees him look, and smiling says, "I set up the cameras, and this is the only dead spot in the room. This table can't be seen, and can't easily be heard." Henry leans in to finish his point.

"The reason your sons are here at the

tournament, is because they have done so well in the game play at SOL and at home. The games' brainwave feedback is designed to work with the medications administered, to alter the brain's neurotransmitter chemistry. Here is the part that no one is supposed to know; the boys' brains gradually adapt, growing new receptor points that allow a higher sensitivity to pheromones. They begin to be able to sense where their teammates are, without sending or receiving any communication through the console. It's as if they can "smell" the other players."

The fathers, listening intently, now leaning forward on their forearms, simultaneously show a mixture of concern and disbelief. "What do you mean, smell the other players?", asks Turner. "You're kidding, right?" Henry sternly looks directly into Turner's eyes, and without blinking says, "This is what I do. I study pheromones and how to communicate on the battlefield without electronic devices. I have been studying Pogonomyrmex, Harvester ants, both for this ability to communicate via pheromones, and for other unrelated genetic traits."

"Other traits?", queries Jim. Henry explains, "Asexual reproduction. I'm not sure how that relates to the boys in treatment, but I have found remarkable similarities between one particular gene in the Harvester ants, and in a single chromosome of some human males. This gene seems to be found only in a small percentage of the population. There is still more research to be done, but it appears that this genetic trait is passed down from Native American and Pacific Rim ancestry. I have isolated it to the 12th chromosome of males with such genetic makeup."

Jim Shaw's mind is racing. All of a sudden, he begins to piece together some of the unusual things that have taken place recently; finding the ancient Comanche papers in his grandfather's chest, the strange encounters with the blue heron, and the ants. He knows it will sound crazy to the others, but he has to tell them.

"OK, listen. This is going to sound nuts, but a lot less crazy than it might have before hearing about your research, Henry." Jim gushes with the story of his grandfather's chest, having desperately wanted to tell someone about it, but being afraid of what would happen if he told the wrong person. This is the time, and the only people he can tell who won't think he is completely crazy.

The other father and the researcher listen to the whole story; of Jim's Comanche ancestry, "The Secret of Ant and Men" tablet and copy, ants being the Ancestors, boys who can see them, Spirit Helpers, and most importantly, how he now knows that Solomon is the human key to all of this. "And one more thing; I never would have told anyone else this, but the other day, I swear to you, a group of ants left a corner of a stone tablet at my feet in the back yard. I kept it, knowing it had something to do with all of this. I just didn't know why, until now."

The three men silently look at the table in front of them for what seems like hours, processing all the information that has been presented. Henry is the first to speak, "My whole mission has changed. Many facts uncovered by my research, that up to this point I had simply accepted as unexplained anomalies, now add up to some very alarming realities. Now I know why the head of the Y12 Center where I work has been so eager for me to narrow down the source of the gene that appears to make patients resistant to treatment. I have recorded the Native American and Pacific Rim connection as only one of many possibilities up to now, not being able to prove or disprove it. Now I understand why it is so important to them. I think they've known all along."

Turner jumps in, "Why would they find that important?" Henry answers quickly, "It's the reproductive aspect. Yes, it all makes sense now. In the ants, we found male characteristics that at first, appeared to be random. Recently, I have narrowed this down to a single gene. This same gene is identical to one found in a very small number of boys with Native American or Pacific Rim ancestry. The reason my superiors are pushing so hard for this specific genetic trait, is because they want to be able to eliminate this resistance gene. If they can control every male with medications and brainwave manipulation, they will have complete control over every aspect of life, even controlling the ratio of females to males, as is the case in the ant world."

Henry continues, unable to stop now, "This is the real purpose of the research, the real purpose for the game. It's not about battlefield communication; it's about genetic manipulation. They can't have boys who don't respond to treatments; that would get in the way of the ultimate goal. And now I know why I've been increasingly under greater scrutiny at the lab. I myself have been given the same medications and game situations, and it has been considered 'ineffective'. I had suspected that it had something to do with my Chinese ancestry, and now I am certain of it. Just as certain that

Solomon's recently discovered Comanche ancestry is the reason for his resistance. I strongly suspect that I will soon be replaced at the lab, due to the perception that my failure to respond to treatment indicates I am not a team player. We have to act quickly."

Turner chimes in, "This is scary. It sounds like you're talking about a conspiracy among many big players, including the military. If that's the case, we can't count on the government to help at all." Henry adds to the gravity of the discussion, "Wait, it gets worse. Have you heard of UNIPHARM? It's a consortium of all the big pharmaceutical companies, and the source for the drugs used in treatments at the SOL Center. They are very concerned about any resistance to the effectiveness of their product. They are aggressively pushing to find the gene that I have already found. I somehow knew that I should not give it to them, but if anyone at the Y12 labs finds my research, they'll instantly know, and I'll instantly be in jail, or worse."

"Even worse, have either of you noticed that the boys are referred to the SOL Center by their school Principals? This is not by accident. I discovered that there is a secret program that recruits school administrators to know how to identify boys who need treatment. One of the signs is that they claim to be able to 'see' ants. Drawing pictures of ants is also a sign to make a referral. Some of the administrators know what happens to the boys; some may not. The bottom line is that the public education system is a partner in this process."

Turner responds, "So, we can't go to the government; we can't go to the military; we can't ask for help from the schools; we can't complain to the pharmaceutical companies. What can we do?" Jim sounds in, "We can't let them get away with it. I can't risk these people finding out that my son has some kind of secret that they can exploit. We have to somehow find a way to disrupt or destroy this machine. Henry, is your lab in the same place as the game results are stored?"

"I think I know where you're going with this", responds Turner. "Henry, if we can get someone into the OWW servers during a tournament, could we destroy the genetic research records too?" Henry thinks for a moment and answers, "Yes, a virus or logic bomb could be uploaded, but there would have to be someone at the control center to override the security measures. I can only think of one person who might be willing to risk his job to help. I'll have to find a way to feel him out and see if he'll help."

Turner follows with, "I still have all the original code I wrote for the game. If I can get my hands on the code that has been added, I might be able to find a back door into the servers. We've got a built-in army of hackers right out there." Turner gestures toward the convention center filled with gamers.

Henry adds, "If we do this, it has to look like hackers simply taking down the game. It has to look like foreign country operatives. We can't risk being detected before the system is completely disabled." Turner jumps in, "That's where I come in. I've got some connections out there, and I know I can get volunteers to penetrate the system and plant a virus that will do the job. And besides, during a tournament, the OWW servers are accepting input from all over the world at one time. It will be much easier to hide the source of such a virus during game play."

Turner adds, "I think the best time to do this will be during the Championship tournament. That's in three weeks, and not only will the best players be there, but the best hackers will, too. Henry, if you'll secure your inside man, I'll arrange for the back door, and will line up some skilled hackers who will likely be invited to the Championship."

Jim Shaw thinks for a moment, and asks, "What do I do with Solomon? Should he be going to the tournaments in between now and then? Should he go to the Championship if he qualifies? The more he plays this game, the more likely they are to discover his genetic trait." Henry argues, "Jim, they don't know what they're looking for, and would have already discovered it if they could. I think the reason for this is that there is no record of any Native American ancestry for Solomon. No one has been able to link that to him, so they will not connect the dots. I think it would be more dangerous for him to suddenly stop playing. It would raise suspicions unnecessarily. I think you should just keep doing the same things you have been."

Turner tosses money on the table for the bill, and the three stand and return to the convention center. Each is thinking ahead to the next three weeks; there is a lot of work to do, and a lot of risk to take. In the chat dialogue box at the bottom left corner of all one thousand players' screens, a message from player "headlessprettyboy" reads, "b rdy 2 prty @ chmpshp".

Chapter 20.

Barbatus addresses the group, "We will not be able to employ our usual chemical camouflage during this battle. Both colonies will be present, and our best advantage today will be that neither colony will be focusing on us as the enemy. If all goes well, the alarm signals will be produced in such large amounts that we will be ignored by both. We can only hope that each colony will be so intent upon destroying the other, that they will ignore us; for a while."

"Time to go", commands Barbatus. "Rugosus and Schmitty, I'm sure our guest will be cooperative and will lay down a very nice trail from his colony to Optera. If he does not, do what you have to do." Rugosus smiles wickedly, "Gladly. He turns to the captive and warns, "Get moving. If you do what you're asked, you'll be released. If not, I'll cut you in half and take only the half I need." The three head toward the P. rugosus colony, to begin laying down the trail to draw its member toward Optera.

"Wheels and Cal", next orders Barbatus. "Quickly take the keys to Optera and lay down a trail to the P. rugosus colony. Move as quickly as you can, and then get back to Optera, in case we need your help." The two take off toward Optera, keys in hand. "The rest of us will move toward Optera, and assume our positions and wait for the action to begin. Let's move out."

The nine remaining ants line up single file, marching toward their chosen staging area, just out of sight of the smaller of the Optera colony's entrances. As they form up in a curved line, in the tall grass, just beyond the edge of the circular dirt mound, Theo approaches Barbatus. "Sir, all of this is being done for me, but if you fail to destroy the colony and what it contains, it will not matter if I survive." Barbatus stares at the young warrior and thinks. "You are correct, Theo. If we fail, all is lost. But, if we succeed in destroying the colony, and lose you, we still fail."

"Then I should be a part of the fight", Theo counters. "This is a difficult decision", Barbatus admits. "I cannot order you to sit completely on the sidelines, but you must stay out of the main battle. Your main goal is to survive. You are still ordered to follow all directions from BA. Is that understood?" Theo smiles as he snaps to attention, and answers, "Yes, sir!"

Rugosus and Schmitty arrive on the outskirts of Optera with their captive, having exhausted his supply of his colony's chemical key. True to the group's word, the captive is released, and immediately turns and retraces his path, intent upon returning to his colony. Schmitty cautiously approaches a temporarily unoccupied entrance opening, tosses in the now empty container for the other colony's keys, and quickly retreats to Rugosus, apparently unnoticed. As the two join their friends lying in wait, Barbatus asks them, "Any problems?" Rugosus answers, "None. The colony member had just enough to reach the outskirts of Optera, and then we let him go. He headed back toward his colony. They should be here soon."

The former captive scurries along the trail he recently marked under duress, and begins to encounter his fellow colony mates, first sporadically, and then more constantly. As he approaches each one, he touches antennae and tells the tale of enemy ants having taken him, and that they are nearby. The pace of the line of ants picks up as they pass the message up and down the now packed trail, of an enemy colony nearby.

At the very same time, Wheels and Cal reach the edge of the P. rugosus colony, and are watching the stream of ants rushing from the mound toward the one they left not long ago. "Gnarly, they're coming out of there so fast, they look like a black river" exclaims Cal, standing up to get a better look. "Cuidado. Get down", warns Wheels. Wheels crouches and walks along the grassy edge of the mound, and when he is on the opposite side from the main opening where the masses are exiting, he tosses the remaining Optera attack keys into the P. rugosus colony side entrance. He returns to Cal, and says "Vamos. We have to hurry."

As the two start back to join the others, the first Optera colony ants are beginning to form a building red stream to the P. rugosus mound. Up to this point, because the renegades have directed each colony on a different trail, they have encountered no opposition, no sign of any resistance to their intended raid. By the time the first defenders begin to notice them, most of the P. rugosus ants are already out on their own attack mission. Most of the large soldiers are still in the colony, since their job is primarily to defend the Queen. The soldiers valiantly stand their ground, but are vastly outnumbered, and are eventually overcome and torn into pieces.

The battle does not take very long. The nursery has been found, and a stream of Optera ants exits the mound entrance, each carrying a captured P. rugosus egg. They will make useful servants, or food for their own young, depending upon the needs of the colony. Soon after, the huge Queen is dragged from the colony by dozens of attackers, and is immediately cut into manageable pieces for transport back to the home colony.

The black raiders are unaware of the fate of their colony. Their sole purpose at this moment is to attack the colony at the end of this trail. As they stream from the trail cut through the tall grass, on to the cleared mound of Optera's entrances, they are met by the same kind of weak resistance that their doomed colony mates are offering back at home. Large, red soldiers are quickly overcome and cut apart. Food gatherers at the opening quickly race downward, sounding the alarm, "Intruders! Protect the Queen!" The message is rapidly passed from ant to ant, and the Queen's Council Sisters are ushered into the safe chamber, just outside the Queen's main room.

Maricopa assembles her team of guards and moves them into position to hold off the attackers. "Defend the Queen with your lives." The guards simply nod in acknowledgment and interlock arms and legs to form a barrier, their jaws opened wide, ready to engage. Maricopa knows they will eventually be overrun, and that the Queen will fall. She already has a plan in place for just this kind of situation. She enters the nursery and commands the nurses caring for the future queen eggs to each pick one up and follow her. "Quickly, quickly. In here." She directs the nurses protecting the eggs into a chamber none have seen before. Inside it, are provisions and many documents, including one very old piece of parchment.

Maricopa directs the elder nurse, "Remain

here for as long as the supplies last, and then you may exit the room and repopulate the colony. You will have to chew your way out. You will be sealed in, so that the attackers will not find you. In addition to caring for the eggs, it is vital that you keep these documents safe, particularly this one." Maricopa holds up an ordinary looking container. "What is it?, asks the nurse. "The document is the only one in existence, and must be kept for the next Queen to use", Maricopa answers. "Seal the room from the outside, and divert the attackers from this passageway, by drawing them toward the nurseries", she orders half of her guards. "The rest of you, come with me. Protect the Queen."

Barbatus sees the masses of black and red ants tangled in battles to the death, and decides the time is right for the group to attack. "BA and Theo, if we are pursued as we come out, we will need your help. The two of you stay right here and make sure no one comes in behind us." He then addresses the other eleven. "Go straight in. Do not engage with any ants of either side, unless they are directly in your path. Fast in and out, that's our goal. Tex and Banshee, take the lead, and do what you do best." The two smile at each other as Tex clanks his huge knife against Banshee's scythe blade.

Barbatus continues to organize the group, "Rugosus and I will be next, and then Patch and Schmitty, then Z and Cal, then Axe, I want you to watch for Bike. We can't afford to lose him." Axe smiles weakly and makes a chopping motion with his weapon. "Wheels, in case things go bad, we'll need to get out fast, so I need you at the rear. Everyone ready? OK, let's go."

As the group nears the main entrance, they

find they must climb over mounds of wounded and dying ants, both invader and defender. The corridors are clogged with motionless ants, but they quickly progress downward, Banshee's scythe efficiently clearing a path through the corpses. Barbatus calls to the two up front, "Turn left at the next split. The Queen's Chamber is just beyond that point. Be ready." The group tightens up their formation, and moves steadily forward, weapons at the ready.

The split is just ahead, and Barbatus says, "Wait. Something's not right. The entrance to the Queen's Chamber should be right here." He points to a wall that is slightly different in color, as if constructed more recently than the walls around it. "Which way, Barbatus?", asks Rugosus. As he asks the question, Maricopa and her guards leap from in front and behind the group, each grabbing one of the team. Maricopa has singled out Barbatus, and angrily growls, "I told you that I would not spare your life." As she says this, she thrusts her stinger toward Barbatus. In a split second, Rugosus leaps between the two, and the stinger pierces his underside.

"No!", yells Barbatus as he deftly swings his long weapon, slicing Maricopa's abdomen in half. The Queen's guards are no match for the weapons of the renegades, and they are swiftly dispatched. As Maricopa dies, she smiles and says to Barbatus, "You have lived today, but you will not live much longer. Your time will come, soon."

Barbatus quickly moves to Rugosus, who is slipping quickly into unconsciousness from the venom, "Rugosus, you should not have risked yourself to save me. I am no longer needed, now that we have fulfilled our mission. I needed you to protect Theo." Rugosus, weakly smiles and almost whispers, "Now you owe me two." At that, he loses consciousness.

"We've got to get Rugosus out of here. Let's move!", orders Barbatus. "What about the Queen?" asks Schmitty. "She'll die without anyone to feed her. Leave her", argues Barbatus. "Quickly, to the surface." Barbatus starts upward with Rugosus slung over his shoulder. The group rises through the corridors, toward the main entrance. As they near the opening, they can sense that they are being followed. "Either run faster, or get ready to fight some more", warns Tex, now at the back of the escaping group.

As they see the others running out of the colony opening, BA and Theo run toward them, weapons drawn. BA slices two pursuers with wild, swinging arcs of his two swords. Just as he turns to check on Theo, one of the injured guards clamps down on a limb holding one of the swords and BA drops it. Too close to get a good angle with his other sword, BA punches at the ant's jaws and struggles to pull away. The flash of the bladed edge of a spear appears an instant before Theo thrusts his spear into the defending ant. The dying ant relaxes his grip, and BA is able to pull free. He picks up his other sword, but it hangs loosely in the injured arm. "Thanks", he offers Theo, who grins and turns to run back to the others.

The group proceeds from the cleared area, into the taller grass, and they stop to rest outside the range of any remaining defenders' ability to sense them. There have been so many alarm signals released during the battle, that the guards who had been chasing the group are unable to distinguish anything but the invaders' and their own chemical keys. They wave their antennae all around at the empty air, trying to sense those they were pursuing. Being unable to follow them, they turn and go back into the doomed colony.

The two colonies' mounds have become killing fields, with contestants battling to the death. To the very last ant, in both colonies, every single one is dead or dying. Even those who were not killed in battle, have been injured so severely that they will soon join their friends and enemies in death. The only remaining living ant in Optera is the Queen, and with no subjects to care for her, she is also doomed.

"What now?", asks Patch. "We have to go to the boy's house", announces Barbatus. "That's where we are going to base now. The tablet is there, the boy is there, and that is where we must defend both. Bike, as soon as we're there, whip up a batch of anti-venom for Rugosus. I hope we're not too late." He is now beginning to feel the weight of his friend, but knows that he owes him his life. "He would carry me. I can carry him."

Down deep inside the colony filled with death, new life stirs inside the eggs which have been saved. And in the corner, in a clay container, the remaining copy has been saved for the next Queen.

Chapter 21.

"Henry...watch this", Clark playfully orders, with that usual impish grin on his face. His body may be confined to a chair, but the prankster inside cannot be contained. Clark has been tweaking the configuration on his tablet computer's wireless settings, and has made it appear to be a rogue network access point. "Any...minute now."

Almost instantly, several men in black suits begin pacing up and down the hallways next to the lab, heads buried in the open laptops they are carrying, occasionally looking up to compare the view around them to what they are looking for on the screen. They circle closer and closer to the two men, as if searching for buried treasure with metal detectors.

"Looking...for something?" asks Clark, almost laughing. "Dr. Shepherd, may we take a look at your computer?" one of the suited men asks, presumptively. "Of course...What are you...looking for?, he asks, barely hiding his amusement. The network security officer looks at Clark and says, "I think you know, Dr. Shepherd." He quickly taps the screen several times, checking the settings, then places the computer back on the mount in front of Clark, and with a stern look on his face, announces, "It seems that your computer was set up improperly again, making it appear to be an access point."

"Gee...I don't know...how that...happened", Clark responds. "It seems to...revert to...that setting...often. Maybe...we should...have it...checked out." The officer quickly answers, "Yes, maybe we should. You know that we have to wait until the tech that is certified to work on your device is scheduled to be in the lab. That should be in a couple of weeks. I'll set it up to be checked. In the meantime, try not to do whatever it is that causes it to change its settings. Good day, Dr. Shepherd."

Clark can barely contain his laughter until the men leave the lab. "I love...messing with...those guys." He has to pause even longer to catch his breath from laughing. "They're so...predictable...Whenever...I'm bored...I make them...think I've set...up a rogue...access point." Henry asks, "You never get in trouble? The network guys are pretty serious about security." Clark answers, "Nah...what are they...going to do...to me?...They let me...do pretty much...what I want." The two laugh a little more, and then Henry turns the conversation to a more serious subject.

"Clark, what happened to Dr. Williams?" Clark responds, "Zeke?...They said he...was 'reassigned',...but something's up...He would have...told me if...he were being...reassigned." Henry grimaces and follows, "Zeke? Funny, I never knew his first name, even though we worked together for almost a year. What do you mean, 'something's up'?"

Clark continues, "I've known Zeke...for quite some...time, and he...would have said...something if there...was a move in...the works...All I know is...that one day he...was telling me all...about some big deal...he had discovered...about negative...side effects of...the drugs being used...on SOL patients,...and how he had...found out that...President Cole had...been taking the same...drugs on an...experimental...basis, and that...there might be some...link between the...drugs and his death...The next thing...I know,...he's gone."

Henry admits to Clark, "I have his storage drive." Clark excitedly answers, "Get...out...You have...his research? Henry replies, "I don't know what's on it. He gave it to me the last day I saw him. I haven't looked at it, since he asked me to keep it for him, but didn't tell me whether it was OK to view its contents."

"We have...to see what's...on it", argues Clark. "Stick it...in that drive." He points to the slot on his tablet computer, and Henry takes the drive from his pocket and inserts it into the slot. The two watch the screen as Clark navigates through the drive by slightly turning his head, moving it up and down, the camera on his computer reacting to the movements of the dot in the center of his forehead, expanding the folders and files one by one. Each layer reveals more and more secret documents that appear to be significantly above either of their security clearances.

"Clark, should we be looking at this?" asks Henry. Clark answers, "Henry,...I think Zeke...was removed...because of this...I think he...was trying to...warn us about it." The two read about UNIPHARM's clinical trials and the unusually high incidences of death, severe illness, and of the high probability of sterility in patients, particularly with one drug; Aggrepax. Internal memos to and from General Green, emphasizing the importance of Y12's "primary objective", make it clear that the purpose of SOL and the ultimate control over its patients is far more sinister than the stated goal of helping them in school.

"I can't believe it, Clark. They even experimented with the President of the United States. President Cole was under the care of his personal physician, now President Anthony, who prescribed him

Aggrepax, despite knowing the dangers."

"They've got top educators involved, the pharmaceutical companies, all levels of government, and even the military has bought in. They want every man taking these drugs and playing the computer game. That's how they plan on controlling the men. The military is on board, because they will get perfectly compliant, highly trained soldiers, who can communicate with each other, and more importantly, be made to unquestionably follow orders automatically, without any electronic devices. By simply adjusting the ratios of the SSRIs and NDRIs, they can make the troops shift from passive citizens to super aggressive warriors."

"And look here; they've been using my ant research to develop asexual reproduction with humans. I've been trying to figure out why they are trying to turn the men into drones, lowering their libido and making them more passive with the drugs and the brainwave manipulation, and making sure that only a chosen few will reproduce. The evidence on this drive proves it. Not only are they trying to control male behavior, they are planning to actually reduce the number of males in the population. This is eugenics! "

The two men continued to quietly look at the dozens of opened documents on the computer screen. Henry turned to look at Clark and said, "Clark, we have to stop this." Clark looks at Henry and answers, "Agreed...How? Henry continues, "I have been talking with some fathers of patients of SOL. One is the original designer of the One World Warrior game." "Turner...Runnels?", asks Clark. "Yes", answers Henry, "and he is covertly recruiting some players he knows, who have the ability to hack into the network and plant a virus. There is one problem." Clark interrupts, "You need...me...You need...a back door...into the...network."

"Yes. Turner said he can find a back door in, if he can get the changes that have been made to his original code", Henry says, describing the plan to have the hackers access the servers during the Championship tournament. "But even with...a back door...they'll be...discovered if...network security...notices the...intrusion." Clark thinks for a moment and says, "I have...an idea...You know...how I just...fooled them...a few minutes...ago?" Henry nods affirmatively, and Clark continues, "We can set...up a wireless...access point...at the...tournament...I can...spoof its...machine access...control name...and security...identifier...to make it...look like...it's my...tablet device....That will...buy enough...time to fool...them into...thinking I've...simply done...it again. They'll be...busy trying...to find me...instead of...looking for...the hackers."

Henry listens intently to Clark's plan, and asks, "Do you think that will work?" "It'll have to", says Clark. "All they need...is about...sixty seconds...to gain access...to the servers...if they have...the right...passwords." Clark smiles and follows with, "And I just...so happen...to have... the passwords...right here...I'll load...everything...on to Zeke's...storage drive...and you can...give it to...Turner."

Henry smiles grimly at Clark and says, "You know that they will find out that we did this. What are we going to do when they find out we were the ones who helped the hackers gain access to the network?" Clark answers, "Hopefully...by that time...the story will...be so public...that they...can't touch us...Either that...or we'll be...seeing Zeke...again soon. Besides...I'll be the...one they...trace this...back to...There's no...way that they...will know you...are involved."

Henry argues, "I can't let you be the only one who goes down for this." Clark says what Henry already knows, "I can't help...in any other...way, and...you can do...a lot more...You have to...stick around...and make sure...this all...gets fixed...Besides...what are they...going to do...to me?" The two men smile at each other, each thinking just exactly what they might actually do to a person who reveals these secrets.

"Mr. Shaw", the voice on the other end of the phone addresses Jim. "We have been going through Solomon's records, and believe that there are some tests that we need to run, to adjust his treatments." The father asks, "What kind of tests?" "Just routine examinations. We have some new DNA comparisons that have been shown to be useful in modifying patient treatment. We have identified Solomon as a potential member of a new group that has been identified as responding to new treatments, and we want to follow up and determine if he is in fact in this group. Simple cheek swab tests are all that is required. Quite routine, and painless."

"What then?", asks Jim. "What happens if he is in this new group?" The caller, trying to deflect the question, answers, "We'll contact you if it turns out that we are right, and then we'll let you know what action is recommended. We'll have the school nurse at

Solomon's school collect the DNA sample. There is no need for you to come in at this time." The caller hangs up as Jim does, and he sits down to decide what it all means.

A few minutes later, Diane Shaw arrives home from the grocery store, arms loaded with bags. Jim jumps up to take some of the bags, and greets her. "What's wrong, Jim?", Diane asks, noticing the look of concern on his face. He answers, "I think they know about Solomon." "What do you mean, know about him?", she asks. "Sit down", he says seriously. "There are some things you should know. Do you remember that old chest that my grandfather left me?" Diane nods yes. Jim continues, "It didn't seem important at the time, but I found out that we have Comanche ancestry. And it turns out that there is a gene that is passed down through males with Native American ancestry that may make them resistant to the treatments that are administered at the SOL Center."

"Is that why Solomon doesn't seem to be changing like the other boys?, his mother asks. "The researcher at the Center, Henry Lee, seems to think so. And Turner Runnels' wife, Lane, has found that this same gene is attracting the attention of a lot of important people. There is a very high likelihood that they are looking for this gene now in Solomon. Diane asks, "What are they going to do with Solomon if they find that he has this gene?" Jim answers, "I don't know, but I don't think I want to take the chance that they aren't going to hurt him. I think we need to get him away from here for a while. I think you should take Solomon to the farm, and not tell anyone where you are going."

"You're scaring me", Diane tells Jim. Trying to keep her calm, Jim responds, "Maybe it's nothing, but I don't think we can take the chance. If it all blows over, no harm done. But I don't think I want them to find him until after the tournament." "Why the tournament?" the mother asks. "There is a plan to get into the computer system of the SOL Center during the championship tournament this weekend, and plant a virus or something that will expose all this drug and game stuff to the media. We need to make sure nobody finds Solomon until after things settle down, one way or the other. I think you two should leave first thing in the morning." Diane nods in agreement, walks to her husband and gives him a hug, and then begins to pack a suitcase for the trip.

Turner has been waiting for his contact to log on to the secure chat site for an hour. This site randomizes the network address of users, so that the location of participants cannot be triangulated. A favorite of hackers, some of them white hats, the ones who are just seeing how far they can get into systems without hurting anything, and some black hats, the ones who don't care what damage they do, this site is one of the few places they are able to communicate with each other, without worrying that they will be tracked down by law enforcement. Traffic to and from the site is routed through a myriad of servers, on multiple continents, and no records are kept at all. Even if a legal entity subpoenaed the chat company, there would be no way to trace users.

He is doing what is called "lurking", waiting for a particular hacker to show up. Finally, in the chat participant list box, at the bottom left of the screen, "headlessprettyboy has logged on" appears. As Turner types his message, it appears next to his screen name of "owwdaddy". He types, "Ready to play this weekend?" The reply is immediate, "rdy 2 prty". Seconds later, headlessprettyboy writes, "u hav port #?"

Turner knows he is asking for the port number that will be used to gain entry into the main computer system during the tournament. Going through the modified code that Clark had provided him yesterday, Turner discovered that the back door he had left open when he originally wrote the program had not been closed. No one bothered to close the port that he had left open, like all good programmers do when writing new code. Turner thinks to himself, "Lazy government programmers, leaving the same port open."

He types in, "2512". The next question comes from the hacker, "ssid, login, pwd?", asking for the unique identifier, user ID, and password to the wireless access point that Clark had given him. Turner quickly types in, "Y12mesh, c.shephard.y12.gov, Y12ProfX@vierIsC00L". The response comes, "nice pwd". Then, another entry, "payload?" Turner, knowing that the files containing the virus and other instructions is too large to transmit in the limited time they have on this site replies, "hand delivered at party". The reply comes, "media?" Turner answers with, "portable drive, but game stations portable drive ports disabled." "ez", brags the hacker.

Turner informs the hacker of the time to begin the hack, "tournament official start". The reply is, "window?" Turner, knowing he is asking how much time it will take for the network security people to be able to track down an intruder, answers, "60 sec". The reply indicating he understands the time constraints comes, "ack".

The final entry from headlessprettyboy, who knows that even though this system is the most secure available, the longer they remain online, the greater the chances that government resources, domestic and foreign, will be able to locate him, is "times up". Turner also logs off, and shuts down his computer.

"Where's Solomon?", Turner asks Jim Shaw, as the two arrive at the team's designated area at the Championship arena in the convention center. "He and his mother are visiting the family farm this weekend", Jim answers. "He's missing the tournament?", asks Turner, incredulously. "After qualifying, and doing so well?" Jim Shaw looks around, making sure no one is able to oversee the conversation, and adds, "Turner, I think you know why he isn't here. I'm very concerned that the government knows about his genetic resistance to the treatments, and that they might try to do take him back to the Center."

At that moment, a small squad of black-suited men are questioning the tournament security personnel, who are pointing in the direction of Jim and Turner. The men quickly approach Jim and the one apparently in charge addresses him, "Mr. Shaw?" Jim answers, "I'm Jim Shaw." "We're here to pick up Solomon", he states in an official tone. Jim replies, "Solomon's not here today. He's with his mother, visiting family." The official stares at Jim for a moment, and then says, "Unfortunate. I'm going to have to ask you to come with me then, Mr. Shaw." "Do I have a choice?", Jim asks. The men stand quietly around him without answering. Jim answers himself, "I guess not", and walks with them toward the main entrance.

Turner Runnels walks up and down the rows of players who are preparing to play. He is very careful to not make eye contact with the one player who will be coordinating the hack today. The hacker is on a different team from his son, but it is not at all unusual for Turner to be seen wandering among players, since he is still officially in charge of the tournaments. Turner has left the details of the hack to his contact, wanting to have plausible deniability after the fact.

As the tournament director walks behind him, the young man with the gray wool cap pulled down over his ears, which are filled with the ear buds of his music player playing music loud enough to be heard by anyone walking near him, initiates his attack. First logging on to his favorite proxy server in Korea, then routing through his favorite hacker bulletin board server in Russia, he uses a back door he planted in an Arkansas bank a few years ago. Skimming amounts from large businesses, in amounts small enough to avoid triggering automated flags, funded most of his equipment purchases, until he decided it was too risky to continue; no need to get greedy.

Now appearing to be an employee at the Arkansas bank, he accesses a Chinese military server, using the credentials he "borrowed" from an individual who had been trying to hack into servers at the Pentagon. It just so happened that a user named headlessprettyboy was in the virtual neighborhood at the same time, and somehow, the penetration attempt was traced back to the server operated by the Chinese

Army. Even though the Chinese government denied any involvement, the Chinese hacker's identification and password were never deactivated.

Scattered randomly across the conference room, a dozen other game players have black dialogue boxes open at the bottom of their screens, with the One World Warrior game playing in the background. Each is on a different team, to make it more difficult to determine his exact location if network security is able to trace the penetration attempt back here. All are poised to flood the OWW servers with a distributed denial of service attack, using their bot network of home and business computers they have collected over the past couple of years. In each of their black dialogue boxes, appears the message from headlessprettyboy, "go".

The young man in the gray wool cap pulls out a vintage stopwatch and clicks it, then rapidly types the login information that had been given to him on the hacker chat room the other day. The credentials are valid, and he is able to log on as the administrator of the wireless access point that has been hidden in a storeroom between the convention center and the servers. "This is too easy", he thinks to himself, without slowing. He then accesses the One World Warrior server that is designated for game data collection, and follows the tree hierarchy that was outlined by his contact, drilling down through nodes, folders, and files. He plugs in the storage drive he was provided by the tournament director when he walked behind him a few minutes ago, and clicks the executable file, initiating the upload.

As the status bar moves steadily to the right,

indicating the files being uploaded, he picks up the stopwatch again. Holding it up to be able to see it and the screen, at the very second the status bar indicates "File transfer complete", he clicks the stopwatch. "59 seconds. Booya." He quickly logs off of each server, in reverse order, then blows his player up in the game with a hand grenade, so that he is out of the tournament. Now automatically logged out by the game server, he shuts down his console and calmly ambles toward the spectator area.

The other dozen who had been attacking the OWW server take similar actions to lose in the game, are shut out of the game, and power off their consoles and join him in the spectator area, to watch the rest of the tournament. As each enters the spectator bleacher section, he nods, acknowledging having escaped undetected.

"Dr. Shepherd", the black-suited security officer addresses Clark, now monitoring game play data upload. "What now?", Clark asks, pretending not to know. "We're going to need to take your tablet computer", the officer demands. "Why?", Clark asks. "The settings are...not changed...this time. It hasn't...switched back since...the last time you...were here." The officer takes the tablet, punches his finger around on the screen a few times, narrows his eyes, and hands the tablet back to Clark. Without saying a word, he wheels around and runs down a hallway toward the convention center, followed by several other offices.

Turner Runnels glances toward the spectator area, and the young man with the gray wool cap raises his head up in the "hey" motion. Runnels repeats the same gesture, and continues walking among active players. As he nears the center of the room, Turner notices a sudden stream of security officers rapidly entering the game play area. Each row of players has an officer walking behind them, and looking closely at their console screens. Turner thinks to himself, "They figured it out faster than I had hoped, but all they know is that it came from the room. They won't be able to figure out which computer it came from."

At that very moment, all the major news organizations, television and radio networks, major city newspapers and national magazines, and even the better known blogs begin to receive instant messages and social network updates, with links to the One World Warrior website. The website's front page has been modified to include links to documents that detail the history of UNIPHARM, its political ties, the goals of the organizations behind it, the clinical trials results of the drugs administered to patients and game players, side effects of the drugs, and how the former President died from complications caused by using the drugs.

As President Anthony is signing some documents at her desk, the television that is always tuned to her favorite cable news network, partially to keep her abreast of the news, and partially just as white noise, crackles with the sound of the breaking news update. "This just in. Startling news about government secret research and your son's health. How former President Cole's death may have been a result of dangerous side effects that were hidden by UNIPHARM and government officials..."

Just then, the Chief of Staff bursts into the office, and breathlessly gushes, "Madam President,

General Green on the secure line." Rebecca Anthony picks up the phone and asks, "How bad is it?" On the other end of the line, General Green answers grimly, "As bad as it can get. Someone got into the game data server, hijacked the website, and uploaded all the documents." "All the documents?" asks the President. The General answers, "Everything." "Who?" asks the President. "At first, it appeared to have been Chinese government-sponsored hackers, but the attack was traced back to players in the One World Warrior tournament. We're trying to figure out exactly who, but there are one thousand players to interview." The President angrily replies, "Forget it. It doesn't matter who did it now. You know what you have to do."

General Green calls General Rogers at the Y12 Center. He picks up the direct line, answering with his usual, "Rogers." "General, initiate self destruct of the complex." General Rogers replies, "Yes, Ma'am. I'll issue the evacuation order, and begin self-destruct in the standard thirty minutes." His superior counters with, "Negative, General. Initiate self-destruct immediately." "We have personnel within the blast area", reports Rogers. "Your orders stand, General", says General Green tersely. "Yes, Ma'am", he replies. General Rogers takes the special red key from his desk, proceeds quickly to the never-opened door at the center of the computer complex, and opens it. Proceeding down the stairs inside the door, he reaches a small room that contains a tactical nuclear device, not large enough to destroy anything larger than a city block, but powerful enough to create an electromagnetic pulse that can wipe out any electronic device within a two mile radius.

The General remembers when this specially designed room, at the core of the computer center, was finished before any other construction began. The inverted cone-shaped room has reinforced concrete walls that are six feet thick, extending fifty feet below the surface, with a bottom diameter of 70 feet. The purpose of the design is to minimize blast damage to the building itself, venting the majority of energy and radiation into the substrata. The exclusive function of this room is to serve as a self-destruct mechanism, for use only as an alternative to having the Center's computer data fall into the wrong hands.

He looks into the retinal scanner. "General Clifton Rogers", the voice synthesizer acknowledges. "Please enter your authorization code." The General punches in the code he has memorized from dozens of drills, and the voice says, "Thank you, General Rogers. Please enter the number of minutes of delay before detonation." He presses the number 1, and then presses Enter. "You have entered a one minute delay. This is less than the recommended minimum safe evacuation period. If you are sure this is correct, please enter your override code." He types in another memorized code and hits the Enter key. "Thank you, General. EMP countdown has begun." Throughout the building, chirping alarms begin to sound, along with bright, flashing halogen lights. The clock displays 59, then 58, and continues to count down. The General races up the stairs and rushes out of the lab and down the hallway to the exit at the back of the complex. The self-destruct program has begun automatically closing and sealing the doors leading into and out of the labs. General Rogers passes through the last door as it closes.

Back in the convention center, game play still not completed, a loud boom is heard in the distance, and the whole room shakes violently, and then everything goes black. Emergency lights flicker on, and then after a few seconds, the backup generators crank to life and the lights come back on in the convention center. All of the game consoles have gone black. People are heard complaining that they cannot get cell service. Music players won't work. All of the sponsor display booths are dead. Turner Runnels looks back up to the spectator area. In the brief darkness, the group of hackers has slipped out. The officers who had been walking up and down the rows of players are now running toward the exits. As they reach the mobile server trailers, the technicians exit, shaking their heads, saying, "Everything's dead."

As news spreads by word of mouth about the problems with the SOL Center, Y12, pharmaceutical drugs, and the former President, people try to log on to the One World Warrior website, but it is no longer available. In its place is a page with a white background that displays "Error 404, Page not found." President Anthony asks General Green, "Is it done?" General Green replies, "Yes. The Y12 Center computers are destroyed, including the mobile units." "What about the remaining copy?" the President asks her General. "It is secure at The Freezer", the General replies. The President then asks, "How many people know of its existence?" The General answers, "Three; General Rogers, you, and myself." The President hangs up the phone and prepares for the onslaught of reporters' questions that she will be denying any knowledge of for the next few weeks.

Henry Lee races up to Turner Runnels and breathlessly announces, "That was an EMP, and it was close. I think it was in the Center. I'm going to check it out." "Be careful, Henry", cautions Turner. "Everything worked as planned. Don't get caught now." "I won't. I'm supposed to be there. There's no reason anyone should suspect anything from me checking out my lab", he responds. Henry runs down the long corridors from the recently built convention center built a quarter mile from the Y12 complex. As he nears the complex, he notices dozens of men dressed in hazmat suits, opening the doors to all of the offices. He slips by unnoticed, and walks quickly to the lab.

Visible behind the glass wall that divides the hallway from the main computer center, he can see Clark Shepherd slumped over in his wheelchair. Henry fumbles with his security card, and swipes it, but the reader is no longer functioning. He finds the manual override lever down and to the right of the card reader, and pulls it up, releasing the door. "Clark!", yells Henry. "Clark, are you OK?" Clark is still conscious, but cannot acknowledge him. The electromagnetic pulse has fried everything electronic, including Clark's breathing mechanism. He is barely breathing, and in great difficulty. "I'll get you out of here", Henry promises, as he grabs the chair handles and pushes. The chair doesn't move. He remembers that there is a switch to disengage the now dead electric motor, allowing the chair to be moved manually, and finds it. He moves as quickly as he can, and finds the closest hazmat-suited worker. Henry says, "We need medical attention, now." The worker directs him to go to the next exit, where military medics are arriving. "We'll take him", a medic tells Henry. "I should go with him", argues Henry. "Not necessary. He'll be taken to a military trauma center nearby, and will be in good hands", insists the medic.

Even though the OWW website went down only ten minutes after all the links to documents were posted, the cached copies on the internet are still available, and the news organizations all immediately copied them to their websites. The documents have been seen by millions of people in only the first hours, and there are already calls for the President's resignation.

At her family's farm, Diane Shaw listens to the news on television, while preparing dinner for Solomon and herself. Word of the conspiracy among all levels of government, and of UNIPHARM's involvement in the death of the former President Cole, facilitated and possibly even caused by now President Anthony's callous disregard for his safety, are being covered non-stop on every channel. The cable news anchor reports, "Lawmakers on both sides of the aisle, in both houses of Congress, are now calling for impeachment, and criminal charges for her involvement in the death of the former President are being prepared by the United States Attorney for the District of Columbia."

She picks up the phone and calls her husband Jim. "Are you watching the news?" Jim answers abruptly, "You shouldn't have called." She replies, "It's out now. They wouldn't come after us now, would they?" "You shouldn't have called. I don't trust them. Pack up and leave, now. Just drive until dark, and then check in to some hotel. Pay cash and don't leave a credit card. Turn off your phone, and don't call anyone. Go buy a throwaway phone at a convenience store, and call me tomorrow. We'll arrange to meet somewhere, after we figure out whether or not it's safe", Jim says impatiently.

Diane Shaw's hands tremble slightly as she disconnects the call and powers off her phone. She calls to her son, "Time for dinner, Solomon. As soon as we finish eating, we have to leave." Solomon has been staring out of the window in his room, at the large bird standing in the field, and he thinks back to that day when he first saw the first one. The voice of his mother snaps him back. "Again? When are we going to see Dad?", the boy asks. His mother answers, "Soon. We'll talk to him about it tomorrow. Eat, and then go grab your things. I'll need you to be on the lookout along the way; you get to pick the hotel to stay in tonight."

Chapter 22.

Wheels runs back to the group, returning from his scouting expedition to the Shaw's house. "The tablet's still there, but we've got two problems." "Problems?", asks Barbatus. "What kind of problems? Report." Wheels begins his debriefing, "The place is crawling with men in black suits. They're going through everything, looking for something." Barbatus interrupts, "They're looking for the boy, or the tablet, or both." The leader pauses for a moment, and then asks, "What's the other problem?"

Wheels continues, "Men all over and around the house, but underneath the house, a huge colony of Solenopsis invicta." Barbatus mutters through clenched jaws, "Invictas. Fire ants. That could be a problem. Bike, how good are you at making up S. invicta juice?" Bike responds, "Get me a sample, and I'll work it out." Barbatus says, "Maybe we can use the situation to our advantage. Schmitty, go with Wheels and grab a 'volunteer'. Do it fast; we don't have much time." Rugosus objects, "I should be the one to go." Barbatus argues, "You're in no condition to go on a raid yet." Rugosus clenches his jaws, but does not object.

As the two approach the house, looking for a telltale trail, the men in black suits are tearing up the interior. "Nothing", mutters the agent in charge. "Has anyone checked underneath the house? Davis, Brooks, check it out." The two agents pull off the vent covers to access the crawlspace underneath the house, and each wriggles through a hole on opposite sides of the house. They painstakingly move from one side to the other, checking every crevice and recess, looking for anything that seems out of place. "Anything?", calls the agent in charge over the radio. "Not yet, sir." "Find something", comes the reply from the head agent.

Schmitty quickly grabs one of the much smaller fire ants, and being very careful to avoid his potent stinger, throws him in a bag, and turns to run back to the group with Wheels. Bike quickly makes the necessary calculations, and starts the process of preparing the chemicals that will be needed to confuse the fire ant colony, allowing their group to safely get near the tablet. "What about him?", asks Rugosus, nodding his head toward the captured ant. Barbatus answers, "Loosen the bag when we leave. He'll eventually escape, but we can't afford for him to get loose until after we get to the house.

"Ready", says Bike to the group. "Let's go", orders Barbatus. The group reaches the edge of the house, and Barbatus orders the chemical keys divided up among four members. "Schmitty, Tex, Banshee, and Axe, each of you grab a bag and go to a different side of the house. Throw the bag underneath the house and run. We'll let nature take its course." Moments later, screams blast over the agents' radios, "Agh! They're all over me! Fire ants!" Both agents crawl as fast as they can through the vent holes, jumping and slapping ants off of their clothing, continuing their screams of pain. "Did you search underneath completely?", asks the agent in charge, not even acknowledging the agony of his two stricken men. The agents, still rubbing the dozens of stings over their bodies, simultaneously answer, "There's nothing under there, sir."

"Up here!", calls one of the agents from the attic. "I found something." He hands the trunk down through the crawlspace hole to another agent, who then brings it down to the agent in charge. "What do we have?", asks the head agent. The one who first discovered the chest describes the contents, as the agent in charge pulls them out, one by one. He stops at the oldest-looking document, the old parchment, and says barely out loud, "Looks like Mr. Solomon Shaw fits the profile." Then, to the group, more loudly, "They'll be very interested in this at the lab. OK, wrap it up. The kid's not here. Let's get moving."

"Sir, we got a hit on the mother's cell phone", reports one of the agents. "Where?", the agent in charge demands. "A farm about 80 miles North of here", comes the reply. "Saddle up. Let's move!", calls the agent in charge, and the line of black vehicles speed away down the dirt road leading to the highway, leaving a plume of dust behind.

As Jim Shaw drives down the road toward his house, he sees the line of black vehicles turn from his driveway and turn in the opposite direction. He quickly pulls to the side of the road to avoid being seen, and waits for them to drive out of sight. As he turns into his driveway, the dust is still swirling in the air. He cautiously steps from his car, looks all around, and walks up to the front door. He finds it open and walks in, to the sight of the house in total disarray. Everything has been knocked off of all the shelves, sofa and chair cushions tossed about randomly, pots and utensils scattered all over the kitchen, every drawer pulled from every cabinet and chest, their contents emptied on the floors. Jim thinks to himself, "They were here for Solomon." Then realizing that the men were also looking for something else, he says out loud, "The trunk!", and runs up to the attic.

"Quick", calls Barbatus, "Get the tablet. We have to get it to the boy's father." The ants pick up the thin, stone tablet, larger in size than all of them together, and carry it from under the house, beside the front porch. As they bring it from under the house, the dust from the string of vehicles leaving is hanging in the air. "They're gone", announces Patch. "They'll be back", promises Barbatus. "They need the tablet. They won't stop looking for it, just like they won't stop looking for the boy."

"They took it. They know", the father says out loud. Frantically, he crawls to the edge of the opposite side of the attic and reaches between the rafters, feeling for the leather pouch where he stored the tablet corner. "It's still here. They didn't find it", Jim breathes a heavy sigh of relief. I've got to find Solomon and Diane", Jim exclaims as he runs out the front door, toward his car. As he steps off of the porch, he sees a group of ants and a small, stone tablet, and stoops down to pick it up. As he does, the ants back away and stand at attention. Jim picks up the tablet, getting a closer look at the inscription cut into it. "This is the original that my grandfather's document was a copy of." He looks down at the ants and says, "You must have hidden it here, and now you have shown it to me. What does this mean?" He looks at the ants, still standing in a straight line, and says, "I wish you could tell me what to do with this."

"Will he know what to do with it?", Rugosus asks Barbatus, who answers, "I don't know, but he is the only one who can care for it now. He has to keep it and his son safe from those who would try to harm them. We have to trust him to do it." Rugosus asks, "Aren't we supposed to keep it with us?" Barbatus thinks for a moment and answers, "Yes, I promised I would, but we can't keep it here now."

Just then, Jim Shaw decides what he has to do. He looks around and finds a shoe box, scoops some dirt in it, and places it on the ground in front of the group of ants. "Get in. I need your help." The ants all look at Barbatus, who is already walking into the box. The rest join him and Jim picks the box up, places it in the seat next to him, and starts up the car. As the engine idles, his cell phone rings, and he answers. "Hello." The other voice asks, "Jim?" He answers, "Diane! Is this phone untraceable?" "Yes", she responds. "I paid cash for it at a convenience store, like you told me to." Jim asks, "Are you two OK? Anyone try to contact you? Did you see anything unusual?" She answers, "No, everything seems fine. We left the farm right after we talked with you. Is everything OK there?"

"They trashed the house", Jim replies. "They were looking for Solomon, and something else." "What else were they looking for?", she asks. "Remember that I told you I discovered my grandfather's Comanche ancestry?", asks Jim. "Yes", Diane answers. "Well, there were some old documents in that chest that I think they were looking for", he says. "What would they want with that old stuff?", his wife asks. Jim answers, "They hold some kind of genetic secret that the government needs as much as they need Solomon. They have all those documents, but they don't have Solomon, and they don't have the original." "What do you mean by the original?", she asks. "I have the original stone tablet that my grandfather's copy was made from", says Jim. "Where did you get it?", asks Diane. "You'd never believe me if I told you", Jim says, looking down at the shoebox full of ants in the seat next to him.

"We have to find a safe place for Solomon, and for this tablet." "Where?", his wife asks Jim. He answers, "There aren't many people we can trust. I can think of one though; a guy at the lab that first told me about all this stuff. His name is Henry Lee. I'll call him and call you right back." Jim scrolls through his phone records and calls Henry's number. "This is Henry", he answers. Jim responds, "Henry, listen, this is Jim Shaw. I need some help." "Is everything OK? Is Solomon safe?", Henry asks. "Yes, for now", Jim answers. "Some government guys showed up at the house, and now they have my grandfather's chest. They must know about Solomon." He continues, "But there's something new. I know it sounds weird, maybe not as weird as it would if we hadn't been through all this, but some ants brought me the original stone tablet that my grandfather's parchment was copied from. It's some kind of old code. I'm pretty sure the ants are trying to get me to help keep it from the government guys."

Henry replies, "Yes, it would have been weird not long ago, but too much has happened. Did you hear about the lab?" Jim answers, "I was walking out of the tournament building, just as the explosion happened. What was it?" Henry explains, "It was an EMP, and the whole lab was fried. Nothing there; no computer records of any sort. There's nothing there that they can trace back to any of the boys, including Solomon." Jim counters, "But somebody still knows about him, and they're looking for Solomon. And now they're also looking for this tablet. What do we do?"

"I've got an idea", says Henry. Give me a few minutes, and I'll call you right back." Henry hangs up and immediately calls a number from his phones contacts list. "This is Shelton", the man answers. "Shelton, this is Henry. I've got some very important things to tell you, and I need a favor." "Shoot", answers Tarver. "OK, you wanted to know what I was doing with the ants in my research? I'm going to tell you everything, and you have to promise that you'll help and not talk to anyone about it, especially any government people." "You know I'm not particularly fond of government people", says Shelton, laughing.

Henry answers, "This is a really big deal, Shelton. Ever heard of the old Indian legends about the beginning of man?" Tarver answers, "You mean, 'The Secret of The Ancestors'? I've heard about it. I figured there must be some science behind it, but that it was mostly legend." Henry responds, "Well, it turns out that it is the genetic code for preserving the males of both species, and there are people who are trying to use it to alter the natural makeup of human reproduction. My research gave them the information they needed, but they still needed the keys."

Tarver asks, "What keys?" Henry answers, "There is a boy who is the human key, and now his father holds the original stone tablet that is the other key that has been protected by ants." "Protected by ants?", asks Shelton incredulously. "I know it sounds crazy, but you'll understand when you see it", argues Henry. "Shelton, I need a safe place for the boy and his family, and for the stone tablet, until all of this is settled. Can we stay at your cabin?" "Sure, as long as I can take a look at all of what you are describing, and if you'll fill me in on all your research." Henry answers, "I will. I have to; you're one of the few I can trust with this information. We'll meet you there in about eight hours." "Meet you there", replies Tarver.

"OK Jim, I've got a safe place for us to go", says Henry. "We need to meet, and then drive in your car. We can't take mine; it's a government issue with a GPS tracking device in it. We're going to West Texas. Can't tell you where until we're on he way." "Got it, Henry", Jim responds. "Meet you at the parking lot of the First Church on Main. We can leave the cars there without anyone checking on them for a few days." "OK. See you in a half hour", says Henry.

Jim calls Diane back on the number that showed up on the previous call. "Hello?", she tentatively answers. "Diane, meet us in town, at the First Church parking lot. We're driving to a safe place in West Texas." "OK", she agrees. "See you in a bit. Jim, I'm worried." Her husband tries to reassure her, "It'll be OK. We've got some good people who are going to help. It shouldn't be too long before this is all straightened out, but just in case, toss that phone and buy another one. I'm on my way." As he turns on to the main road, Jim rolls down his car window and pitches his phone into the creek.

"I don't like this", says Rugosus. "We have a much better chance on our own." "Our job is to protect the tablet, not ourselves", argues Barbatus. Rugosus counters, "What about the kid?", nodding over at Theo. "Our fates all depend upon keeping the tablet out of the wrong hands", states Barbatus. The group of thirteen stand surrounding the tablet, lying flat on the dirt in the center of the shoebox. The car pulls to a stop in the church parking lot. Theo is the first to see the boy and asks, "Is that him?" "You've never seen him yet, have you?", says Z, just waking up from the nap he took during the drive. "That's the boy. The human key", confirms Barbatus.

As Jim pulls into the church parking lot, he places the shoebox on the seat behind him. Henry locks up his car with his phone on the front seat, and walks over and gets in on front passenger side. Jim and Diane embrace next to the car, and then she takes the right rear seat, behind Henry. Solomon gets in next to his mother, and noticing the box beside him, looks down into it. "It's them. These are the ones." Diane asks, "What do you mean 'the ones'?" Solomon answers, "The same ants I saw at school. You know, the ones I drew." His mother asks, "How do you know they're the same ones?" The boy answers, "I can see them. They're the same ones. They've been waiting for me. What's this?", reaching for the tablet. His father chimes in, "I wouldn't exactly call it waiting. They've been pretty busy. They brought me that tablet. It seems to be very important to a lot of people, and we need to make sure that we don't let the wrong people have it. That's why we're driving out in the middle of nowhere and staying for a few days."

Diane swivels her head back and forth between her husband and her son, her mouth hanging open, not sure if they are joking, or delusional, or if this is all real. Too much has happened for this to be a simple prank, and the people who have been trying to find Solomon are very real. She decides to just wait quietly to see what will happen next. "I hope Jim knows what he is doing", she thinks to herself.

As the sun begins to fall beneath the mountain tops on the horizon, Jim slows the car, the odometer mileage slowly approaching the turnoff point from the highway. Henry says, "There it is. This is the road to the cabin." "Here?", Diane asks. "There's not a town within a hundred miles of here." Henry smiles and answers, "That's the point, isn't it? The guy we're meeting uses this cabin when he does research out here on, guess what, ants." Nearing the end of the twenty minute drive down the bumpy dirt road, the dim lights in the windows of the mud and stone cabin slowly grow brighter and larger. The car stops just outside the front door. As the four exit the car, the lawn mower engine hum of the propane fueled generator drowns out the chirping of the insects, and the door opens, light spilling out into the darkness. Shelton has been here just long enough to get dinner started for the group.

Henry introduces the family to his fellow researcher, "Shaw family, this is Dr. Shelton Tarver." Jim sticks out his hand and introduces his family, "Jim Shaw, my wife Diane, and my son Solomon." Tarver takes his turn, "Shelton. Nice to meet you all. I've heard a lot about Solomon. Sounds like you've had a bit of excitement." "You don't know the half of it", answers Jim. "Let's go in and get settled", offers Shelton. "Look at these ants", says Solomon cheerfully. "Let's see those", Shelton says as the two of them walk into the cabin, each with a hand on the box. "What do we have here?" asks Shelton.

"If anyone can figure out these ants, it's

Shelton", Henry says with certainty, as the group sits down at the table. "Why do these ants keep finding me?", asks Solomon. Shelton answers, "I've been studying ants for as long as I can remember. I've been looking at ants since I was younger than you are." Tarver looks down into the box and observes the variety of ants collected. "This is very unusual. You've got what appear to be thirteen ants, all of different species. I see two P. barbati, but the rest are all individuals from species that are often in competition with each other, and from a wide variety of geographical origins. I've never observed ants from different colonies, much less different species, able to be near each other without fighting. You've got a P. rugosus, a P. bicolor, a P. apache, a P. schmitti, a P. wheeleri, a P. texanus, a P. comanche, a P. badius, a P. desertorum, a P. californicus, and a P. occidentalis."

The ant expert looks even closer at the group in the box. "Fascinating. In addition to the apparent lack of animosity between what should be warring species, these ants actually appear to be a cohesive unit. They are lined up as if in formation. That's impossible, of course, but they appear to be a group." He squints tightly as he leans in even closer. "What's this? They have some kind of unusual coating or covering." He pulls a magnifying glass out of his backpack, and peers into the box. "Impossible. They have what appears to be some kind of fabricated covering over their exoskeletons; almost like an armor. And, yes, it can't be anything else. They are holding weapons. They have constructed weapons! This is amazing!" Shelton is almost giggling in delight, completely lost in his study of the ants.

Jim startles Shelton back to the group, "Dr. Tarver, these are no ordinary ants." "What do you mean?", asks Shelton. Jim explains, "They apparently are on a mission to protect this tablet", pointing to the small stone tablet in the box. Shelton picks up the tablet and studies it for a moment. "I've seen this before, in old Native American artifacts. I can't quite read it, but it looks like it is a petroglyph of some sort. The figures appear to tell a story. It looks familiar; I think I've seen this one before, or a copy of it, at the university's museum. It's quite possible that this is the original of the copy I have seen. If so, it has great historical significance."

Jim interrupts, "Shelton, I know what the tablet says. My grandfather left me a copy of it, and a description of what it says. He was the grandson of the famous Comanche chief Santana, and he described in great detail how boys with this lineage are not only able to see the ants, but are the actual key to the survival of the human race." Jim went on to describe the legends of the destruction of the Earth, how the ants protected the chosen few men, and how a new tablet with the new genetic code was written and destroyed each time. "The tablet is called 'The Secret of the Ancestors', and it is the framework for the genetic makeup of this generation of humans. Note that there is a corner missing. This corner", as he holds up the corner of the tablet he has been keeping in his pocket.

"Somehow, these ants, this tablet, and Solomon, are all essential to the secret of the genetic code. That is why they are after Solomon." Henry jumps in, "Of course, it all makes sense. The Generals and the President are trying to be able to reproduce females without needing men, as their way of protecting the human race the next time it is destroyed. They're trying to avoid the destruction of the planet, but what they're doing is actually going to cause it. Once they eliminate the need for sexual reproduction, there will be out of control genetic mutations and disease, and humans will slowly die off. If they find Solomon, they're going to actually cause what they are trying to avoid."

"Hold on there", says Shelton. "Is that what you've been using the ants for in your research?" Henry immediately answers, "Evidently, yes. But I didn't realize what the research was being used for until recently. I wondered what they wanted with pheromones and ant asexual reproduction. I discovered it too late to help one of my fellow researchers, but it was his information that tipped me off to something being wrong. As soon as we figured out what was going on, we worked up a plan to publicize the real reason for the research with a computer virus. We were racing the military, or the government, or both, to expose the plot before they could figure out Solomon is the key. When the information came out, General Green had the lab computers destroyed with an EMP. The information is out now though. It's only a matter of time before those responsible will be held accountable."

"Had I known what it was being used for, I never would have agreed to participate", says Shelton angrily. "But, one good thing has come of it; I would never have learned of the apparent intelligence of these ants, had this not all taken place. I would like to keep this group and study them further, after this all has passed. I think some very big things can come from this."

Henry replies, "I don't think anyone would mind you studying the ants, Shelton. But first, we need to make sure that the tablet is moved to a safe place. Can you think of such a place?" Tarver thinks for a moment, and smiling says, "The safest place is often the most public one. Why don't we put it in the university's museum? I can commission the School of Anthropology to do testing on it. That will keep it safely under environmental controls while they date it and try to decode it. It will be months or years before they figure out what it says and publish any papers on it. That should be plenty of time for all this to be settled."

Shelton continues to study the tablet, then comments, "Well Jim, one thing is for sure; this isn't Comanche. There is no written version of the Comanche language. That's the main reason they were used as code talkers in the World Wars; there was no written copy to decode the spoken words. This must be something far more ancient than any of the more modern tribes. Maybe the Anthropology fellows can figure it out."

Henry adds to the discussion, "If that corner is the key to the code, I think we have to keep them in separate places, just in case one is found." "I agree", adds Jim. "I think Henry should keep it; Shelton is going to know where the tablet is, and I will be concentrating on keeping Solomon safe. The key has to be kept separate from the other two." The three men nod in agreement, and Jim hands the corner piece to Henry.

Rugosus asks Barbatus, "What are we to do? How are we going to protect the boy, if we remain here when he leaves with his family?" Barbatus responds, "Our job is to make sure that the tablet doesn't fall into the wrong hands, and that the boy is safe. The tablet will be in good hands at the university museum, the corner key is being held by the young researcher, and the boy seems to be safe now with his family. But don't forget that we also still have been charged with keeping Theo safe. I think he will be much safer with us. No one will be able to find us with the old man."

Rugosus adds, "Don't forget that we never did find any of the copies of the tablet in those colonies when we defeated the Queen. Maybe we can hitch a ride back with him and see what we can find. Barbatus agrees, "That has been on my mind, too. We must find a way to make sure that no copies remain. The only way to do that will be to go back into those colonies. If we can somehow get him to dig up the colonies for us, it will be much faster. Perhaps the old man's shovel will be useful to us after all."

The next morning, Shelton has breakfast already prepared for the entire group when they wake. "Coffee?", he asks, waving a half filled mug in Solomon's direction. Solomon grimaces and says, "No thanks." "Don't worry. I'm sure there's some milk in the refrigerator." Jim sees the large portable phone on the small desk in the corner, and asks Shelton, "Is that what I think it is?" "The satellite phone? I keep that out here in case I need to call in to the office in town. No cell towers anywhere near here", Tarver explains. "If you're going to call someone, you should keep it short, so that our location can't be triangulated", Henry cautions.

"I'm going to call Turner Runnels. He's in this with us, and can help us figure out if it's safe to come back yet." Jim pulls out the business card Runnels gave him at the tournament, and then punches in the numbers for his cell phone. "Hello?", he answers. "Turner, I need to ask a favor of you", Jim appeals. "Who is this?", Turner asks. "It's Jim Shaw", he answers. Turner excitedly replies, "Jim! You're OK. Where are you?" "We're out West, but I can't tell you exactly where right now. We don't know who's listening in. What is going on there now? Has anyone been looking for us?" Turner answers, "Everyone. The school, the SOL Center, and other guys who I can only assume are government agents."

He continues, "But, they all seem to have disappeared since the Senate hearings have started. The top military brass have been called to testify at the impeachment proceedings." Jim responds, "Impeachment? Of the President?" "Yes", Turner answers. "She's up to her eyeballs in this mess, and the press have been covering the SOL, Y12, UNIPHARM, and One World Warrior link non-stop since the explosion at the tournament. It seems that there is a whistle blower that was actually in the computer complex at the time, who has testified against General Green and the President, and who has verified the information that was leaked to the Press. Is Henry with you? They're looking for him to testify, too"

Jim says, "Henry's right here with me. I'll put him on the phone after we're finished. I was going to ask you if we could stay with you for a few days until this all smoothes over, but is it possible that we could go back to our own home?" Turner answers, "Why don't you plan on coming here first, and I'll go out and take a look at your house and see what is going on there. I'll let you know what I find out when we meet at my house." Jim sighs and answers, "Thanks. We'll be there in about eight hours. Here's Henry."

"Turner", Henry calls into the phone. "I heard something about impeachment. What's going on?" Turner fills him in, "What I can determine so far is that General Green was the one who set off the EMP, evidently at the direction of the President. She denied it all as a partisan attack by her political enemies, but there was someone who was in the lab and who has provided evidence of their involvement. He is testifying at the hearings, and has mentioned your name as someone who can also testify to the accuracy of his story." "Clark!", Henry says without thinking. "Yeah, Clark something", answers Turner. Henry then explains, "Clark Shepherd was there when the EMP went off. I had to pull him out. I was afraid he wouldn't survive. I'm so happy to know he is doing well enough to testify. So they want me too, huh?"

Turner replies, "Yes. I'm surprised they haven't found you yet. I think you should report to some neutral government official, like maybe your Senator's office." "That's a good idea, Turner. That's exactly what I'll do", agrees Henry. "We're heading out right now. It will take us all day to get back. If anyone asks about me, just tell them that I'll be there today. I'll call again when we get there."

So, are you heading back?", Shelton asks. "It'll be a long day. Eat up first." "Thanks, Shelton. We appreciate your help", offers Jim. Shelton replies, "My pleasure. And I got something out of it, too. This tablet, and these ants; I've got a lot of research to do now." Henry, Jim, Diane, and Solomon finish up their breakfast, toss their few bags into the car, and back away from the cabin. They wave at Tarver as they pull away on the drive back down the dirt road to the highway. "Maybe we can catch up with the news on the radio", Jim says, as he clicks on the car radio. "...Senate hearings resume approximately ten minutes from now. Stay with us for live coverage of the impeachment proceedings..."

Chapter 23.

"The Honorable Senator from Oklahoma has the floor" announces the speaker, as she pounds the gavel, calling the hearing to order. Senator Bill Hopper leans toward the microphone in front of him and begins, "General Green, you've already been debriefed by the National Security Agency on the classified aspects of your testimony, so we'll be concentrating here on the declassified facts of the Y12 Center's relationship with UNIPHARM, and how this relationship might have been influenced by President Anthony's position in several organizations tied to Y12, and the SOL Center."

He continues, "General, what was the purpose of the Y12 Center?" The General answers, "The Y12 Center has been one of the world's foremost research centers in the areas of transferring military technology into civilian uses. Hundreds of products we all use everyday, began as concepts developed for military use. The Y12 Center conducts research, tests technologies, and translates that into working prototypes. The Center holds tens of thousands of patents on military and civilian products in use today, as well as those that will be used in the future."

"Thank you, General", replies the Senator. "I would like to know more about the research that the Y12 Center has been conducting on the drug Aggrepax. What can you tell me about the relationship between the manufacturer of Aggrepax, UNIPHARM, and the Y12 Center? Specifically, how and why did UNIPHARM get approval to conduct trials of their drugs on the U.S. military? Was there a bidding process that was open to all major manufacturers? If not, how did UNIPHARM win this contract?"

General Green answers, "There was no bidding process. The President at that time was President Cole. President Cole instructed the FDA to award the contract to UNIPHARM without bids. The Y12 Center entered into a contract with UNIPHARM to perform clinical trials on the proprietary combination of SSRI and NDRI drugs that was named Aggrepax. " The Senator interrupts, "So this very dangerous project, was initiated outside the control of Congress, solely on the instructions of the President?'

He continues, "General, for those of us who are not fluent in medical terminology, will you please explain what SSRI and NDRI drugs are? Also, is it typical that a government research center is asked to perform clinical drug trials?" General Green folds her hands together on the table in front of her and responds, "I'll answer the last part of your question first. While new drug trials are typically conducted in hospital or university medical research labs, this is not the first time that the Y12 Center has contracted to conduct such trials. In cases where drugs are to be used in combat or other military settings, it is appropriate that the trials be conducted using military personnel as test subjects. This trial was coordinated with the cooperation of top education experts, the combined branches of the U.S. Armed Services, and the FDA."

The General begins to answer the other part of the question, "Selective Serotonin Reuptake Inhibitors, SSRIs, and Norepinephrine-Dopamine Reuptake Inhibitors, NDRIs, affect different parts of the brain and the neurotransmitters released by those parts of the brain. NDRIs cause levels of Norepinephrine and Dopamine to remain in the bloodstream longer, causing a stimulant effect. SSRIs do the same with Serotonin, causing a calming effect. By varying the levels of combinations of these two types of drugs, desired levels of alertness or focus were achieved. From these results, two varieties of Aggrepax were developed; one for civilian use, and one for use by the Armed Forces.

She continues, "The primary purpose of Aggrepax was to treat symptoms of ADD/ADHD in young men, in both military and civilian life. The civilian version of Aggrepax contains a balanced SSRI and NDRI content, to help present an acceptable compromise between the anti-anxiety effects of SSRIs and the anti-depressive effects of NDRIs. The military version, Aggrepax-M, is formulated with higher levels of NDRIs, heightening alertness, reducing sensitivity to pain, and increasing aggression. From the beginning, the specific combination of drugs used in Aggrepax was formulated with input from pharmaceutical companies, physicians, educators, and the military. An important part of the testing protocols of Aggrepax was the incorporation of a computer simulator game system. The Army purchased a battlefield simulation game company and its product, One World Warrior. During the trials, synergistic benefits became known, which provided additional value to this combination of Aggrepax administration during game play of One World Warrior."

The Oklahoma Senator leans in and asks, "Understanding that much of this is still classified, what can you tell us about these synergistic benefits?" The General replies, "I cannot be more specific than that research was being conducted on battlefield communication. The declassified name for this technology is the Swarm Intelligence Project." The Senator quickly follows with, "It has been reported that this communication did not use any equipment or devices; that it was done chemically somehow. Is this true?" "I am not at liberty to discuss the classified aspects of the research, Senator", argued the General. "I understand, General", responds the Senator.

He continues with his questioning, "General, there are reports of hallucinations in users of Aggrepax. What can you tell us about that?" The General leans over to listen to her aid's comment, and responds, "In testing the various levels of SSRI and NDRI balances, there were cases of Serotonin Syndrome that occurred in higher levels than anticipated. One of the side effects of chronic high levels of serotonin is hallucinations. What is not classified about the research results, is that increasing serotonin levels is a key element of the Swarm Intelligence Project. It was necessary to see what level of SSRI produced the desired results, while assuring the safety of the test subjects. I can assure you that civilians were not subjected to risks that military volunteers were. Civilian safety was at all times a high priority."

The Senator pushes further, "One other aspect that has surfaced after the lab explosion, is that research on asexual reproduction was being conducted. What purpose would the military have for conducting research on human reproduction?' The General pauses for a few seconds, leans over once again to consult with the aid, and answers, "That's classified information, Senator, and I am unable to discuss it."

The Senator counters with, "But there have been sexual side effects from the drug that have been found; isn't this correct?" The General responds, "Yes, Senator. The research has indicated a higher than normal rate of impotence and loss of libido in patients receiving the civilian version of Aggrepax. This is a known side effect of SSRI drugs, and does not appear to be as pronounced in the military version, due to its lower levels of this class of drugs." "Well then, why are civilians not given the same version as the military?", asks the Senator. The General answers matter-of-factly, "It was determined that the level of aggression produced by the military version would not be acceptable in civilian settings."

"One other question, General", states the Senator. "Was President Cole being treated with Aggrepax when he died?" General Green scowls at the Senator and answers, "I think that's a question for his physician." The Senator immediately follows with, "And that was the present President Anthony, was it not?" "I believe that it is correct, Senator", she answers.

Dierdra Willingham cannot tear herself away from the Senate hearings on television. As painful as it is for her to face the reality that she has been a part of the process of sending boys to a place she now fears was not what she had hoped, she still wants to believe that she was doing the right thing to help them. "What are these boys going to do now? Where will they go to get the treatment they need?", she asks herself. "I'm already hearing teachers complain about boys who seemed to be doing well after going to the SOL Center, and now are back to their old behaviors; restless, distracted, and disruptive. Some are even reporting boys with new piercings, and even some self mutilation marks. Something has to be done, and soon."

The Principal picks up the phone to call her friend Rosalind Burlington, whom she met many years ago at a National Organization for Women meeting. The two struck up a friendship and Dierdra has been more than happy to help Rosalind in any way possible. Dierdra also met Rebecca Anthony through NOW, where she realized that they all had the same world views. Dierdra jumped at the chance to be involved in the development of the SOL Center, and was elated when Rosalind was hand selected by then Vice President Anthony to be its Director. She never questioned the methods used or the numbers of boys treated by the Center. She trusts the mission of the Center and the objectives of her friends, and knows that the world will be a better place when their plans are carried out.

Rosalind is now working from home, after the SOL Center was temporarily shuttered after the EMP blast. "This is Rosalind", she casually answers. "Rosalind, this is Dierdra. Do you have a minute?" "Good to hear from you, Dierdra. I'm swamped with contacting all the parents of patients, but I need a break. What can I do for you?" Dierdra begins, "I'm concerned about all of the boys I referred to the SOL Center. What is going to happen to them now? How will they continue to receive the medications they have been prescribed? What do I tell the parents of my students?"

Rosalind answers, "Their family doctors will be able to get them prescriptions. That should not be a problem. Dierdra, there are some issues with the SOL treatment protocols that I have been weighing for the past few weeks, but I've been so busy with running the Center, that I haven't had the time to really investigate them." "What kind of issues?", asks Dierdra. "You've heard about the potential safety issues with the drugs, haven't you?" Rosalind asks her friend. "Sure, but I assumed that those were in situations where other drugs were combined, or they had underlying conditions or something. Why?", asks Dierdra.

Rosalind explains, "It appears that there are some dangerous side effects to Aggrepax, which is the final version of the combination of drugs that we've been testing at SOL. We've known about this for a while, and have been adjusting amounts, frequency, and exact ratios for a while now. What we found is that a small percentage of the boys don't require the drugs after the first few weeks of treatment. It appears that for a certain group of patients, the feedback from the computer game and the interaction with the other players causes the patients to be able to modify their brain waves, independent of the drugs. They don't need the drugs to communicate with the other players, once they learn to tap into this apparently natural ability."

Dierdra responds, "If they no longer need the drugs, why do they need to stay at the Center?" Rosalind answers, "We have a contractual arrangement with UNIPHARM to finish the protocols, whether or not the patients demonstrate improvement. That's what I've been agonizing over; it appears UNIPHARM is more interested in refining the pheromone sensitivity aspect of the trials, than it is in finding effective treatments for the boys' conditions. From what I've seen, it appears that the SOL Center was never about helping boys overcome learning deficiencies; it's always been about developing battlefield communications for the military, and more importantly, being able to control males."

Dierdra asks, "What do you mean, control them?" Rosalind answers, "Dierdra, you and I met through organizations whose missions have always been to correct the world's problems by taking power away from men and having women run things." "Yes, and we agree that this is a worthwhile goal, right?", responds Dierdra. Rosalind replies, "I've always believed that women could do things better by making better decisions, not by mentally handcuffing men. The disturbing facts about how this program works are that we are essentially turning males into second class citizens, controlled by a ruling class of females. How is that better than what we've accused men of doing to women in the past?"

Dierdra asks, "So what is next? With the SOL Center closed, we won't be referring any more students there. What happens to education? What do we do to help these boys learn? How will teachers run their classrooms?" Rosalind answers, "You'll teach them; like we used to. Dierdra, here is the part where I need your help. I will be appearing to testify in the impeachment hearings soon. There are very powerful forces involved in all this, and they have a lot at stake. There exists a very real possibility that I may be targeted by these forces because of what I know, and for what I might reveal."

"What do you mean? Why would anyone try to stop you from testifying?", asks Dierdra. Rosalind explains, "I have been very involved in the detailed planning and day to day operations of the SOL Center. I have been exposed to very privileged meetings and conversations with General Green and even the President. In short, I know too much. I know about President Anthony's associations and why the people with the money behind this project are doing what they are doing. Did you ever wonder why UNIPHARM was willing to give away its drugs? They're not doing it because they're nice; they want to corner the market by having everyone permanently on their products. The heads of government will then owe their position and power to UNIPHARM, and the consortium will essentially control the world."

Dierdra responds incredulously, "President Anthony is a good woman. She would never go along with such a sinister plot." "Rebecca is a different woman than when you and I first met her", argues Rosalind. "She is the most dangerous of zealots; one who has the power to turn her convictions into reality. I was a witness to her rantings about how she would never let the world go back to the way it once was. She once told me that she would rather work toward her world goals while in the background, but once she assumed the position of President, she was forced to accelerate everything. The first meeting with General Green and myself after assuming office, she said that she feared that she could not be elected after President Cole's term ended, and that she could no longer afford to be patient and wait for things to progress according to the original plan. That is the reason why UNIPHARM was given fast track approval for Aggrepax, and why the real reason for President Cole's death has been hidden from the public."

"Hidden?", asks Dierdra. "It has been slowly leaking out in the press that President Cole might have had a bad reaction to a drug. They just don't know which one." Rosalind counters, "Yes, but what they don't know is that President Cole was actually the first patient of then Dr. Rebecca Anthony to be prescribed the new drug, Aggrepax." "The one the boys have been prescribed?", asks Dierdra. "Yes, but what makes it unforgivable is that even after knowing what happened to President Cole, Rebecca allowed UNIPHARM to get approval for the drug for use in children. What nobody knows, yet, is that over the past few months of his life, President Cole was experiencing stronger and more frequent hallucinations; he believed that he could see ants everywhere", answers Rosalind.

"Ants? Is that why we were asked to identify boys at school who talked about ants, or who drew pictures of them?", asked Dierdra. Rosalind answers, "Yes. It appears that the hallucinations are one of the side effects of Aggrepax. Seeing ants is one of the indications of resistance to the drug. Whenever a male exhibits this symptom, it is an indication that he will not be easily controlled by the drug. And this is the real reason for why I might be in danger; I know the real purpose for the drug. The purpose is to control men, to control all aspects of their lives; by prescribing different medications, men can be made compliant, or passive, or aggressive, as in the military situations where different versions of the drug are prescribed."

"I don't know what to say", says Dierdra. "I feel as if I've been punched in the stomach. What have I done? I've been sending these boys to be turned into zombies. What can I do?" Rosalind answers, "First, I'm sending you the originals of all the documents I plan on presenting to the Senate in my testimony. If anything happens to me, please deliver them to Senator Hopper of Oklahoma. He already knows the outline of what they contain, just not the details. Second, if you do not hear from me again, I want you to tell all the parents of the boys. I'm including a list of all the patients that have been treated at SOL. They need to know." Dierdra argues, "Of course, but nothing is going to happen to you."

Turner Runnels has been working almost non-stop over the past few days. His contacts in the Army, asked him to head up the restoration of the game servers. "We have been ordered to hand over control of OWW to civilian management and oversight, and you are the only name that was mentioned", the General had told him as he was asked to resurrect the system. He quickly arranged for server farms to be located in unused warehouses at a nearby National Guard base. All the data that had been contained on the Y12 computers has been lost, but the OWW portable server farm containers were shielded from EMP damage, and were physically separated from the Y12 Center. Though all of the trailers' electrical circuits were fried, destroying all computer components contained within them, all game play data had been stored on shielded solid state hard drives. The choice of solid state drives over magnetic drives was made because of their faster speed, not resistance to power fluctuations, but one of the security features designed into the portables was a fail-safe system to physically disconnect the servers from the electrical grid, in the case of an "event".

Within nanoseconds of the impending pulse being detected, sensors triggered switches in guillotine-like connectors, physically cutting the wires and isolating the drives from the pulse.

Starting from scratch with his original code, and with the data recovered from the salvaged drives, Turner already has the One World Warrior game at 80% capacity, and it will be near 100% within 24 hours. "Randy, see if you can log on", Turner says to his son. "I'm in!", reports Randy. "Thanks, Dad." Turner asks his wife, "Lane, how long has it been since Randy took any of the medicine?" His mother answers, "It's been about a week now, and I can't tell the difference." Turner thinks for a moment and asks, "I wonder if the game itself is affecting the boys' brains? Maybe they don't need the drugs at all." Lane answers, "Well, from what we know now about Aggrepax, no boy should be on it, so hopefully, you're right. We'll see."

Turner asks his wife, "What are you going to do about UNIPHARM? Are you going to testify?" She responds, "I have to appear, but I cannot testify against a former client." "Even though their drug could have hurt your son?" Lane answers, "I have taken an oath to never reveal confidential client information." "But I haven't", counters Turner. "Luckily, the information that was sent out from the Y12 computers should be enough to bury the drug, and the company, but if I am called to testify, I'll tell them everything, including what you and I have discussed." "You can't do that", argues Lane. Turner angrily retaliates, "If you won't, I will."

"General", announces the guard outside the

hospital room door, as he snaps to attention. "I'm here to see Clark Shepherd", says the General, authoritatively. "Yes sir", responds the guard, as he steps aside and opens the door. The General removes his hat as he paces into the brightly lit room, and he addresses his injured researcher, "Dr. Shepherd; you awake?" Clark Shepherd moves his head as far as possible to see his visitor, but is forced to look out of the corner of his eyes to see the General. "General Rogers...Good to...see you." Clark's tablet computer has been mounted to a metal frame over his bed, so that he can use it while on his back. He has been watching web reports of the impeachment trial, and using his head to control the pointing device, pauses the video.

General Rogers begins, "Clark, I want you to know that I had no idea you were still in the lab. I was given orders to initiate the self-destruct sequence with only a one minute delay. I knew there were people in the lab, but I had assumed that everyone else could make it out before the doors closed. I am deeply troubled by the way this has all been handled."

Clark listens without blinking, then asks, "So every...one else...made it...out OK?" "Yes", answers the General. "You were the only one within the blast area. It was limited, due to the size of the device, and the construction of the self destruct room. The EMP was the primary purpose; the building's structure was relatively unaffected. The lab was completely destroyed however, including most electronic devices, such as your chair and life support systems. Sorry about your old tablet; I trust this replacement is satisfactory?"

"Yes...it's fine", responds Clark. "Sir I've...been called...to testify...in the Senate...hearings."

"Yes, I know", replies Rogers. "You just tell them the truth. You haven't done anything wrong, and all of the information that has been leaked to the press cannot be linked to you or any other lab employees. It all points toward me. I'm the one who will take the fall for General Green and the President." "But General...I've seen what's...on William's...storage drive...I know what...they are...planning...and that...you were...just following...orders", argues Clark. "Thank you Clark, but as a doctor, I should have recognized what they were up to a long time ago. Because I did not, I sent quite a few good men off to places where they won't be heard from again, for a long time. I suspect that I will very likely join them soon. With all this out in the open, I am no longer useful, and the powers that be will want to get me far away from the public eye. I will almost certainly end up at "The Freezer"."

"The Freezer?", Clark asks. "What is...that?" General Rogers answers, "I went through all of Dr. Williams' files, and found references to it, and looked into it. It is a top secret storage facility, located at a base at the center of Antarctica. It is where we keep anything that we don't want anyone to see. The staff are supposed to be assigned for two year stints, but no one knows anyone who used to work there. Williams indicated that there was an automatic uploading of all Y12 and SOL data to this location in Antarctica."

"Why are...you telling...me this?", asks Clark. The General answers, "If anything should happen to me, I want someone to know about this 'Freezer', and that there may be individuals stationed there against their will. If I disappear before your Senate testimony, you should assume that I have been sent there, and I would ask that you reveal the existence of the facility in the hearings. I'm certain the President has a lot of secrets hidden there."

Chapter 24.

"The scheduled witness is not able to appear", announces the Majority Leader. "The Director of the SOL Center, Rosalind Burlington, was aboard a private aircraft that crashed on its way here last night. All aboard are presumed deceased. We will take a short recess, so that the next witness can be contacted and our schedule moved up one slot." A hushed collective murmur fills the room and then subsides, as the Senators move toward the exits and to the hallways for media interviews.

"Senator Hopper!", the aide puffs as she runs up to meet the exiting Senators. "This package was delivered this morning. It's marked as urgent. It's from Rosalind Burlington." The Senator stops abruptly and argues, "That's impossible. She was in a plane crash last night." He opens up the envelope and begins to read the cover letter. Quickly placing the documents back in the envelope, he walks rapidly toward the Majority Leader's office.

"General Rogers", announces the leader of the security detail. "General Rogers, please come with us." "Under whose orders?", he counters. "General Green sir, under the authority of the President of the United States", comes the reply. "I was expecting you", the General says under his breath. "Am I allowed to take anything with me from my office?" "All your personal effects have already been collected", the security officer answers. "Come this way." The group marches outside, where a helicopter is waiting, its engine running and blades spinning. The General and two of the security officers enter the aircraft, and it immediately powers up and lifts off, tilting forward and roaring away.

After a thirty minute flight, they arrive at the military base, where a cargo plane is taxiing toward the tarmac. The group files across the tarmac from the helicopter to a portable ramp, straight through the door, passing through a bulkhead to an isolated section with only three jump seats. One of the guards motions for the General to take a seat. The General sits down in the middle jump seat and asks, "I don't suppose you can tell me where we're going?" "No, sir", comes the answer. He responds, "Doesn't matter. I have a good idea, anyway."

As he shifts in his seat, acting as if he is adjusting his seat belts, General Rogers deftly slips a tracking device from his pants pocket to a harder to find smaller key pocket on the inside of his pants. When he had seen the guards approaching his office, he knew he had only seconds to decide if he would risk being discovered with a bug, and luckily, the guards had not been instructed to search him. The General settles in and fastens his belts, as the two guards take seats on each side of him.

"When are we leaving?", asks General Rogers. One of the guards answers, "We are waiting for our primary passenger to arrive." General Rogers smiles grimly and asks, "When is she supposed to be here?" The guard simply stares at Rogers without answering. He wonders if it is a good thing or a bad thing to be on the same plane as the person who is sending him off to parts unknown. "At least with Green on the plane, we won't have an accident on the way."

Rogers smiles uncomfortably at the thought of what might happen if he did not have such protection
.

"Senator Hopper", announces the Majority Leader, "Do you wish to reserve any of your time?" "No, Senator. I would like to take the full time allotted, since this will be our last witness before the President appears before us."

"Dr. Shepherd, I want to thank you for appearing before us today. I know that it is difficult for you, and that we appreciate you enduring this process so soon after your injury. I trust that we have accommodated your needs as much as possible?" Clark Shepherd nods slightly and answers, "Yes, Senator...everything is...acceptable." The Senator begins, "Dr. Shepherd, earlier today, we were made aware of evidence regarding the purpose and methods used by the SOL Center and the Y12 lab where you were employed. Have you been made aware of this information?" Clark answers, "Yes, Senator."

The Senator continues, "And you have provided us with information that allegedly was passed to you by a former colleague named Dr. Zeke Williams?" Clark responds, "That is correct...Senator". The Senator holds up two sets of documents, "Dr. Shepherd, we have provided you with electronic copies of these two sets of documents. Are you able to access them?" Clark slightly moves his head to bring the documents up on his tablet computer. "Yes, Senator...I am able...to access both." Senator Hopper follows up, "One of these sets was provided by you, from a portable storage drive that you have testified was given to you by Dr. Williams; is this correct?" "Yes,

Senator", replies Clark. The Senator then asks, "And the other has been provided by now deceased SOL Director Rosalind Burlington; have you had the chance to review that information?" Clark answers, "Yes, Senator...They appear...to contain...essentially...the same...information." The Senator continues, "Dr. Shepherd, can you testify to the accuracy of this information?" Clark answers, "Senator...I can only...tell you that...what I provided...came directly...from Dr. Williams...I cannot...verify what...is purported...to be from...Ms. Burlington." "Thank you, Dr. Shepherd. No further questions. I yield to the Senator from Arizona", announces Senator Hopper.

The Arizona Senator smiles and addresses Clark, "Dr. Shepherd, you do agree that the information in each of these sets of documents, implicate President Anthony in the matter of the death of the former President Cole, isn't that right?" He responds, "Senator,...that is what...they appear...to show...If the...allegations...they contain...are factual...they would...indicate that...the President...was involved...from the...beginning." The Senator smiles and says to Clark, "Thank you, Dr. I yield the remainder of my time to the Senator from New York."

"Dr. Shepherd, were you ever present during any discussions between President Cole and Vice President Anthony, or between President Anthony and General Green, or at any time during any of the discussions that are detailed in the documents that were submitted as evidence from Dr. Williams or Dr. Burlington?" Clark answers, "No Senator, I was not." Senator Bower smiles and continues, "Thank you, Dr. Shepherd. We thank you for enduring the hardship of coming here and appearing before us." Two military medical staff personnel walk down from the back of the chamber, help Clark pull away from the witness table, and accompany him up the aisle and out of the Senate Chamber.

The Majority Leader pounds the gavel and calls, "These hearings will adjourn until tomorrow, when President Anthony will appear." She walks down the steps behind the long, elevated desk, and into the hallway that leads to the Senate Armed Services Committee meeting room. As she enters the room, Senator Hopper is already seated, along with all the other committee members, as well as the Joint Chiefs of Staff. As Chairman of the JCS, General Green is seated at the head of the table, and announces the beginning of the meeting. "Ladies, Gentlemen, thank you for attending. We are meeting under unpleasant circumstances today. The impeachment trial of the President has created a situation in which we need to make some decisions regarding the makeup of the JCS."

The General continues, "Because of the cloud that has formed over the allegations made against her administration, and because of my personal involvement in the Y12 Center and the consortium formed with UNIPHARM, the President has asked for my resignation as the Chairman of the Joint Chiefs of Staff. I have tendered my resignation, and she has accepted it, effective immediately. Vice Chairman General Ben Longarrow will be assuming all duties of Chairman. Chairman Longarrow, members of the committee, good luck." General Green stands, and the rest of the members stand as she leaves the meeting room, accompanied by her aides. One of the aides talks to her as the three swiftly walk down the hallway, "Your plane is waiting. All arrangements have been made for your visit to your specified destination."

General Green, never breaking stride, and continuing to look straight ahead asks, "What has the flight crew been told about the trip?" The aide answers, "They have been given the coordinates, and have been instructed to destroy the flight records upon their return, as per standard resupply mission instructions. We have arranged for the base staff rotation to be modified, so that the flight will appear to be a standard semi-annual resupply and staff rotation mission. All staff not directly related to sensitive materials storage will be rotated out when you arrive." "Thank you, Colonel", General Green replies as the group nears the bottom of the steps, where the olive colored limousine waits for them, the driver standing by the open door. The General gets in the car, followed closely by her aides. The driver closes the door behind them and then slides into his front seat. The car speeds away toward the military base, to the waiting transport plane.

As the replacement staff file on to the plane and find their seats, the flight crew are reviewing the flight plan and going over the pre-flight checklist. "Long flight, Major", says the number two pilot. Normally, only two pilots are required for the standard crew of five, but a third pilot is assigned for these long distance resupply missions. Major Lowrey, the pilot, calls off to the rest of the flight crew, "Navigation?" The navigator answers, "Course entered and locked." "Flight engineer?" The engineer responds, "All systems, check." "Loadmaster?" The answer comes,

"Cargo secured, waiting on three high value passengers." Major Lowrey discusses the flight plan with the other two pilots, "Co-pilot Kershaw will be flying the first shift, then O'Grady, you'll get a turn and will be landing at Diego Garcia, since you are based there. We'll be taking on fuel there, and I will fly the final segment in. The landing is a bit tricky where we're going, and it's my bird."

At that moment, the General and her aides arrive, and quickly walk up the ladder and take their seats. The loadmaster announces over the intercom, "All passengers are now aboard and secured." "Thank you, Tech Sergeant", responds the pilot. "You are cleared for takeoff", the tower radio voice announces. The flight crew smoothly slides into gear, reflexively flicking switches, turning dials, and sliding throttles into precise position. The passengers, some sleeping, some reading, some staring at the windowless walls, are settling in for the long flight. General Green opens a manila envelope and begins reviewing its contents. She briefly scans each document in the stack and returns them to the envelope. After closing the fastener, she writes her initials and the date and time on the back of the flap. The outside of the envelope is marked "Top Secret, Y12 Cold", which indicates that they are to be stored in the most secure vaults of the facility that she expects to call home for the next few years.

"Madam President", begins the Senate Majority Leader. "We regret that we are here under the present circumstances, but thank you for arranging your schedule to be here." Rebecca Anthony smiles and responds, "Quite all right, Senator Bower. I think we would all like to get this behind us as quickly as possible." "Thank you for your cooperation, Madam President", responds the leader of the Senate, a member of the same political party as the President, and one of her closest friends and political allies. "Mr. Hopper, do you wish to begin with your questions?" "Yes, I do, Ms. Bower. I take it we're adopting a less formal air today?" After a few muted chuckles from the audience, and the Majority Leader's barely hidden frown at being called out for her break in protocol, the Senator from Oklahoma continues, "Madam President, I also regret that we are here under these circumstances, but we all have an important job to do, and I intend to carry out my duties in a thorough, but fair manner." The President forces a smile and says, "I understand, Senator. We all want this to be handled in a fair way."

Shelton Tarver walks out of his cabin with the box of ants in his hands, and just before he gets to his truck, out of the corner of his eye he spots something out of place. As he looks up, only feet away to his left, at first what looks like a several feet high sapling tree, is a huge bird. As Tarver and the bird lock eyes, he stops in his tracks. The bird leaps into the air, and with huge up and down sweeps of its wings, flies off toward the main road. Blinking as he watches the bird fly away, he thinks to himself, "Wow, I haven't seen one of those since I was a boy. That's a heron, I think. It's supposed to be a good omen." "Hear that boys?", he says to the ants in the box.

The ants watch as the heron surprises the old man and flies away. Banshee speaks first, "Is that the same one we saw at the boy's house?" Barbatus replies,

"It may not be the same bird, but it is the same Spirit Helper. It means that we are to go with this man and protect the tablet. He will take it where it will be safe. We will stay with him." Barbatus scans the formation, and each of the other twelve nods in agreement.

Hopping in and starting up the old truck, Shelton begins the long drive to the Van Ross University campus, the box containing the ants and the tablet on the seat next to him. He has taken the lid off of the box, and cannot keep from constantly looking at the ants inside. "Very unusual", he thinks to himself. "They are not trying to escape; they are just standing there, as if in formation." As he turns into the driveway to the parking lot, his thoughts turn to how he will explain to the Dean of Anthropology how he came to possess the tablet. Now muttering to himself out loud, "He already thinks I'm some kind of Indiana Jones caricature; he'll probably think I desecrated some Indian burial ground for it."

"Let's see what you've got here", says Dean Roy Hunter as he peers into the open box. "Hey, it's got ants all over it." "Never mind them. I'm studying them. What's the tablet about?", Shelton asks. "Let me get a magnifying glass", says the Dean. "OK. Let's take a look", he says as he looks closer. After a few moments, he looks up at Shelton and asks, "Where did you get this Tarver?" Shelton answers, "Roy, you would not believe me if I told you. You're going to have to just trust me on this one. I came by it legitimately." The Dean says argumentatively, "This is a very old piece, and if it is as original as it first appears, an extremely important discovery."

"It says this is 'The Secret of The Ancestors'.

It refers to itself as the 'Fourth World' tablet. It says that there have been three worlds of men, and tablets, before this one. It tells of how each of the previous three worlds were destroyed; by fire, by ice, and by flood, and how each time, The Creator allowed a chosen few to go below to live with the ancestors. It appears that it is referring to ants as the ancestors. It goes on to say that each time the world was destroyed, the old tablet, along with its key, was destroyed, and a new one written. The key and tablet are always hidden apart from each other, so that no one could possess them both."

He continues reading and translating, "Along the edges, there is a string of what looks like genetic code. This must be what is referred to as the human key. They must mean the human genome. The last paragraph is rather ominous; it says that the Fourth World will be destroyed by the tablet itself. I wonder what that means?" Shelton answers, "From what I can tell, this tablet is supposed to be kept out of the hands of the wrong person. Who that is, I don't know. For the time being, I think the best thing to do is to keep it here with you. Until we know more, keeping it in here will keep it out of the public eye until you figure out exactly what it is and what to do with it."

"Madam President", Senator Hopper begins. "Let's start with your relationship with UNIPHARM. When did you first begin working with them?" Rebecca Anthony leans in to her microphone and answers, "I first worked with key pharmaceutical company executives when I gave a series of lectures at various medical conventions on my research on treatments for attention deficit disorders. I presented my findings and the tool I developed for measuring such disorders, the Anthony Rating Scale. Through these contacts, I was asked to become involved in international women's issues with The National Organization for Women and the United Nations Development Fund for Women."

The Senator interrupts, "And that is when you met UNIPHARM head Geraldine Zoecker?" The President responds, "Yes, that is correct. But at that time, she was the head of the largest Swiss pharmaceutical corporation. UNIPHARM came about later, as a result of the combining of resources of all of the largest international drug companies. UNIPHARM was formed to realize the potential economies of scale in research, testing, manufacturing, and marketing of the world's most needed and useful drugs."

"At that time, what was your relationship with Lawrence Cole?", the Senator asks the President. She answers, "I was then Governor Cole's personal physician." Senator Hopper continues, "Did you prescribe any medications to then Governor Cole?" President Anthony responds, "I cannot discuss specific medical histories of my patients." The Senator, now growing more irritated, argues, "But, President Anthony, that is the heart, pardon the expression, of this inquiry isn't it? The autopsy of President Cole revealed extremely high levels of the components of Aggrepax in his bloodstream. We can only assume that as his personal physician, that you prescribed that drug to him. That is a safe assumption, is it not?" "Again, I cannot discuss specifics of any patient's medical history", she repeats.

The Senator presses on, "Madam President, you have been provided with copies of the documents that have been entered as evidence in this trial, from Y12 and SOL personnel?" "I have", answers the President. "And in that evidence, are there copies of hand written notes, in your handwriting, which detail the SOL Center treatment records of President Cole, and his progress during this treatment, which includes drugs similar to Aggrepax, and then subsequent treatment with the final versions of Aggrepax?"

The President leans over to confer with her attorney and answers, "I cannot confirm nor deny the legitimacy of the evidence. If any of the notes in evidence are actual patient records, I cannot comment on them." The Senator, growing more and more impatient, continues, "And the series of reports, with the initials of "RA" in the bottom corner of each page, chronicling his steadily deteriorating health, and the negative side effects he was experiencing, apparently due to the drug being administered, are you able to comment on them?" She again leans over and discusses with her attorney before answering, "I must assert the necessity for doctor patient confidentiality on any such evidence."

The Senator pauses for a moment, staring unblinkingly at the witness, then proceeds. "Very well. Let's move on, shall we? UNIPHARM received streamlined approval for Aggrepax. Who authorized the FDA to allow this without the standard trials?" The President answers, "UNIPHARM has a special relationship with the FDA, which allows them to use their own clinical trials as the basis for approval. Because of the classification of the drug as a national security priority, the trials were conducted on an accelerated basis with volunteers from the U.S. Armed

Forces."

The Senator presses for more, "Madam President, who directed the FDA to grant UNIPHARM this special status?" She deliberates with her counsel once again, and answers, "The Senate Armed Services Committee, upon the recommendation of the Joint Chiefs of Staff, instructed the FDA to suspend the normal testing requirements in this case." "Are you saying that General Green, the Chairman of the JCS, and Senator Barbara Bower, the Senate Majority Leader and Chairman of the Armed Services Committee, are responsible for allowing UNIPHARM to administer an unsafe drug to the President of the United States?"

The Majority Leader bangs her gavel over and over, calling "Order. This hearing will come to order!", over the cacophony of whispers and hushed conversations that have erupted. "I move that the Senate excuse Madam Bower from these proceedings, pending her future appearance as a witness before this matter", Senator Hopper proclaims almost gleefully. The Majority Leader, clearly shaken, bangs the gavel a few more times and announces, "This hearing will be in recess until further notice."

Away from the still open press microphones, the two Senators lean in toward each other for a private conversation. "I'm not taking the fall for her, Bill", Barbara Bower growls to Senator Hopper. "Rebecca Anthony has been in charge of this from day one, and made it clear that anyone who got in her way would pay the price. I've been a team player and have stood aside as I watched what she's been doing." Senator Hopper insists, "You know you are going to have to step down as Majority Leader until this is finished, and that you are going to have to testify against the President." "Yes, I know", she sighs heavily. "Don't worry Barbara", answers Senator Hopper. "I have been made aware of some interesting information that will settle all of this soon."

The blindingly white frozen base is almost void of activity as the transport plane taxis up to the main building. The Tech Sergeant swings open and secures the door, and the blast of antarctic air immediately fills the cabin interior. The main group of passengers remain seated while General Green and her aides are the first to exit the plane. At the bottom of the portable ramp, the base commander, only distinguishable from the other crew in their fur lined hooded parkas by his authoritative posture, shakes mittened hands with General Green and motions to the nearest airman to take the General's bags. The group quickly moves inside the nearest Quonset hut style steel building, among the dozen or so similar curved roof buildings, all shaped like tin cans cut in half lengthwise. "General Brooks", the incoming General begins. "Thank you for the warm reception." The two laugh a little at her joke, and the commander of the base answers, "We didn't expect our staff rotation for another few months. Anything I should know?", knowing that whatever the reason, it would be on a need to know basis, and he didn't need to know.

General Green replies, "No, Frank. Nothing I can tell you, except that I am relieving you of command." "Forgive me for asking General, but why you? The Chairman of the Joint Chiefs of Staff?", General Brooks asks incredulously. "I resigned as JSC

Chairman, and have been reassigned as base commander of this facility, at the direct request of the President. I am your replacement", General Green says with a tight smile. "Yes Ma'am", General Brooks answers sharply as he straightens and snaps a salute. "I relinquish my command." "Thank you, General Brooks", responds General Green, matching his salute. "Godspeed, General." As his hand returns to his side, General Brooks answers, "Good luck to you, General."

Chapter 25.

Shelton Tarver thinks back to his last conversation with Roy Hunter before he left the tablet at Van Ross. "I wonder if this is going to be a waste of time, looking around for more clues about the tablet and any secrets it might reveal. Oh well, it certainly can't hurt, and being out in the field is what I enjoy most anyway. I just wish we didn't have all this mess hanging over our heads."

Shelton pulls off the county road, on to the dirt road where he and Henry had found the original batch of ants. It seems so long ago; before he knew all of what has since transpired. "OK, boys. Let's see if you can find your way home." Shelton stops the truck where the road ends and the desert begins, gets out of the truck, carrying the box containing the band of thirteen, and walks slowly in a zigzag pattern, looking for landmarks to remind him of where he had originally poked around on that first mound.

Barbatus alerts the group, "We're here. Saddle up." The ants adjust their armor and gather their weapons as Tarver watches the group form a line and march out of the box he has placed on the ground next to the mound. "We'll stick together until we reach Optera. There's no telling what we'll find, if anything, after all this time."

Shelton lingers just behind the group, following out of not only his curiosity, but to protect his investment in his find. A lifetime of studying ants never prepared him for how a group of sentient insects will change everything ever known about history and biology. "I have to find out if these are the only ants like this, or if they all are."

There is a lot of time to think while walking slowly behind the ants. "As a scientist, I have to be aware that I am imagining this. Even though others appear to have seen what I see, it could be some kind of mass hysteria or other phenomenon, and I must maintain as much objectivity as possible. I have to see where this leads."

The ants walk in single file across the sandy desert, where they eventually reach a clearing with no grass and small pebbles piled up around the opening to a nest. "This is it.", announces Barbatus, recognizing his former home.

"Tex, Banshee, you take the lead and I'll follow you. The rest of you wait here for now." Rugosus objects, "Wait, I should be first in. Besides, I've got a score to settle with that bunch." "I want to settle all this more than anyone, but you might be right. I need you to take up the rear and watch my back."

As the group of four descends through the winding tunnels down into the deserted colony, they find no signs that anyone has lived here for a long time. Tex, first to reach what used to be the nursery says, "There's a wall here that's newer than the rest of the tunnel. It might be where they hid the tablet."

The four attack the wall and break a hole large enough to enter the chamber one by one. Barbatus is first to go in. Banshee follows while Tex waits at the entrance and Rugosus watches the tunnel behind them. After a few minutes, Barbatus comes back to the entrance and says grimly, "It's empty. There used to be a large number of eggs here, but they are gone, and the food and other storage cells are broken open and empty. If the scroll copy of the tablet was ever here, it's gone now. We have some tracking to do."

As they reach the surface, the group members waiting anxiously wait for a report. Barbatus angrily states, "Nothing. Look around for a trail. What we're looking for has been moved. Banshee, you're the best tracker, see what you can find." Banshee begins casting around, kneeling down to look closely at the tracks left behind, squinting and looking off in first one direction and then another, trying to get inside the head of the ants they are tracking and outguess which path they took. Banshee looks at Barbatus and says, "They appear to have left in three groups, and deliberately made all three trails look the same, to make it hard to figure out which one carried the future Queen eggs. They might have split up the eggs to establish separate colonies. There's no way to know which one has the scroll."

"We'll split up then.", Barbatus states sharply. "Tex, Banshee, and Wheels, take Bike with you. You're the fastest, so you follow the oldest trail in the center. Patch, Schmitty, BA, and Axe, you take that trail on the left. Rugosus, Cal, Z, Theo, and I will take the right trail."
Don't go into the colony alone; we'll need to go into one colony at a time, at full strength. Just scope out the colony you find, and we'll meet at sundown."

Barbatus' group heads down the third trail with Cal in front, followed by Barbatus, then Z, then Theo, with Rugosus following closely behind, scouring the horizon to the sides and rear for any surprises. The trail grows fresher and fresher, easier and easier to follow. "We're getting close, dudes", announces Cal. The group stops behind clusters of dry grass and peer at the new colony between the yellow blades.

They lie motionless as Barbatus studies the new colony for hours. He watches the traffic in and out of the entrance, looking for any signs that this is not just any ordinary colony. "The quantity of food being stored is far larger than what the colony needs for itself and there are many more guards than what should be expected. "Something's up in this colony. They appear to be hunkering down for a siege or long period of protecting the Queen. I'm pretty sure this is it, but let's rendezvous with the other two groups and see what they have to report. We'll take the most likely candidate first."

As the three groups gather back at the point where the three trails began as one, Barbatus asks for a report from the other two. "What did you find, Tex?" Tex answers, "Ours was the oldest, and it looks like it's just an ordinary colony. No unusual numbers of guards, and there were only a few food trails leading away from the entrance. I can't be sure, but it doesn't look like anything special."

"What about you, Patch?" Patch answers, "Abandoned. Maybe attacked and pillaged. Hard to tell, but it's empty." Barbatus responds, "They wouldn't leave the scroll unprotected. The colony we found is heavily fortified. We'll start there. Bike, be ready to whip up some chemical keys for the colony when we get there and capture one of them. Patch, check everybody's armor. Everyone, make ready your weapons. Let's get going."

The Queen of New Optera, a direct descendant of

the Queen of Optera meets with her Council. "The attack will come soon. Make preparations to defend the colony." Her new Protector answers, "Yes my Queen. All is ready."

The Queen pulls aside her Supreme Queen's Sister and tells her, "No one but you must know. There are two copies of the scroll. One is here in my chamber, and the other is in the colony we created to look like an abandoned shell. The other copy is buried deep inside. You must go there with only your most trusted aides and remain there until you hear from me. If you do not hear from me, you are to take the scroll to the remaining colony and hide it there. Tell no one what you are doing until my death. Only then are you to tell the new Queen what she holds."

The Supreme Sister agrees, "Yes my Queen. But what does the scroll contain?" The Queen narrows her eyes and answers, "The future of our species. It contains the secret to controlling both the Ant and Human worlds. With it, we control our own destiny. Without it we lose all control. But it is only part of what is needed to control the world. It is useless without the key."

"What is this key you speak of?", asks the Supreme Sister. The Queen answers, "It is one ant. An ant that contains the genetic code that allows him to resist the control detailed within the instructions on the copy of the original tablet. One day that ant will come to seek the scroll. We must capture him when that day comes."

"I understand, my Queen", promises the Supreme Sister. "I will do as you ask." The Queen looks back at the Supreme Sister and commands, "Now go. Protect the secret." The Supreme Sister responds, "Yes, my Queen.", and turns to gather her security detail and leave the colony.

The Queen watches her leave. Staring through the wall in an almost dream like state, she says to herself, loud enough for anyone to hear, "One day, a Queen will possess both the copy of the tablet and the key, and then we will finally have a perfect world."

The group gathers at the crossroads, having determined that New Optera is most likely to contain the scroll. Barbatus lays out the strategy of attack. "First, we will capture a colony member for Bike to use to make our masking agent." The group members each nod in acknowledgment. "Next, we divide into two groups for the actual attack. Z and Cal will remain with Theo just out of sight of the entrance. We might need you to help us escape, if we even make it back to the surface." Some of the ants look down at that thought, while others stare straight at Barbatus. "We will capture the colony member as they return to the colony at sundown. Bike will have the masking agent ready by morning. We attack from the East side of the entrance at sunrise."

The capture of the colony member for his chemical keys is uneventful, and Bike whips up his batch of the masking agent that will help hide the team from detection by the colony guards. Barbatus calls the group into formation and orders, "Patch, check everyone's armor. We need every advantage we can get." In the hour before sunrise, the group marches to within sight of the colony entrance, then waits in the tall grass for the signal to proceed. Barbatus lays out the plan. "Rugosus and Schmitty will lead with me.

Axe and BA, you must keep our escape open from the rear. Finish off anyone you see still moving as we move through the colony. Tex and Banshee, I need you immediately behind our point group. There will be many colony defenders which will be wounded but still fighting as we move quickly to the Queen, and they will be dangerous. Finish them as we pass. Wheels, you stay with Bike and Patch. We cannot afford to lose their skills. If things go badly, get them to Z, Cal, and Theo as quickly as possible, and do whatever necessary to keep Theo hidden away, with or without the scroll. Any questions?" No one says a word. "Good", says Barbatus. "Time to go."

There are no guards at the entrance at this time of the morning. The colony is still cool from the damp evening. The group is almost half way to the Queen before workers preparing to go out and collect food are encountered. The workers pass by the raiders without recognizing any danger. Bike has once again done his job. The tunnels widen as they near the Queen's chamber. Barbatus walks swiftly in the middle of the tunnel, with Rugosus on his right side and Schmitty on his left, the three walking side by side, taking up the width of the passageway. Tex and Banshee follow immediately behind, also side by side. Bike and Patch follow them closely, with Wheels tucked in behind them. Axe and BA look nervously behind them as they walk together at the rear. All ten tighten their grips on their weapons, while trying to remain loose and ready for action.

"Halt!" shouts a guard at the main entrance of the Queen's chamber. Before he even finishes his command, Rugosus dispatches him with one swift swing of his blade-tipped staff. Almost instantly, two more guards are upon them. Barbatus swings his identical weapon downward between the two defenders and runs straight forward between them. Schmitty and Rugosus quickly lunge forward and impale the two guards, then quickly withdraw their weapons and rush forward behind Barbatus. Tex kicks the wounded defenders as he passes them, and Banshee quickly removes each of their heads with two efficient swings of his scythe. The rest of the group rushes forward through the tunnel, hugging as close as possible behind the leaders, to avoid creating any gap in the attacking formation.

"This way", Barbatus commands, recognizing the familiar design of New Optera, laid out similarly to his old colony. "The Queen's chamber will be just ahead." Immediately, a dozen guards appear from both sides of the tunnel in front of them. Before Barbatus, Rugosus, and Schmitty can react, Tex and Banshee are already slashing at the guards. The defending guards are threatening to divide the attackers, with Bike and Patch being two of the weaker fighters. Axe steps forward, wildly swinging his axe, cutting in half all of the guards on one side, while BA stabs and slashes the guards on the other side. The group is intact as they reach the main door to the Queen's chamber.

"Axe, break down the door", Barbatus barks. Axe steps up and breaks the door with two massive swings of his axe. Barbatus, Rugosus, and Schmitty rush through the open doorway. Inside are the Queen, two of her Queen's Defenders, and a handful of guards. Tex and Banshee quickly dispatch the guards, while Rugosus and Schmitty press the points of their blades to the necks of the Queen's Defenders. Barbatus demands of the Queen. "Where is the scroll?" The defiant Queen responds, "I don't know what you are talking about." Barbatus growls, "I am from old Optera. If you will not tell me where it is, there is no need to let you live, and I will find it anyway." The Queen smirks at Barbatus who does not yet see the object she has pulled from behind her cloak. Rugosus sees the flash of the dagger from the corner of his eye and instinctively lunges to protect Barbatus. The blade finds a gap in Rugosus' armor, and it sinks deep into his neck, almost completely severing his head. He falls to the floor motionless.

"No!", Barbatus screams, and immediately swings his weapon, cutting the Queen's immense abdomen from the rest of her body, killing her. Schmitty cuts off the heads of the other two Defenders and says to Barbatus, who is cradling the head of the motionless Rugosus, "He is dead. We must go, now." Barbatus gently lays his friend's head to the floor, and turns to leave with the others.

Suddenly, guards appear from the sides and rear of the attacking group. "Go, go!" yells Schmitty, and the group rushes back to the entrance, led now by Axe and BA, each swinging his weapon in a maniacal frenzy. Wheels, Bike, and Patch quickly follow behind, cutting off the heads of any wounded guard still able to attempt to stop them. Schmitty grabs Barbatus by the arm and runs through the colony, with Tex bludgeoning any still moving injured colony members, and Banshee removing the heads of any pursuers with wide swinging arcs of his scythe.

The nine group members fall down in the tall

grass as they reach their waiting comrades, chests heaving from the effort of the escape. "What happened? Where's Rugosus?", asks Theo. Schmitty answers, "He didn't make it." Barbatus adds, "He died protecting me. It should have been me." Schmitty answered, "You know you would have done the same for him. Any of us would." Schmitty thinks back on a time when he did not think of Rugosus as anything other than lazy and selfish, and now regrets ever having considered him as anything other than the brave and loyal friend he has grown to know.

"We failed", laments Barbatus. "We did not get the scroll." Bike replies, "We still have Theo. He's even more important than a copy of the tablet." Barbatus narrows his eyes and says, "Theo is important, but if the scroll falls into the hands of a Queen who then captures Theo, the world is doomed. Now it is even more important that we keep Theo safe."

As Shelton Tarver watches the ant battle from up high, he does not notice that he is being followed by a half dozen armed agents in dark suits. The agent in charge calls to him from twenty or thirty yards back, "Mr. Tarver!" Shelton jumps at the booming voice, totally unaware he was not alone. He glances around at the six men and answers, "I'm Shelton Tarver. Who are you, and what are you doing out here?"

"Who we are is not important. We are here on a classified mission, under the direct orders of the President of the United States. We are to watch as you dig up the colony that contains the scroll." Shelton innocently asks, "What scroll?" The agent unforgivingly responds, "We are to observe you digging up the ant colony with the scroll and then accompany you back to the Y12 Center for debriefing and consultation with the Center's staff."

Tarver thinks to himself, "Y12. That's where Henry works. Maybe he can straighten this out, if he's not in trouble with these same guys." Now talking to the agent he answers truthfully, "I still don't know what you're talking about, but there are three colonies in this clearing. I have no idea which one you are looking for."

"Then you will dig up all three, and we'll take them all to the Center", answers the agent expressionlessly. He then tosses a shovel and a seventeen gallon galvanized steel tub at Shelton's feet and adds, "Hurry up. We've got a long drive ahead." Tarver bends down to pick up the shovel, and notices the group of twelve ants standing in a straight line, facing him. He leans over and whispers, "Run. Get away from here." He stands back up and jabs the shovel into the ground next to the largest of the three colonies.

Barbatus recognizes what is happening and commands the group, "We have to go. The agents will be looking for the scroll. They aren't looking for Theo. We must find another abandoned colony and trust that whoever is looking for the scroll will not be able to find the human key. Whatever happens, we cannot let anyone find Theo."

Shelton watches out of the corner of his eye as the ants file off away from the clearing. As he digs up the first and largest colony, he considers the possible outcomes of being taken to a secret government facility. "Nothing good can come of this. What is this scroll they keep asking about? I wonder if it has anything to do with the tablet at the University? At least I know someone on the inside. Maybe Henry will be able to tell me what's going on."

He places the entire mound in the big tub, and places a burlap bag over the top and secures it with wire. Two agents pick it up and place it in the back of one of the two large black SUVs waiting behind the men, their engines still running. He digs into the earth around the other colony, which looks almost abandoned, but still with apparent ant activity. He secures it in the same way he did the first one, and looks at the remaining colony entrance.

"This one looks completely abandoned.", Tarver announces. "Dig it up anyway. We'll let the Center's researchers figure out which one they are looking for." He digs up the third colony and places it in another tub in the same manner as the other two. The agents pick up the tubs and place them in the back of the SUV.

The head agent then tells Tarver, "OK. Time to go. Get in the car." Shelton complies without a word, getting into the back seat. Two agents get into the SUV, one on each side of him, and the two vehicles quickly turn around and head back toward the main road, raising clouds of dust behind them as they rumble along the bumpy road.

The twelve ants walk for hours, and as the sun begins to set, Tex whispers almost in a shout, "Look. It's that bird again." Directly in front of them is a Great Blue Heron, standing with its head straight up into the air, motionless. As the ants approach, the great bird leaps into the air, and with slow, rhythmic flapping of its wings, he flies into the sunset. Bike is the first to say what they were all thinking, "That's that Spirit Helper again, isn't it." Barbatus agrees, "Yes. He was telling us that this is where we will hide Theo. Look, there is another cluster of colonies over in that clearing under where he was standing."

Just like the group of three colonies they fled from earlier in the day, one of the colonies is very active and well populated, one is smaller and less populated, and one appears to be abandoned. Barbatus knows what to do. "We will move into the abandoned colony and recruit members from the other two colonies to build up our forces. With Bike's masking agents, we can enter either colony at will and take whatever supplies we need. We can stay here almost indefinitely, and provide better protection for Theo than we could around the humans."

As the group enters the abandoned colony, Barbatus surveys the tunnels and chambers for security and defense strategy. "Welcome to your new home. I propose we name it after our fallen comrade, Rugosus. I propose we call it 'New Rugosus'. Any objections?" The group loudly and unanimously agrees. The twelve can finally rest for a time before they must settle in and build up this colony of their own. New Rugosus is now the best hope for protecting the secret that Theo contains.

Seated at her desk, going through electronic mail, General Green sees that she has received a secure communication from President Anthony. It is a message from the President's account, formatted to self-destruct exactly sixty seconds after being opened. The message reads, "General Green. Special Forces in route to your location. All records to be destroyed. Link found between ant and male human DNA. Agents dispatched to collect biological samples and archaeological artifacts. You are free to disclose all in testimony."

General Green knows that this means the President is prepared to go down with the ship. She has always said that the long term goal is far more important than any public office. "With the ant DNA and the ancient artifacts containing genetic codes, the scientists at UNIPHARM will eventually figure out how to use them to achieve our objectives", she thinks back on what Rebecca Anthony predicted. Her mind races as she works through the steps of the shut down process she will initiate in the coming moments.

The two black SUVs hurriedly enter the rear entrance of the now almost abandoned Y12 Center. The three tubs, each containing an excavated ant colony, are taken to the lab where Henry Lee has been restricted, guarded by more men in black suits.

"Shelton!", Henry calls as the lanky professor is brought in, each arm firmly in the grasp of a black-suited guard. "Hello, Henry", answers Tarver. "Under the circumstances, I guess I should be happy to see you. Looks like we'll be working together on Pogo colonies again."

The head agent gruffly directs the two, "The President has directed me to observe you two searching through these colonies, and that I should personally take possession of the scroll and any other significant objects you find in them. Now get to it."

Henry and Shelton look at each other and begin to talk about the best way to approach the search through the colonies. "How about I dig first, and you sift, Henry", suggests Tarver. "What are we looking for, anyway?, he asks. Henry answers, "I have been informed that we are looking for a 'scroll' of some sort. I have been given no other information. I can only assume that any type of scroll will be inside some sort of container, so I guess that is what we will need to look for."

Both men know exactly what they are looking for, but it is not in their interest to let the black-suited men know that they have any inside information. Shelton digs down into the busiest colony, scooping the dirt into the sifting pan Henry is holding. Henry then sifts the loose dirt through the screen to another tub below, revealing any rocks, ants, or hopefully, whatever contains the scroll. Henry carefully wipes his hand over anything that does not go through the screen, and then dumps the ants and whatever else is left into the bottom tub.

This continues for a couple of hours, with Shelton carefully scooping dirt into the screen, and Henry even more carefully sorting through the dirt and ants. "Let's switch for a while, Henry", suggests Tarver, and Henry takes the trowel and takes his turn at digging in the dirt. After another half hour, as Shelton is sifting through the dirt Henry has plopped on to the screen, he asks, "Hey, look at this." Henry comes over to take a look, as well as the head black-suited agent.

"This looks like a piece of sandstone, but it's lighter than a rock would be, and has decorations on it. The three men take turns picking it up and carefully inspecting the object, then the head agent takes out a pocket knife and cuts it open. He turns it upside down over the screening pan, and a small tubular piece falls out of it. He picks it up, unrolls what appears to be a document of some sort, and then rolls it back up and puts it back in the sandstone jar, and places it in a padded container he had been carrying in his suit pocket. "Thank you gentlemen. Our job here is finished. I have been instructed to remind you that everything you have seen here remains classified, and that you are still bound by your contracts. I trust that you will honor your commitments."

The agents all quickly exit the lab and drive away in the black vehicles, leaving Henry and Shelton standing next to the two remaining tubs of ant colonies.

After a few moments of uncertain silence, Henry says, "Well, I guess this means that the President has the scroll. It won't do her much good without the key, but I didn't feel like telling those guys that." Shelton responds, "I wonder why they didn't make us dig through the other colonies? Was there only one scroll?" Henry cocks his head to the side and says, "You know, I haven't considered that there might be more than one. Let's look."

The two sift through the second colony carefully, looking for a similar item in this tub with fewer ants, but more activity than the third one. After a couple of hours of study, finding nothing, Shelton says, "Looks like we might be wasting our time. Maybe they knew there was only one. That last colony looks dead. Surely it's empty." Henry argued, "Let's check it. I don't want to leave anything to chance, and if there's another scroll, we can't afford for it to fall into their hands."

With Shelton digging again and Henry sifting, almost to the bottom of the tub with the apparently dead colony, Henry feels a hard object on the screen and starts wiping away the loose dirt. "Look! I think it's another one." Henry picks up the oval rock with drawings on the side, and they see that it looks almost identical to the earlier one.

Shelton quickly orders,"Don't crack it open. We know what's in it, and it will be much better preserved if it's not exposed to air. Leave the container sealed and I'll take it to the University to be safeguarded with the tablet. No one will look for it there."

As Shelton walks into the School of Anthropology lab at Van Ross University, Roy Hunter excitedly meets him at the door. "Shelton Tarver, do you comprehend what you have discovered? The tablet you brought me is one of the single most important pieces we've ever studied. Not only is it historically significant, but it very well might turn out to be one of the greatest scientific finds in history."

"You'll like this then", replies Tarver, holding the small container between his thumb and forefinger. "Hold on to your hat. This was found inside of a Harvester ant colony, and even though I haven't opened it yet, I'm willing to bet that it has almost exactly the same story on it that the tablet tells."

"Let me see that", the Dean gasps. "I need to get this into the lab, so that it can be opened under controlled conditions and fully documented in real time. This will prove beyond a shadow of a doubt that it is authentic and will remove any possible claims that it is a forgery."

"You're right, of course", answers Tarver, "but you can't publish anything about it." "What do you mean, Professor Tarver?", asks the Dean. Shelton replies, "There are a lot of powerful people out there who will do anything to get their hands on this information. I don't know when it will be safe to reveal the existence of these pieces. I don't know if it will ever be safe."

"For now, study it, document it, prove it is what it seems to be, and sit on it. I promise that you will get credit for discovering it, if and when it is safe to tell the world it is here."

Chapter 26.

It has only been one month since General Green was reassigned to the base known as "The Freezer", but she has already started to feel the crushing daily sameness and monotonous cold. "I better get used to it, because I'm going to be here for a while", she thinks out loud.

The compound is laid out in a circular pattern, with eight main corridors radiating out from a central hub. Below the surface level, primarily occupied by construction equipment and Snow Cats and other winter terrain vehicles, there are seven lower levels, each smaller in diameter than the one above it. The lowest of the eight levels is where the secure storage facility is located.

As General Green travels down each level, at each security checkpoint, she presents her credentials and either looks into a retinal scan or presses a finger on to a fingerprint reader. The security checkpoints are unmanned, and a chip inside the ID card is read by scanners in the corridor walls. Access is granted automatically, with a handful of monitoring personnel centrally located on the second level below the surface. The exception to this protocol is The Freezer itself, occupying the eighth level. This level, in addition to similar security measures, also has two armed guards posted around the clock, with shift changes staggered so that only one guard is relieved at a time.

The armed guards do not move at the approach of General Green except to salute, but remain at attention, looking straight ahead. While they do not look directly at her, they are keenly aware of her rank and title, and when she presents her credentials, one of the guards leans over to carefully view it. He nods in acknowledgment of her clearance, and the two snap their hands down to their sides as she passes between them.

General Green walks down the hallway to the secret storage facility. As she reaches the first door, it automatically slides open, releasing a rush of pressurized air outward. She steps inside the air lock, and the door closes behind her. The lock repressurizes, and then the internal door opens. The air inside is the same temperature, but is extremely dry, the humidity controlled by its own environmental system.

"Good morning, General Green" a voice volunteers from the back of the storage lab. General Green continues between rows of sliding drawers, filled with decades and decades of varying levels of secret documents, records, and evidence. She does not know what is stored in any of these drawers, and does not have any interest in any of it, with the exception of the one box of files and genetic samples which came with her on her flight here.

"Good morning, General Rogers", she answers. "I trust that you have everything in order." "Yes, General", responds Rogers in a professionally cool manner. It takes all of his military discipline to treat his superior with respect, but being a good soldier is all he has left.

"And Dr. Williams?", inquires General Green. Rogers answers, "Dr. Williams has been continuing his research through the files, and has been very cooperative." Even as he says this, Rogers thinks of how he will use the information Zeke Williams has shared with him about the true nature of the research that had been gathered from the Y12 research and stored here at The Freezer.

General Green reinforces her concern by following up with, "I trust that the two of you will maintain the secrecy of any classified information you come across, and that you will, of course, notify me immediately should you discover anything that appears to be a possible national security issue." "Of course", Rogers quickly answers. "The General should be advised however, that if I am called to testify as to my knowledge of this facility or the contents of any documents stored here, I will truthfully answer any questions asked of me, and if the question is about a classified matter, I will only provide the answer to the appropriate authority."

General Green narrows her eyes, her lips pressed tightly together, clearly understanding Rogers' message; he will no longer cover for her. She grits her teeth, smiles grimly, and answers, "Understood, General. Do your duty. That is all I ask of you." She then turns on her heel and marches quickly away to her quarters.

"Cliff", Zeke Williams addresses Rogers, as they are now much more familiar, having spent every day together for the last month in this isolated, frozen prison. "Do you think she knows that we know everything?" Rogers answers, "Yes, Zeke. I am certain that she suspects we know enough to take her down. She will not go down without a fight, so we need to make sure that we have everything documented."

Williams responds, "Everything in this room is a

disaster for Green, the President, and anyone involved with Y12. I have to tell you something, Cliff; I saved most of what I discovered on a flash drive back at the lab, and slipped it to Henry Lee. He has it all."

Rogers answers Williams, "I know, Zeke. The same information has been presented to the Senate impeachment committee. We need to make sure these documents are preserved, in case there is any question as to the authenticity of the documents that have been presented so far."

Williams jumps in, "Cliff, what we know could bury them all. Too bad we're stuck here. Nobody even knows we're here." Rogers smiles and says, "They know we're here, and they're coming for us. I planted a tracking device on myself before our flight here. All we have to do is stay alive until they come get us."

"Yes, General", the security officer answers. "Security Protocol Zero Minus Forty is now in effect." General Green nods to the officer and says, "Initiate Code Deep Freeze now." "Acknowledged, General. Countdown initiated on my mark." The security officer places his key into the lock on the right side of the panel, as another officer places his key in the lock on the opposite side of the panel, eight feet away.

"Five, four, three, two, one, mark", and the officers simultaneously turn the keys. At that moment, sirens begin blasting throughout the complex and lights flash on the walls, signaling the order to evacuate the lower secure storage levels.

As the two officers from the eighth level arrive up from their posts, the senior officer reports, "General, there are personnel remaining in the secure storage room." The General replies without emotion, "Acknowledged, Colonel. Proceed with shutdown of the storage facility." "Yes, General", snaps the officer, and the two proceed up the levels, followed by General Green, along with the security personnel from each successive level.

Just as the security personnel and General Green reach the surface level, they are met with a heavily armed group of Special Forces, who have the entire staff at gunpoint. The soldiers are dressed in black, with full body armor under their parkas. The smell of smoke from the flash bang grenades, thrown as the rescue began, still hangs in the upper half of the room. As they check off each person in the room, the elite soldiers use zip ties to restrict the movement of the staff. Even General Green is arrested, as well as the security officers assigned to her.

The team leader of the soldiers checks each name on his list, and then says, "There are two unaccounted for. Where are General Clifton Rogers and Dr. Zeke Williams?" General Green does not answer, but the security officer assigned to the lowest level room answers, "They are locked in Level Eight. Only General Green has the access code."

"General Green, you will accompany me to the lower level and you will enter the code to open the secure storage room and release the two personnel.", commands the team leader. General Green stares straight ahead and makes no move to comply.

"General Green, I have authority from the Chairman of the Joint Chiefs of Staff to force you to comply, using any means necessary." The team leader gives the General a moment to consider, then adds, "I have been ordered to inform you that you will be called to provide testimony as to the function of this facility and the President's role in it, and will be offered retirement instead of a court martial, but only if all personnel are recovered safely. You have thirty seconds to comply, or this offer will be rescinded."

General Green lowers her head, and then nods in agreement. The team escorts her down to the panel in front of the doors at the lower level. She enters the code, and the rescuers use the keys that were taken from the security personnel to turn off the alarms. The doors open, and warm air rushes in, causing the two inside to stand up from where they were seated together, huddling on the cold floor. "General Rogers? Dr. Williams?" commands the Special Forces officer. "Yes", they each answer. "I have been ordered to ensure that you will appear in front of the U.S. Senate. Come with me."

The rest of the Special Forces officers carry out the entire contents of the secure storage room, and load the boxes and the staff of The Freezer on the waiting plane. The engines had been running the entire half hour of the operation, and as they were brought to full power, the ice crackled as the skids slide across the air strip. The plane climbs quickly, leaving the abandoned base, lights still shining on all the snow cats and other surface vehicles.

Zeke and Rogers look at each other, relieved that they were not left to die in The Freezer, but not looking forward to the upcoming days of testifying against their President. They know more than anyone that powerful forces were working to keep the information they were about to share from being publicly released.

As the plane makes a wide turn to head away from the lights of the base, General Green, no longer confined by the zip ties, reaches down to gently push in a folder that is protruding from the slightly open top of her briefcase. As the folder slides from view, the label with the name, "S. Shaw" disappears. She looks straight ahead for the rest of the flight, her face empty of any signs of distress.

The House of Representatives chamber is packed full of photographers, with electronic flashes blinding the members like continuous lightning. The members are unusually quiet, and there are no empty seats, not even those of the usually fashionably late senior members. The chamber is far from silent, however, with every square foot of space occupied by members of the media or official staffers.

The Speaker gavels the House into order. "The Chairman of the Judiciary Committee now has the floor." "Mr. Speaker, the Judiciary Committee reluctantly presents the following Articles of Impeachment of the President of the United States", the Chairman reads from the official declaration distributed to each member of the House of Representatives.

"Article 1. Exceeding the bounds of the powers of the Office. President Anthony is accused of conspiring with foreign entities to endanger the lives of U. S. citizens, by knowingly subjecting them to dangerous substances without properly established testing protocols, and deliberately circumventing existing safeguards to protect against such unsafe practices.

Article 2. Behavior grossly incompatible with the proper function and purpose of the Office. President

Anthony is accused of administration of said unsafe substances to former President Cole while acting as his personal physician. President Anthony is also accused of subsequently conspiring to cover up the true nature of President Cole's death.

Article 3. Employing the power of the office for an improper purpose or for personal gain. President Anthony is accused of assisting foreign and domestic organizations in circumventing health and safety laws and regulations, failure to disclose her close association with these organizations prior to, or after assuming the office of President, and failing to report the receipt of fees, honorariums, campaign donations, and assurances of future employment by foreign entities, specifically UNIPHARM, the international pharmaceutical conglomerate created in part with the assistance and guidance of the President, before rising to the office of President.

Mr. Speaker, I respectfully present to this body, these Articles of Impeachment of President Rebecca Anthony."

The House explodes into chaos, and the Speaker bangs his gavels repeatedly. "Order! The House will have order." The din calms to a murmur, and the Speaker continues, "The vote is to determine whether this body will present the Articles of Impeachment of the President to the Senate for a trial. Those in favor of presenting the Articles of Impeachment, vote 'Aye'." A resounding "Aye!" is heard throughout the hall. "Those opposed, vote 'Nay'." A far smaller number of dissenters is heard, and even those seem unwilling to be seen voting this way. When the electronic vote totals appear on the big board, the vote is far beyond the simple majority required to send the Articles of Impeachment to the Senate.

The Speaker bangs his gavel again and pronounces, "The Ayes have it. The House will present the Articles of Impeachment for President Rebecca Anthony to the Senate immediately following the closure of this session." He lifts the gavel and slams it loudly, ending the session.

The Senate begins the trial of President Anthony by calling General Green, who has been granted immunity from prosecution, in exchange for her early retirement and full cooperation with the investigation.

Henry Lee, now in charge of the newly reopened Y12 Center, watches a room full of consoles with young men playing One World Warrior. Turner Runnels has been managing a team of programmers to rewrite the code, to take out the government's ability to manipulate the brainwaves of players. The banks of servers recording game results are still behind the dark glass walls, but no longer are the volumes of game results sent to secret government back up servers. There are still tournaments almost every weekend, but the Y12 Center has been converted to a military only facility. The civilian treatment center for attention disorders has been permanently closed, after UNIPHARM disbanded and funding for non-military research ended.

Clark Shephard still monitors game play, but is now the head of OWW game play results analysis and data translation, working closely with General Ben Longarrow to refine the still secret Swarm Intelligence Battlefield Communication Project. Henry, Clark, and General Longarrow have been meeting almost daily, close to finalizing field tests on taking players who have excelled in the game, and replacing standard communication equipment in the next Pacific Alliance War Games.

General Longarrow walks in while Henry and Clark are pouring over the current game results being displayed on Clark's tablet. "Well, are we ready?" Henry jumps visibly, startled by the General's sudden appearance. Clark answers, "Yes...General. We are...ready...for the...games tomorrow." The General responds, stern faced, "Good. I don't need to tell you that we need to see some positive results from these games. I'm getting a lot of pressure to prove Y12 is worth the investment. If we don't come through with an overwhelming outcome, there will likely be reduction in funding at best, and at worst, the elimination of the Swarm Intelligence program entirely."

The General continues, "These war games will be simulating what will happen in the event of a nuclear detonation in the lower atmosphere, producing a wide EMP, which would totally destroy all conventional communication equipment, as well as most, if not all, weapons systems. Our most likely enemy in the world will undoubtedly use such a weapon in a potential conflict. This enemy has overwhelmingly superior numbers, which we can currently offset with our technology. Subjected to an EMP, we would no longer have such an advantage. Gentlemen, your research, what you have been developing here, means the difference in winning or losing our next major world conflict."

Henry and Clark briefly look at each other, and Henry says, "General, we have found some very promising results. I'd like for you to sit with us and observe game play for a while, to familiarize yourself with what to expect." The three huddle around Henry's computer station with multiple monitors creating a panoramic view of the battlefield. From this desk, they can see the virtual positions of the whole company of simulated soldiers, each one on the screen representing a player in the room beyond the glass wall.

As the three scan back and forth from the screens at the desk to the players in the room, the General narrows his eyes and asks, "What are they doing without their headsets on? I thought the headsets were essential to the game." In fact, none of the players have on their headsets. They lie unused to the side of the computer consoles, and the players are feverishly working the keyboards, moving their virtual partners around the battlefield, without uttering a sound.

The General repeats his question, "What is going on? Why aren't they using their equipment? How are they playing the game?" Clark answers, "We have...found that...after being...exposed to...the game and...Aggrepax...they no...longer need...headsets to...communicate...with others." Henry adds, "They seem to intuitively move toward the most effective position. The entire company moves in unison, toward the objective, without any verbal communication at all. They are clearly communicating in some way, but just how, we don't know."

The General asks cynically, "How is that possible? Is this what you have been trying to tell me about the ants?" Henry smiles and answers, "Yes, General. It seems that over time, the drugs the players have been using, in combination with the feedback mechanism of the game, have somehow tapped into the players' brains' ability to receive and transmit communication via pheromones, just like the ants. We're not exactly sure yet how it works, but it works."

The General bursts through the doors into the glass walled room, and puts his hand on the shoulder of one of the players. "Son, how are you communicating with your team mates?" The player looks up at the General and answers, "I'm not sure, General." The General, asks again in an irritated tone, "How do you know where they are?"

The player, with a confused look on his face, calmly answers, "I can smell them."